Chocolate a'la Murder

A PERFECTLY PROPER PARANORMAL
MUSEUM MYSTERY – BOOK 4

KIRSTEN WEISS

Cover Art: Dar Albert

Visit the author website: https://kirstenweiss.com

Misterio press / paperback edition June, 2020

ISBN-13: 978-1-944767-59-4

CHOCOLATE A'LA MURDER

one

I adjusted the Aztec priest and frowned.

Afternoon sunlight painted the black-and-white floor tiles. Black pedestals dotted the room. Displayed on each was a different aspect of *The Magic of Chocolate*.

I shifted a gilded cocoa pod on the *Chocolate Alchemy* pedestal, so it leaned against a dusty alchemical beaker.

Normally, the tiny Gallery room in my paranormal museum was filled with quirky local art. This weekend, the San Benedetto Wine and Visitors Bureau was kicking off Wine and Chocolate days. Since the local wineries had the wine side handled, I was going with a chocolate theme at the museum.

And I had no chocolate.

My stomach butterflied, that feeling of nerves and excitement common to the self-employed. This would be okay. I had an amazing if odd museum, with ever-changing exhibits that kept me on my toes. An amazing and definitely-not-odd boyfriend. Plus, amazing friends—Adele and Harper. The chocolate would arrive in time.

"I've got it!" Harper hurried into the room, her olive cheeks dusky-rose from exertion.

I wished sweat made me sexy like it did my friend, the Penelope Cruz clone. I could feel the grit clinging to my damp forehead.

Harper carried a picture frame beneath her arm, and my shoulders slumped. For one relieved moment, I'd thought she'd come bearing chocolate. But Harper was a financial planner, not a delivery girl.

"Sorry I'm late." Chest heaving, she adjusted the lapel of her pinstriped pantsuit. "Am I too late?"

"You're right on time. I was just finishing up." Knotting my brown hair into a ponytail, I motioned around the room.

She handed me the ornately framed poster. "You didn't get it from me," she said. On the hand-drawn poster was a modern witch's perspective on chocolate.

"Of course not," I said. "You were only doing me a favor and picking up a framed ..." Spell? Meditation? Whatever it was, the poster looked spooky, written in Harper's elegant script and bordered by a cabernet-red mat and black frame.

Harper was a secret strega, a classical Italian witch. But she kept that aspect of her life firmly in the broom closet. It didn't fit her high-powered, financially savvy image.

She shivered, her expression becoming a careful blank.

"Harper?" I asked, suddenly alert.

Slowly, she turned and walked to the pedestal closest to the door to the museum proper. On it, a whisk from Mexico called a *molinillo* stood upright in a ceramic jar. Used for mixing Mexican hot chocolate, the molinillo was a thing of beauty. Decorative geometric shapes had been whittled into the pale wood and burned black for contrast. A feminine hand had been carved at the top of the spindle. Beside the display, a tent card read: *Haunted Molinillo—Rattles When a Lie Is Told.*

Circling, Harper bent toward the pedestal and slipped her hands into the pocket of her pinstriped blazer. "What have you got here?"

"A molinillo. I can't believe I found one that was haunted."

She glanced from me to the molinillo. "I'll say." Abruptly, she straightened. "My name is Adele Nakamoto," she deadpanned. She stared intently at the display. "Strange. It's not rattling."

"That's because it's not a very important lie." I pushed a wisp of hair behind my ear. Was my witchy friend sensing something I hadn't? "And besides, I know you're lying. The molinillo doesn't need to give me a warning."

Harper arched a brow.

"Okay," I admitted. "I don't know why it's not rattling, but that's the legend."

She tugged on her plump bottom lip. "What's its story?"

"It's a little vague. My collector—"

"Herb? You're trusting him after the cursed cowbell incident?"

"In fairness," I said, "the riot wasn't his fault." And Herb wasn't exactly *my* collector. He was *a* paranormal collector who occasionally dropped by the museum peddling his wares. "Anyway, I got lucky. He turned up with a haunted molinillo right when I needed something chocolate-themed." Which, on reflection, seemed somewhat suspicious. "I'll change the sign so it's clear only important lies set off the molinillo."

Harper pointed to a corner of the Gallery, where I'd arranged a red-velvet canopy above a round table covered in a star-spangled black cloth. "What's happening there?"

"A fortune-teller's coming in to do chocolate scrying for customers." I bounced on my toes. It was going to be awesome. I'd been promoting her all over town. Though it worried me a little that Harper hadn't seen my flyers and advertisements. I was also a little concerned about melted chocolate being used during the scrying process and the potential for burns. But the fortune-teller had assured me she had it handled. "She's also promised to read with the chocolate tarot cards," I said. I'd be giving everyone who bought a ticket to the museum a single chocolate tarot card-of-the-day as a free gift.

"Are the cards actually made of chocolate? Because that sounds sticky."

Sticky and delicious! "Sadly, no. They're paper and ink, just chocolate-themed." As a confirmed cacaophile, chocolate tarot cards were something I could get behind.

Harper turned to the shelves on the wall opposite the windows. Aside from one that was filled with the boxes of tarot and oracle cards, they were empty. "And the empty shelf space?"

I hung her framed offering over a small ebony table between the shelves. "Actual chocolate, if it ever gets here. The delivery man's late. He was supposed to arrive this morning."

"Where are you getting the chocolate?"

"From Reign."

Harper whistled. "That new place? Good stuff. I've been giving their chocolate away as thank-yous to my clients."

I nodded. Reign's chocolate was expensive and beautiful, but it tasted just okay to me. My favorite was still See's Candy, a West Coast institution. That *I Love Lucy* scene with Lucy and Ethel working the chocolate conveyer belt? Filmed at See's.

"Listen," Harper said, her expression turning serious. "I'm thinking of—"

"Where is it?" Our friend Adele Nakamoto, chic in a slim, ice-blue skirt and ivory blouse beneath her Fox and Fennel apron, bustled into the Gallery. She looked around wildly. "Is it here?"

Harper pointed to the black frame.

Adele tossed her head and a wisp of ebony hair floated free from her chignon. "That's not chocolate. Where's the chocolate?"

Uh oh. "It hasn't arrived yet," I said, fighting a reflexive cringe.

She planted her fists on her slim hips. "But I need it now. Twenty retirees are going to arrive in my tearoom in fifteen minutes, and they expect Reign chocolate." Adele's tearoom, the Fox and Fennel, was conveniently located right next door to the museum. "Plus, Allie is out sick, and our main oven stopped working this morning. I've already had to cancel my appointment with the caterer. This week has been a disaster. Even Pug has a cold."

"Oh no," I said, frowning. Adele's pug was sweet as a sugar cube—I cut a glance at GD—unlike some animals I knew. The black cat sneezed, turned, and sauntered into the main room.

"You've hired a caterer for your own tearoom?" Harper asked.

"No, for the wedding!" Adele paced, her apron strings flying out behind her. "Dieter and I are getting married in three months," she wailed, "and we haven't even finalized the menu."

Easygoing Dieter Finkielkraut and uptight Adele Nakamoto seemed an unlikely couple at first glance. But

I believed they had what it took. Unfortunately, Adele was caught in the iron grip of the bridal-industrial complex.

"Let me see what the holdup is." Hastily, I pulled my cell phone from the back pocket of my jeans and called the chocolate shop.

No one answered.

After the fifth ring, a machine picked up. I left a message and pocketed the phone. "I'm sure they'll call back." Preferably before Adele went nuclear.

"Will they? You don't know that." Adele's fingers dug into her ebony hair. "Twenty retirees!"

Ignoring my pleading look, Harper backed out of the Gallery. "I'd help you with your little chocolate problem—"

"Little!" Adele's eyes bulged.

"—but I've got a client meeting." Harper turned and sprinted into the museum's main room. The bell above the front door jangled.

I smiled tightly. "It's fine." *Jussst fine.* I brushed off my hands. "The delivery's probably on its way, but I'll go to Reign and pick up some chocolate in the meantime. Leo can run the museum without me." My assistant would have no trouble managing things. The place was depressingly empty this afternoon; Wednesdays are not boom times for paranormal museums.

"How much do you need?" I asked Adele as I walked past her into the main room. It smelled of old objects and furniture polish, and I inhaled a calming breath. I checked the black crown molding for spiderwebs and found none. Freestanding shelves displayed haunted objects and creepy dolls. On the opposite wall, a door disguised as a bookcase led to Adele's tearoom. I loved that secret door, and not just because there were scones on the other side.

Leo, seated behind the glass counter, poured over a college textbook. His thin frame hunched in a comma shape beside the antique cash register. My assistant's black leather jacket hung over the back of his tall chair. He glanced at me and flashed a grin, and then his head dipped again to the book.

"I need the amount of chocolate I ordered," Adele said, waspish. "But if I can get seven of each of their bars, it will get me through the retirement party."

"No problem," I said lightly. "Leo, do you mind watching the museum while I'm away? I'll be gone for about thirty minutes."

"Yeah ... sure." His dyed-black hair fell forward, hiding his eyes. The heater whirred behind him.

"He's got an exam coming up," I said in a low voice to Adele.

"Education first," she chirped.

Leo attended the local community college, and he had bigger things in store than working at a paranormal museum. But I hoped I had a couple years left before my goth assistant moved on to greener and less haunted pastures.

The museum's ghost-detecting cat meowed from the haunted rocking chair in the opposite corner. GD Cat rose rolled, stretched, and yawned. The old wooden rocking chair swayed beneath the black cat.

"Thank you, thank you, thank you." Adele pressed the spine of a book on the bookcase. The case pivoted outward, opening into her tearoom.

I grabbed a handful of postcards off the counter. "Wait—"

But she'd already vanished through the secret door. It snicked shut behind her.

I sighed and returned the postcards for my *Magic of Chocolate* exhibit. Last night, after a few glasses of wine from her family's vineyard, Adele had agreed to stack them on the counter in the Fox and Fennel. I could give them to her later.

I glanced around the main room one last time. Everything was in order. Haunted photos of murderers stared down at me, their black frames gleaming. Rows of shelves containing haunted objects gleamed, dust free. From high atop a wall pedestal, a bronze skull seemed to wink.

"See you in thirty minutes," I said.

"Mmph," Leo grunted, not looking up.

I strolled through the bookcase and down the tearoom's elegant, bamboo-plank hallway to the alley. Spring in San Benedetto could be iffy, and this was one of those days that couldn't decide what it was going to be. Fog hung low in the sky. But it was warm enough for me to shrug out of my Paranormal Museum hoodie, exposing my museum T-shirt beneath. When you're self-employed, fashion takes a back seat to advertising.

I drove down Main Street in my vintage red pickup. Yes, I could have walked, but there was a chance I'd be returning with a massive chocolate delivery, and for that I needed wheels.

I slowed in front of Reign. A burly, red-headed man in jeans and a slouchy blue T-shirt picketed in front of the chocolate shop's windows.

Huh. Was a strike the cause of the late delivery? The chocolate shop didn't seem like a big enough business to have organized labor.

Frowning, I turned the corner, looking for parking. I found a spot on the street beside the bank and walked back to Reign.

"Reign, unfair! Reign, unfair!" The man bobbed his sign, decorated with the single word: *UNFAIR!* He marched back and forth on the brick sidewalk.

Adele would kill me if I let a single picketer stop me. Averting my gaze, I scuttled past the man and through the glass door into the shop. The aroma of chocolate stopped me in my tracks. Tension dropped from my shoulders. Chocolate might not be magic, but it was great aromatherapy.

The shop's cinderblock walls were painted light gray and glistened with a dreamlike sheen. A long, polished wood counter the color of dark honey stretched across the back of the store. Driftwood displays showed off jars of sauces and bars of chocolate wrapped in simple brown paper. Colored crowns in varying colors decorated the top of each bar. Rows of chocolate-covered fruits and nuts and truffles infused with wine lined a glass case on the counter.

My mouth pinched, and not with delight. No salesperson stood behind the chic counter. Was the guy on strike supposed to be manning the front of the store?

The heady scent of chocolate twined around me, and I told myself not to freak out. If I had to wait somewhere, this wasn't a bad spot. An artisanal chocolate shop beat a paranormal museum, hands down. Of course, if I owned a chocolate shop, I'd probably be fifty pounds overweight instead of my usual ten.

Ignoring the temptations along the way, I marched to the cash register and rang the bell.

No one responded.

"Hello?" I called, leaning across the counter.

Silence.

If I returned empty-handed, Adele would have an aneurysm. And I needed chocolate for the museum too.

Settling in to wait, I picked up a brochure and scanned through it.

After years spent working with European chefs and chocolatiers, friends Atticus Reine and Orson Malke began making hand-crafted, ethically sourced, single-origin chocolates in their San Francisco apartment. They opened their flagship branch in San Benedetto, close to the organically grown nuts and other ingredients which complement the subtle flavor of the cacao.

Their pledge? To forever change the way you look at chocolate bars. Because our craft chocolates are made in small batches from select beans, our chocolates are as complex as a fine wine. Sign up for our Chocolate of the Month Club and make sure you get the best of our chocolates when they're made.

Mouth watering, I flipped past the photos of the owners to the page with wine and chocolate pairings. It listed wines from local vineyards, as well as a logo that proclaimed Reign an associate member of the Wine and Visitors Bureau. Plot 42, owned by Adele's father, was on the winery list. No wonder my friend was hell-bent on including Reign chocolates at her tearoom.

Something metallic clanked in another room, like a heavy door closing.

My head jerked up. "Hello?"

No reply.

My scalp prickled, and I fisted my hands. I needed to get a grip. This was an innocent chocolate shop, for Pete's sake. The counter guy was on strike outside, and an owner would have to show up eventually. I needed to stop thinking like I was in a haunted museum and lose the paranoia.

I returned to studying the brochure. I'd done a lot of research prepping my *Magic of Chocolate* exhibit, and the story of the cocoa bean and what people had done with it amazed me. How did the Mesoamericans figure out that the slimy cocoa bean could be fermented and turned into such a delicious drink? Casanova had drunk chocolate daily, believing it to be an aphrodisiac. The tryptophan in chocolate is part of serotonin, a chemical in the brain connected to sexual arousal.

Not that I needed help in the romance department. I was still in the honeymoon stage of a relationship with the sexy Detective Jason Slate. No outside stimulants were necessary. But the honeymoon would end sometime. I hoped it wouldn't end with the sort of painful discovery my last relationship had.

Folding the brochure, I jammed it into the rear pocket of my jeans. *Where was everyone?* "Hello?"

Silence.

Oh, come on! I couldn't wait here all day. Not with Adele tapping her expensive shoes while waiting for my return.

I edged around the counter. A long, rectangular window in the gray cinderblock wall behind the register looked into the kitchen. I peered through the window and saw metal racks and metal counters and tall machines. Something in the kitchen whirred softly. But there was no one inside.

This was getting ridiculous. The store was open. The door was unlocked. The guy on strike couldn't be the only employee working today.

Fuming, I pushed open the swinging door to the kitchen area and leaned inside. Metal racks of cooling chocolates were stacked high on wheeled carts. "Helloooo?"

No response.

Suddenly uneasy, I sidled into the room. Gleaming

metal countertops with massive metal bowls. Black rubber fatigue mats on the floor. At the back, beside a glass-fronted wooden room, a well-lit hallway that cut along the left side of the room.

Promising-looking boxes sat stacked against the wall in the hallway, beside a closed office door. Were those our order? Maybe someone was in the office and couldn't hear me?

I probably shouldn't be in their kitchen, but Adele and I needed our order. I headed toward the open hallway.

The whirring sound grew louder behind me.

Hair prickling the back of my neck, I froze, then looked over my shoulder.

In the kitchen, a man lay supine on the floor beside two narrow metal vats. The vats angled downward, chocolate dripping onto his face and chest.

two

"Oh my god," I whispered. Dizzy, I stepped around the chocolate pooling on the floor and knelt beside the slender man. He wore a brown Reign apron, so he must work here, but I couldn't recognize him beneath the chocolate covering his face. His chocolate-coated beard looked obscene. "Sir? Are you all right?"

His arm was one of the few parts of his body that wasn't covered in chocolate. Not having any better ideas, I grabbed his wrist and felt for a pulse.

There wasn't one.

My breath came in quick gasps. "Dammit." I fumbled in my jean pocket for my cell phone and called for help.

"911, what is your emergency?"

"This is Maddie Kosloski," I stammered. "I'm at Reign Chocolate on Main Street. There's been an..." Accident? Murder? "There's a man lying on the floor in the kitchen. I can't find a pulse. I'm alone here, and I don't know what happened."

"Is he breathing?"

"Um." I studied his unmoving form. "No. But ... he's covered in chocolate." My gaze darted around the gleaming kitchen.

"Excuse me?"

"Melted chocolate. He fell beneath some vats, and the chocolate's all over him."

"Hold please." The dispatcher clicked off.

"Wait! What …?" Was there a special dispatcher for chocolate-related emergencies?

"Hello," a man said. "This is Emergency Medical Services. Can you tell me what's happening?"

I repeated my story.

"All right. Do you know CPR?"

"Yes, but—"

"Your friend may be choking, or even drowning. I need you to clear his air passage with your finger and turn his head sideways. Can you do that?"

"He's not my—" *Not important!* "Yes. Yes. I'm putting the phone on speaker." I set the phone on a dry spot on the thick black floor mat.

Steeling myself, I parted the man's jaw and reached inside. I felt more squeamish about the process than I wanted to admit, but I did it anyway. I didn't have much choice.

When I was done, I heaved the man onto his side. A glug of chocolate dribbled from his mouth.

"Okay," I said, relieved that was over. "I did it. His throat is clear." I wiped my hand on my jeans.

Far off, a siren wailed.

"Good work," the medical dispatcher said. "Now you're going to need to perform CPR."

I stared at the chocolate-smeared face. *Oh boy.*

"Fine." My voice cracked.

Unwrapping my Paranormal Museum hoodie from my hips, I wiped chocolate off the man's mouth with a sleeve. I winced and pressed my mouth to his, then breathed into his mouth.

His lips were warm and slippery beneath mine.

I turned my head and sucked air in. The damp bristles of his beard tickled my cheek. Involuntarily, I licked melted chocolate from my lips. My stomach made a quick, unpleasant bolt toward my throat. *Keep it together, Maddie.* Grimacing, I repeated the process, punctuated by bouts of chest compressions.

"What's happening?" the dispatcher barked, his voice thin over my cell phone's speaker.

"Nothing," I panted, tasting the bitter sweetness of dark chocolate. Oh, God, it was delicious. And that was so wrong for so many reasons. I shuddered.

"Keep at it," he said. "You never know."

The bell over the front door jingled.

"Police," a woman called out.

My shoulders crumpled inward but I kept up the CPR. I knew that voice.

"Back here," I shouted, my breathing ragged from the compressions. "In the kitchen."

Detective Laurel Hammer strode into the kitchen and stopped short. Tall, blond, and muscular, she stared down at me, her ice-blue eyes crackling with … surprise? Annoyance? With my old high school bully, it was hard to tell. In her view, I'd never been an innocent. Over time, her attitude toward me hadn't relaxed. It had morphed into anger.

She gave herself a little shake, her short hair settling in place, then dropped to her knees on the other side of the fallen man. She grasped his wrist, pressed two fingers to his neck, and shook her head. "What have you done?"

Defensive, I sat back on my heels. "The dispatcher told me to—"

"Save it." Her neck muscles corded. "I'll take the chest compressions. You keep up the mouth-to-mouth."

I blinked, then bent my head to the fallen man's. We worked until the paramedics arrived a few minutes later and let them take over. I backed away, my knees groaning.

"And for God's sake, wipe your face," Laurel snapped. "You look like a fat kid let loose on a hot fudge sundae."

"I'm not fat!" It was only an extra ten pounds. Roughly, I wiped my mouth with the back of one hand, but I couldn't escape the taste of chocolate. Dark, delicious chocolate. I fought a gag. *Wrong. Wrong!*

I turned, feeling sick, and raced down the hallway. There had to be a bathroom down here somewhere.

"Hey!" Laurel shouted. "Where are you going?"

I ducked into a unisex bathroom and splashed water on my face. The heady scent of chocolate turned my stomach. In the mirror over the utilitarian sink, chocolate streaked my mouth and chin. Brown streaked my bare arms, and I was willing to bet if I looked hard enough, I'd find it dotting my black T-shirt. I looked like Count Chocula after a particularly messy snack.

Grabbing a paper towel from the bin on the wall, I scrubbed my face.

"Thanks for disappearing on me." Laurel appeared in the open door and glared. "Getting rid of the evidence?"

"I don't feel so good."

"What happened to that guy's not catching. I doubt the victim was poisoned."

"Victim? Is he …" But of course he was dead. In my heart, I'd known he was gone.

"He's dead." The detective glanced down the hallway and nodded at someone beyond my vision. "What are you doing here, Kosloski?"

"Adele and I placed a big chocolate order last week. It was supposed to be delivered today, but it was late. When we tried calling Reign, no one answered. We thought the easiest solution was for me to drive here and collect whatever I could. No one was at the counter, so I walked into the kitchen and found … him." I imagined the body and angled my head. Something wasn't right.

No kidding, something wasn't right. A man was dead.

"Did you recognize him?" she asked.

I tasted a bit of chocolate behind my front tooth and my stomach rolled. "Are you serious? Under all that chocolate? I mean, he was wearing a Reign apron. It looked like one of the owners, Atticus or Orson. They both have beards like …" I swallowed, remembering the man's chocolate-covered bristles against my chin. "They look a lot alike."

Laurel's blue eyes narrowed. "You seem to know a lot about them."

"Their pictures are in the brochure." I waved vaguely toward the front of the shop, my sense of not-rightness growing.

"Did you see anyone?" she asked.

"Only the guy out front, picketing."

"What guy?"

I rubbed my forehead. My hand was sticky, and I dropped it to my side. "One of the employees, I think. He was red-haired and about my age, or maybe younger."

"Thirty-five?"

She *knew* I was a year younger than her. "Thirty-three. He was wearing jeans and a blue T-shirt." I squinted. "I think he might have been the cashier, but I'm not sure. I've only been here twice before."

"And yet you managed to find a dead body and mess up the crime scene. Again."

"I didn't know he was dead," I bleated, as if that made it any better. "And the dispatcher told me—"

"Use your head next time."

Laurel had been right there beside me giving him

CPR! Or at least, we'd been together until I cut and ran. But if I'd stayed, I would have really messed up the scene.

I cleared my throat. "I did hear something when I was waiting by the counter. It sounded like a door closing in the back."

"When was this?"

Time had done weird, *Star Trek* dilations since I'd entered the chocolate shop. Had I been here an hour? Twenty minutes? "It was only a minute or two before I went into the kitchen, I think. And then I called the dispatcher right away. Does that help?"

Her nostrils flared. "Does it sound like it helps?"

Detective Jason Slate, tall, dark, and commanding, appeared in the bathroom doorway behind Laurel. He wore his detective's uniform, a navy business suit that he filled to perfection.

At the sight of my boyfriend, relief cascaded through me. I sagged against the bathroom's tiled wall.

"Laurel, what's …" His gaze met mine and he took a half-step back. His brown eyes, flecked with gold, widened. "Maddie?"

"I didn't know he was dead," I wailed. "I tried to fix it."

"Did you break it?" Laurel asked.

"I didn't mean that," I said. "I just found him there. What was I supposed to do? Ignore the dispatcher and let him die? I didn't know he was already dead." But what if he hadn't been dead when I'd found him? What if he was dead now because I'd done bad CPR? What if I hadn't cleared his throat properly? What if he could have been saved? Bile swam up my throat. I raced to the nearby toilet and made it just in time.

Someone gently pulled my hair back from my shoulders.

I fell sideways, half onto my butt on the cold bathroom tiles.

Jason knelt beside me and placed a gentle hand on my shoulder. Warmth seemed to flow through his broad palm. "Hey, you okay?"

"Yes," I said weakly.

"Because you're green," he said.

"I think it's the smell." Normally I adored the scent of chocolate. I'd even bought a cocoa-based perfume once. Now the smell clung to me like a nauseating miasma.

"Laurel, will you give us a minute?"

The detective's mouth twisted. She nodded and stepped from the bathroom.

"What happened?" He wrapped his hands around mine.

I ran him through everything. "I didn't mean to find a body again." I hiccupped. "What's wrong with me? Why does this keep happening? You don't think he was murdered, do you?"

Jason lifted me to my feet, his hand remaining on mine, firm and calming. It was all I could do not to lay my head on his chest. One of the best things about Jason was his even keel. He was a good man to have nearby in a crisis.

"It's too early to say, but I think it looks like an accident," he said. "He probably slipped, hit his head, and knocked over those vats on the way down."

I frowned. "But there are rubber mats beside them. They're non-slip."

"Maddie, we don't know what happened yet, and a good detective doesn't make assumptions. We don't have all the facts. In fact, we hardly have any facts."

But I wasn't a good detective. I wasn't a detective at

all. I was a paranormal museum owner, and I had a very bad feeling.

three

The next morning, I sat behind the glass counter in my museum. Fog pressed against the windows, sinking the museum in gloom. I unfolded the local paper. The death of the chocolate maker, Atticus Reine, was front-page news.

PROMINENT BUSINESS OWNER DEAD

Atticus Reine, co-owner of Reign Chocolate, was found dead in his San Benedetto shop yesterday. Investigators believe foul play may have been involved. Authorities say he suffered a head wound caused by an unknown trauma. The body was found, covered in chocolate, by a hysterical customer.

"The investigation is still in its preliminary stages," said San Benedetto Detective Laurel Hammer. "Detectives and the medical examiner's office are still looking into it. We're asking anyone with information to come forward."

Colleagues, family, and friends were shocked by the chocolate maker's death. Orson Malke described his business partner as "a brilliant chocolate maker and good friend. We're all devastated."

Atticus Reine and his partner were at the forefront of the bean-to-bar chocolate movement. Reign Chocolate roasts ethically sourced raw beans to create "two-ingredient" chocolate—cocoa and sugar. The company adds local organic ingredients to create simple and elegant confections.

The exact cause of Mr. Reine's death is still being investigated.

"I'll bet not everyone's devastated," I muttered to the bronze skull on the pedestal. I should have stopped to talk to that picketer.

The skull didn't reply.

But I had real sources, if I wanted information. Penny Beauvais might have some useful gossip about the murder. As president of the Wine and Visitors Bureau, she knew community members even remotely connected to wine. And Reign Chocolate had been an associate member of the Bureau.

GD, sprawled beside the tip jar on the counter, rolled onto his back and meowed.

"Nice try." I wasn't going to be fooled into a belly rub. The cat hated them and was looking for an excuse to sink his teeth into his favorite and only chew toy: me.

My cell phone rang, and I checked the screen. It was my mother.

"Hi, Mom."

"Madelyn, this is your mother."

"Yeah, I—" My mother would never understand caller ID. I rolled my eyes. "Hi."

"Has Shane spoken with you recently?"

"No. Why?" Shane was my overachieving brother who worked for the State Department. He lived a charmed life, getting sent to all the posh posts. I'd be jealous, but I was happy staying put in California.

"Oh, nothing. I was just wondering. Melanie's seeing someone new. An Italian count."

And that was my wunderkind sister, the opera singer. "And you wanted to know if Shane had a new girlfriend?"

"Is it wrong to be interested in your children's love lives?"

"Um. Yeah." Wrong in so many embarrassing and uncomfortable ways.

"Now, about that detective you're seeing ..."

The bell over the front door jingled.

"Sorry, Mom," I said hurriedly. "Customer. I've got to go."

"Make lots of money, dear! Bye!"

Relieved at the interruption, I pocketed the phone and looked up.

Harper, natty in a sleek caramel-colored jacket and suede pants, strolled into the museum. She looked around. "Slow day?"

"It's Thursday morning," I said by way of explanation, folding the newspaper.

She nodded toward it. "Tell me you weren't the hysterical customer who discovered the body."

"I was not hysterical." I grimaced. "Until Laurel arrived."

"Ohhhh. No." Harper's brown eyes widened. "She didn't arrest you, did she?"

"No, but I could tell she wanted to." Laurel and I had a long and tangled and public history. Needless to say, I was one hundred percent innocent. Mostly.

Harper braced one hip against the counter. "What did Jason say?"

"Not much. He can't really talk about cases." And I hadn't spoken with him since we were at Reign yesterday. I was trying not to be bothered by that. We had a date scheduled for tonight—a surprise he'd been dangling in front of me for weeks—so maybe he figured he'd fill me in then. Besides, even if the police did now think foul play was involved, I couldn't be a suspect, could I?

"I knew Atticus," Harper said quietly. "He and his wife were clients."

"I'm sorry. I had no idea."

"They were a fun couple."

I rotated a pen between my fingers. "I don't suppose he had any life insurance?" I asked, fishing.

She shot me a look. "You know I can't talk about that."

My cheeks burned. Of course she couldn't. That sort of thing was confidential.

"But they didn't have any children," she said neutrally.

I straightened. Harper wouldn't have taken them as clients if they had kids and didn't have life insurance. Her own parents had died when she was young, and they'd had nothing in place. Her grandmother had raised her. Money had been tight, and Harper had never forgotten the worry and hardship.

"There are other kinds of insurance I recommend," she continued, bland. "In business partnership arrangements, I like to recommend buy-sell insurance. That way, if one partner dies, the other partner gets an insurance payment to buy out the deceased partner's spouse."

"That sort of thing would make lots of sense for business owners like Atticus and Orson," I said.

"Mmm," she said, neither confirming nor denying. "Was it true he was covered in chocolate?"

"He was lying beside two chocolate vats. Not huge vats—probably five gallons. They'd tipped over."

"Melangers," she said.

"Huh?"

"They grind the cocoa beans into a liquid. It takes hours. Maybe days. I can't remember. I got a tour of the kitchen when Reign opened. But the melangers tip so the chocolate can be poured out for the next stage in the process."

A chill crawled up my spine. Jason had seemed to think that the melangers were accidentally knocked over. But if it was murder, had someone dumped the chocolate onto Atticus intentionally?

"Could his murder have been random?" Harper asked. "A robbery?"

"I don't know," I said slowly. "The cash register was closed. Nothing looked disturbed, aside from, you know." *The chocolate-covered body.* But a robbery in San Benedetto, especially one that ended in a murder, would be a very bad thing.

"If someone were to get this buy-sell insurance," I said, "how would it work?"

"Well, you would have to have a business partner."

"Which I don't. I'm just curious. For my future paranormal museum empire."

"Financial education is important," my friend agreed. "If one were to get buy-sell insurance, one would have to value each partner's share of the business. The insurance would cover the other partner's share."

"So, if you and I were partners, and our paranormal museum was valued at a million dollars—"

She raised a brow.

"A hundred thousand dollars," I amended.

Harper stared.

"It *could* be worth that someday." I flipped my ponytail over one shoulder. "I need to pick a number."

"If the museum was worth a million, and we were equal partners, I'd have insurance on you for half a million. You'd insure me for the same. Then, if I died, you'd get the half million, so you could buy the business from my hypothetical husband. That way, you wouldn't have to worry about my imaginary husband trying to tell you how to run the museum, and he'd get a quick payout."

It was easy cash. And it would give Orson a motive for murder. Atticus's wife, too, since she'd ultimately get the money when Orson bought her out. Of course, the victim's spouse was always the prime suspect.

"Who has an imaginary husband?" The bookcase creaked open and Adele clacked into the museum on three-inch heels.

"No one," Harper said quickly.

Adele flushed. "Maddie, I hate to ask, but did you get any idea what happened to our chocolate delivery? My father didn't get his either, and he's supposed to start wine and chocolate tastings at Plot 42 tomorrow."

I hung my head. "Sorry. The only people I talked to were the police."

She blew out her breath. "This is a disaster. No one's answering the phone at Reign. I've been promoting our chocolate as part of Wine and Chocolate Days. Everyone's asking about it, especially after the M-U-R-D-E-R."

"Who are you spelling it out for?" I asked, bemused. "Harper? I'm pretty sure she can read."

"Since kindergarten," Harper agreed.

"For the C-A-T." Adele placed her hands over GD's ears.

"GD isn't exactly sensitive to death. God knows how many mice he's massacred." The cat left them for me and only me on my chair. Leo never got a dead mouse surprise. I knew it was intentional.

"But killing mice is a cat's job," Adele said.

GD's green eyes gazed up at me, and I swear they

were filled with disappointment.

"The point is, customers have been understanding under the circumstances," Adele said. "But I feel like I've been engaged in false advertising."

"I know." I glanced toward the Gallery room at my right. It had everything for my *Magic of Chocolate* exhibit but the chocolate. "We may need to come up with an alternative plan."

Adele wrung her hands in her Fox and Fennel apron. "I suppose I can make some calls to other chocolate wholesalers."

"Look," I said, "Leo's going to work in the museum this afternoon. Why don't I swing by Reign again and see if they're open? Since no delivery man came by yesterday, I assume our chocolate is still at the shop." Besides, the museum got busy on Fridays and the weekends. If I didn't have premium-priced chocolate in the Gallery by tomorrow, I'd lose sales.

Adele smiled. "Thank you. I'm sure with everything that's happened, they're too busy to think about deliveries. Maybe you could just bring back the delivery yourself? It would take some pressure off them. And me."

"Sure. You know how I am," I said, marveling at her newfound Zen and waiting for the other stiletto to drop. "Always thinking of others." Plus, it was a great excuse to go back and snoop.

Harper narrowed her eyes at me.

"Now," Adele said, "about the wedding." She whipped a folded sheet of paper from her apron and spread it on the glass counter beside GD. "As you can see, we're here." She pointed to a spot on the timeline. "And we need to get all these things done before the big day."

GD sneezed and hopped from the counter. He ducked beneath the rocking chair. I thought he had the right idea.

Adele parceled out tasks, argued herself out of and then back into almond favors, and got our opinions on how to ensure people didn't give inappropriate toasts.

When she finally left through the bookcase, Harper gave a pained cry and fled the museum.

I sagged on my tall chair. Detail-oriented Adele was going to make sure her wedding was perfect, even if it killed us.

Shaking myself from my stupor, I grabbed the feather duster and walked into the Fortune Telling Room. This was my favorite part of the museum, filled with relics from America's nineteenth-century spiritualist movement. I stopped in front of a tall piece of wooden furniture that looked like a wardrobe but was a spirit cabinet. Turn-of-the-century mediums would sit locked inside to perform their ghostly conjurations as "proof" they weren't cheating. Since no one could see what they were doing inside the cabinet, this made it even easier for these early ghost whisperers to cheat.

I dusted the framed vintage Houdini poster beside the cabinet, then opened the doors.

A narrow, bespectacled man in a bow tie sat on the bench inside. "Hello."

I shrieked, leaping backward and dropping the feather duster. "Herb!" I willed my heart to slow. "What ... ? How did you get in there?" I'd been in the museum all morning, except for the few minutes when I'd slipped next door to sneak a blueberry scone from Adele. Had he been waiting here the whole time?

"I had to make sure the coast was clear," he whispered. His eyes bulged behind coke-bottle glasses.

"We're alone, aren't we?"

Grinding my teeth, I scooped up the feather duster. The paranormal collector had supplied most of the exhibits in my museum. He was also freakishly paranoid about police, a stance I couldn't understand since as far as I could tell, he was on the up and up. "The coast is clear," I said. "No police."

"It's not the cops I'm worried about." Herb leaned forward and peered from the cabinet. "It's the public."

"Why? Is an angry mob on your tail?" Because it wouldn't be the first time. I crossed my arms, the feather duster sticking out behind me like a misplaced tail.

"It's the molinillo. I heard you were the one who found that dead chocolate maker at Reign."

"Ye-es," I said, baffled. What did that have to do with the molinillo?

"Last December—"

I brandished the feather duster like a duelist. "Don't say it."

"We have to consider the possibility—"

"No, we don't."

"It may be cursed."

"I told you not to say that!" Last December, one of the supposedly-cursed objects in my museum had started a town-wide panic.

"It's a supernatural molinillo," he hissed. "For chocolate making. And now a chocolate maker is dead. Connect the dots."

"There are no dots. It's a coincidence. They do happen."

He adjusted his thick glasses. "In the world we work in, they don't," he said portentously.

We? Good God. I *was* in Herb's world now. "Right. Let's back this up. You told me the molinillo is haunted, not cursed, and it rattles when someone lies."

"Well, yes, that's what I told you."

My eyes narrowed. "What's that supposed to mean? Is there something you *didn't* tell me?"

"Well ... What I told you is what was told to me, but I wasn't able to verify it from the original source. You know how stories can get distorted. And since the original owner in Mexico died, people might think it's—"

"If you tell anyone it's cursed—" I stepped closer.

Feathers brushed Herb's nose and he reared backward, bonking his head on the rear of the wooden cabinet. "Ow! I won't! What do you take me for? But I do think it's worth taking extra precautions. Now, that shaman friend of mine, Xavier, is back in California. For seven hundred dollars, he can perform a binding spell—"

"Seven hundred?! It was five hundred last time." And that had been way overpriced. I'd only paid because ... long story.

"He *was* nearly killed."

"You can't blame me for that," I groused. "And *nearly killed* is an exaggeration."

"Be that as it may, he's got a right to be cautious."

"I will not hire Xavier for another exorcism." The last time I tried one, I'd turned it into a public event to get more publicity. It had gone badly. Understatement. "It's your duty to make sure your buyers have all the facts about the objects you sell and their haunted histories." Paranormal collectors had to have some code of ethics, didn't they? "If you really think it's cursed, I want to know why. I want details, Herb. Names. Dates. Contact numbers."

Herb's shoulders slumped. "Fine. I'll see what I can

dig up on the molinillo. But if you want Xavier, let me know. A binding ritual wouldn't be a bad precaution."

"No to the exorcist."

"Shaman."

"Whatever."

He shut the cabinet doors, barricading himself inside.

I blinked. Was Herb planning on apparating out of the spirit cabinet?

Leaving that mystery for another time, I returned to the main room, hoping for clients and a chocolate delivery.

Neither came.

four

Still trying to think positive, I drove through a caul of fog to Reign. I parked my pickup on the street beside a plum tree. Its spring flowers had made way for small, burgundy-colored leaves. They hugged the silvery bark, dripping with moisture.

I shrugged off my museum hoodie and scanned the brick sidewalk.

The picketer wasn't there today. An *Open* sign hung in the chocolate shop's lit window.

Not bothering to lock my vintage truck's door, I strolled inside the shop. The heady scent of chocolate flooded the silvery room.

My stomach twisted. Had chocolate-tainted CPR ruined my love of the bean? I clamped my lips shut and hurried to the vacant wooden counter. Angry voices—male and female—drifted from the kitchen and echoed off the dove-colored cinderblock walls.

"Hello?" I called.

The voices fell silent.

A tall, willowy woman with hair like honey strode through the kitchen's swinging door. She didn't wear an apron over her skinny jeans and matching ivory sweater. And she wasn't wearing a hair net either, so she couldn't be an employee. She braced her slim hand on the cash register. "Yes?" She smiled warmly. "How can I help you?"

"Hi, I'm from the Paranormal Museum."

"Oh?" Frowning, she adjusted a pyramid of chocolate bars wrapped in brown paper with purple crowns. They were displayed beside a piece of driftwood, and she snapped a picture of the arrangement with her phone. "Sorry. Atticus usually ..." She exhaled shakily. "I'm late with our social media promotion."

"Um, Adele Nakamoto from the Fox and Fennel and I put in a bulk order for chocolate," I continued. "It was supposed to arrive yesterday, but it never turned up ..." I trailed off.

A broad-shouldered man in his mid-thirties emerged from the kitchen. He wore a baseball hat over his wavy brown hair, and a beard net over his chin. "The museum? You're Maddie Kosloski, aren't you? The one who found Atticus."

The blonde behind the counter gasped.

The man hurried around the counter, wiped his palms over his brown apron, and stuck out his hand. His brandy-colored eyes moistened. "Orson, Orson Malke. I heard you did everything you could to save him. Thank you."

His hand engulfed mine, his grip firm but not crushing. He stood close enough for me to smell his piney aftershave, to see that his eyes were red-rimmed and watery.

"Anybody would have done it," I said. "I'm sorry I was too late."

"What did you ... ? What happened?" He released my hand. "The police didn't tell us much."

"I stopped by to see about our chocolate delivery," I said. "No one seemed to be here, so I began to walk back to the office. That's when I saw Atticus. He was in the kitchen, beside the melangers."

The woman's face paled. "How awful. We could tell

from the police tape where—" Her phone buzzed, and she glanced at the screen. "Where the police had blocked off the kitchen."

"I'd gone to the Wine and Visitors Bureau," Orson said. "They wanted some specially decorated chocolate squares. Normally Atticus dealt with promotional issues like that. But he was flooded with marketing work, what with the Wine and Chocolate Days. As you can imagine, they're a big deal for Reign."

"Orson is the real chocolate maker." The woman walked from behind the counter and brushed against him possessively. "Atticus was the marketing genius behind our success." She stuck out her free hand. "Lola Emerson-Malke."

"My wife and media star," he said, smiling fondly.

And another possible suspect. She could have killed Atticus for the insurance money just as easily as Orson. As Orson's wife, she would benefit too. But did they need the money?

"Not quite a star." Lola's mouth trembled. "Atticus was determined to make my husband and me known on social media. He said it's all about building an online community." She flipped her longish hair over her shoulders. "So, you're the woman who runs the Paranormal Museum. I've heard so much about it."

I was afraid to ask what. "I've been focused on marketing and social media myself. In fact, this month I'm promoting a *Magic of Chocolate* display in my Gallery." I waited a beat. When the couple didn't respond, I said, "But I'm missing the chocolate?"

Orson winced. "Right. Your order. Sorry about that. It's ready in the back. I'll get it for you now."

"Thanks," I said. "If you haven't delivered the order for Plot 42 yet, I can take that off your hands as well. I'm headed out that way."

"Thanks," he said. "You're a lifesaver." He strode behind the counter and disappeared into the kitchen.

"Plot 42?" Gaze drifting to her phone, Lola shifted her weight, her thumbs skimming across the keypad.

"The Nakamoto family vineyard," I said. "Adele Nakamoto mentioned that her parents hadn't received their delivery yet. They start wine and chocolate tastings tomorrow."

"And you're connected to them how?" Her arms dropped to her sides.

I scraped my hair back. Did she think I was trying to steal their chocolate? But coming so soon after Atticus's death, I couldn't fault her suspicion. "Literally. There's a secret passage between my museum and Adele's tearoom. We've been friends for years."

Her phone buzzed and she glanced at its screen. "Sorry, it's just—"

"It's okay," I said quickly.

The swinging door from the kitchen bumped open and Orson backed through. He rolled a dolly stacked with cardboard boxes. "Have you got a car?"

"A truck," I said. "It's out front."

"I'll help you load these." He followed me onto the sidewalk and hefted the boxes into my truck bed. "The boxes are labeled," he said. "A 42 for the winery, and the other is your joint order with the tearoom." His brow creased. "Did you and Adele decide how you were going to split them up? I didn't see any notations in our files, or I would have packed them in separate boxes."

"Yeah, don't worry about it. We went in on the order together. We've got it figured out." I shut the truck bed with a clang. "If Atticus was in charge of marketing, what was he doing in the kitchen yesterday?"

"I don't know. He was supposed to be manning the front counter while I was dealing with the Visitors Bureau. But there are all sorts of reasons he could have gone into the kitchen." Orson's face creased, and he blinked rapidly. "Atticus was ..." He cleared his throat and looked toward the kitchen.

Sympathy squeezed my chest. "I'm so sorry for your loss. Please let me know how I can help. I can't imagine what you're going through, losing a friend and partner and trying to keep a business going."

He looked down the wide street and adjusted his ball cap. A mail truck trundled past. "I don't know how I'm going to manage. I always did the chocolate-making myself, but I relied on Atticus for most everything else. He was a marketing genius. And now one of our counter workers, Sam, had left and was picketing outside."

"Left? What happened?"

Orson's face tightened. "Not everyone's cut out for this business," he said shortly.

"I could put the word out if you need counter help," I offered. "My colleague may have friends at the local community college who could do the job. And Ladies Aid is a surprisingly good source. Someone always has a grandkid or niece who's looking for work."

The chocolate maker smiled crookedly, but I couldn't forget the flash of anger I'd just seen. "Counter help would be great," he said. "If you find anyone, tell them to call me at Reign." He extracted a card from the pocket of his brown apron and handed it to me.

Eyes glued to her phone, his wife stepped from the shop. "Orson? Would you mind helping me with something?" Her voice sharpened. "If I'm going to take over Atticus's job—"

"I'll be right there." He waved to her. "And thanks

again, Maddie." He trotted into the store and the glass door closed slowly behind him.

I drove down Main and beneath the adobe arch that marked the exit from San Benedetto's downtown (such as it was). On the other side of the railroad tracks, the buildings turned industrial, and then I was in the vineyards. I whizzed past gnarled, bare vines sunk low in fog. Mustard flowers sprouted from the thick greenery between the rows.

My tires crunched on Plot 42's gravel drive. I parked between a picnic table and weeping willow. The door to the nearby barn/wine tasting room stood open, brown grapevines climbing the faded wood. Orange and yellow mums bloomed beside the brick path to the barn, spots of cheeriness in the fogbound gloom. A chalkboard sign leaned against the dull red wood. In elegant pink script, it proclaimed, *Yes, We're Open!*

I hefted a box labeled *42* from my truck bed and lugged it into the barn. A wall of barrels stacked in metal racks by the open door hid a storage area. Upright barrels formed makeshift tables at random intervals on the cement floor. A long, polished wooden bar ran along the right side of the room. Three thirty-something women leaned against the bar and sipped from fat wine goblets.

A fourth, behind the bar, glanced up and raised her chin. "Hi, can I help you?" Her smile was bleak. Two long brown braids dangled over her shoulders. She wore a blue denim shirt and rows and rows of tiny, multicolored beads around her neck.

I clunked the box onto the far end of the bar, away from the tasters. "Chocolate delivery for the Nakamotos."

She blinked, paled. "I should have picked up that delivery myself."

"Sorry. I hope I didn't cause a mix-up. Adele asked me to collect the chocolate for her parents, and I thought—"

The woman shook her head, her blond braids swinging. "No. It's not ... It's fine." She spun away, one hand gripping the edge of the bar, her knuckles whitening.

Mr. Nakamoto, slim and gray-haired, strolled into the barn and stopped short. "Maddie! What are you doing here?"

I glanced at the woman behind the counter. "Adele asked me to drop off your Reign chocolate."

His gaze tracked mine. "Uh, thanks. That will be fine. India, do you want to take a break?"

India's chin quivered, grief cracking her porcelain face. "No thanks. I'd rather keep working."

Had India known Atticus?

Mr. Nakamoto whisked behind the counter. Grabbing the box, he ducked, hiding it from view beneath the bar, and then he popped up.

I gestured with my thumb. "There's more in my truck."

"I'll get it." He strode outside, and I followed.

Peering into the bed of the vintage pickup, he said, "That's more than we ordered."

"Some of those are Adele's and mine. The ones labeled *42* are for the winery."

He stacked two boxes on top of each other. "India is—was—Atticus Reine's wife."

"Oh." Pity and guilt about the man I hadn't saved twined in my gut.

"She insisted on working today. Said it would keep her mind off things. I'm not sure it was a good idea, though."

"And then I brought in a box of chocolate from her husband's shop and reminded her of her loss." I wished one of the Malkes had mentioned that the widow worked here.

"It's not your fault. And she's tough. India will get through this."

"How long has she been working at the tasting room?" I asked.

"Three weeks. She said she needed to work or she'd go crazy, and she couldn't work with her husband because they'd kill each other." He winced. "She was joking."

"Of course," I said quickly.

He hefted the boxes and retreated into the barn.

Thoughtful, I shut the tailgate, which was slick with damp. The poor woman. India was too young to be a widow. Yet I couldn't help but wonder where she'd been when her husband had died. The newspaper article had said her husband was struck a blow to the head. With the proper implement, anyone could have used enough force. I hadn't noticed any bludgeoning instruments in the kitchen at Reign. But my attention had been elsewhere. Sickened, I swallowed, remembering.

India strode from the barn, her movements elegant and tense. Shielding her eyes from the watery sunlight, she beelined for me. "Maddie Kosloski?"

I walked to meet her beside the green-painted picnic table. "Yes?"

"You were the one who found Atticus. My husband."

"Yes." I glanced at my tennis shoes darkened by the thick, damp grass. "I'm very sorry for your loss."

She gulped. "Was anyone else there?"

"Anyone else?" Startled, I looked up. "No. I was surprised the shop was empty. Someone was picketing outside, though. A man named Sam, I think?"

Her expression darkened. "Sam Reynolds. It's because of him that my husband—" She snapped her jaw shut.

"Was working the counter that day?"

She nodded, blinking rapidly. "Sorry. I shouldn't ... He probably had nothing to do with it," she said unconvincingly. "But did you notice anything strange?"

A vision of the dead man flashed into my mind, and I felt myself blanch. There had been something almost contemptuous in the scene, the way the chocolate had been splashed across Atticus's face. "Two of the melangers had tipped, so chocolate was everywhere. But aside from that, no. I assumed the melangers tilted when your husband fell."

"Maybe." She gazed over her shoulder at an outbuilding covered in grapevines. "You tried to revive him, they said."

"I tried." And failed. I stared harder at my darkening shoes.

"Thank you for that. At least someone was there, someone tried ..." She blinked rapidly. "They're cruel, you know?"

"Who?"

"Everyone. The public. Reign was becoming known, thanks to Atticus. He and Orson had a name. And people thought that the success, the money, made us hard, impervious. People thought they could demand and push and criticize. But Atticus wasn't hard. He was a person, a good person, and he cared. He cared about so much."

I didn't know what to say, and so I said nothing.

"This wasn't random," she continued, her voice high

and thin. "Someone killed my husband, someone who knew him. This was personal. And the chocolate …" She gasped and raced into the barren vineyard.

I wavered, wondering if I should go after her.

She squatted, head hanging, between the rows of gnarled vines and dug her bare hands into the earth.

I looked at my own hands, then got in my truck and drove off into the fog.

five

Gray, fog-soaked twilight leaked through the Gallery windows. I stacked pyramids of Reign chocolate bars on the black-painted shelves, organized by nation of origin. The wrappers were a flat brown, the ink color of the crowns varying by country. A bag of Reign's chocolate-covered almonds slipped to the tile floor. I returned it to its shelf and adjusted another pyramid of chocolate-covered caramels in brown boxes. I didn't usually sell food; there was never a shortage of quirky art to fill the Gallery. But I was sure this would sell. Chocolate—even high-priced chocolate—was nigh irresistible.

Unfortunately, the thought of chocolate now made my stomach flip. I had to get over my squeamishness at some point, though. Right?

The bell over the front door jangled.

Half hopeful, half irritated by the interruption, I peered through the door to the main room. I had my date with Jason tonight, and a new customer would delay the closing time.

But it was my ex-boyfriend, Mason Hjelm, who ambled into the museum. Tall and muscular, with a mane of blond hair he kept in a ponytail, Mason wore his usual work uniform—jeans and a black Harley Davidson tee. He owned the motorcycle shop next door, so we couldn't avoid each other even if we wanted to. A small part of me wanted to. We'd ended things on good terms, but it was … complicated.

I straightened away from the boxes.

My ex said something to Leo, seated behind the counter. Leo angled his chin in my direction.

Mason strolled into the Gallery and jammed his hands in the front pockets of his jeans.

I fiddled with an arrangement of chocolate bars from Belize. "Hi, what's going on?"

He smiled, his Nordic eyes crinkling. "Why does something have to be going on?"

"It's a small town. Something's always going on."

He scanned the Gallery, the pedestal displays, the shelves filled with Reign chocolate. "What's all this?"

"For Wine and Chocolate days. It's our new *Magic of Chocolate* exhibit."

He quirked a blond brow.

"I *am* an associate member of the Wine and Visitors Bureau. I may as well take advantages of their promotions."

He peered at my haunted molinillo exhibit and quickly stepped away. "How's Adele?"

"In the throes of wedding planning," I said, curious. Usually Mason was better at getting to the point. And while he was always friendly, he also wasn't one for idle gossip.

"I suppose she's driving you and Harper crazy?"

"Driving herself crazy is more like it. Planning a wedding is a lot of work." Enough to make me consider eloping. I shifted my weight. "How's the bike shop?"

"Good." He looked out the square windows. A motorcycle roared past on the street outside. "Good."

"Well. That's good." I eyed him. "Was there something you wanted to tell me?"

His head snapped around. "What?"

"The reason you stopped by," I prompted.

He rubbed the back of his neck. "Oh. Right."

The bell over the front door jingled, and we both glanced toward the main room.

Jason, sexy in a blue business suit, walked into the museum. He looked around, spotted us, and strode into the Gallery. Touching my elbow, he kissed me on the cheek. "Hi, Maddie. Mason."

"Jason," he said.

I smothered a nervous laugh at the rhyme.

"Hi. What's going on?" Jason asked.

"Nothing," I said. "Mason just dropped by—"

"To see the new exhibit." My ex motioned toward the molinillo. His hip bumped the pedestal, and the molinillo rattled, rolling in its wooden bowl. "It looks great. I'll have to bring Belle by some day."

I frowned. "I thought she didn't like the paranormal."

Mason backed out of the Gallery. "It's chocolate. Who doesn't like chocolate?" Turning on his booted heel, he hurried from the museum.

Huh. That was weird.

Jason rubbed his hands together. "Are you ready?"

"For our date? Absolutely. Let me lock up." I shuffled Leo out the door, double checked GD's food and water supply, and turned out the lights.

We stepped onto the brick sidewalk, and Jason watched me lock and bolt the front door. Detectives are big on security, but I wasn't fussed about burglars. Everyone knew we live-streamed video of the museum at night. That way, people could watch for ghostly activity or just laugh at GD's antics. I swear, that cat understood what the webcams were for, because he spent hours preening in front of the cameras.

Jason checked his watch. "I think we have time to walk."

"Where are we going?"

He grimaced. "I wanted to leave the surprise for the last minute, but under the circumstances, you deserve a heads-up."

"A heads-up?" I asked, taking a step backward. "Are you taking me to the police station? This isn't another interrogation?"

He laughed shortly and looped his arm over my shoulders, pulling me close enough for me to feel his body heat mingling with my own. "That wouldn't be much of a date." Then he cocked his head as if considering the possibility of my arrest. Both of us knew it wasn't totally out of the question, not if his partner had anything to say about it. "Ah, anyway. We're going to Reign."

I stopped beside a plum tree. "The chocolate shop?" My heart skipped a beat. Jason and I had worked on paranormal research together before. Was he finally going to bring me into a real police investigation?

"Since you love chocolate so much, I booked us a chocolate-making class two months ago." He gave me an abashed look. "I figured they'd cancel the class, but it's still on. I hope your mother doesn't mind me taking you to a murder scene."

"Oh," I said, disappointed. Of course he wouldn't bring me into his policework. It was probably illegal. Certainly unethical. Teaming up had been a crazy idea. "What does my mother have to do with it? Has she been harassing you?"

His eyes glinted. "Come on. Your mother isn't the type."

"You don't know my mother," I muttered.

"I know you two are close, and that's all I meant. After what happened, I wouldn't blame you if you didn't want to go ahead with the class."

"No," I said quickly, taking his hand. "It was a great idea. I love chocolate." Good thing the molinillo wasn't nearby to rattle at the lie. I'd *loved* chocolate, past tense. Before I found Atticus's body.

Gently, Jason squeezed my shoulders, drawing me against him. My heart thumped faster. I hoped he couldn't feel it.

"Good," he said. "I admit, I'm looking forward to more time in that shop."

Ah ha! A joint investigation! "No leads?" I asked innocently.

"None I can discuss."

My heart shrank. Why did I keep coming back to us working together when I knew it could never happen? But if my boyfriend keeping his work and personal life separate was the only downside to our relationship, it was a downside I could live with. "I met India, Atticus's wife, today," I said casually. "She works at Plot 42."

"I know," he said. "She told me she grew up in the Midwest and likes being back in farm country."

"Oh? I read that her husband and Orson had lived in San Francisco."

"Yes, that's where India and Atticus met. And why were you reading up on Atticus and Orson?"

"For my chocolate research. Reign's my supplier for the Gallery." Okay, that was a weak excuse. I hurried on. "Did you know that cocoa was used in religious ceremonies as early as 2000 BC? The Aztecs used the seeds as currency. And Montezuma drank cups of chocolate as an aphrodisiac."

"I'm taking you to the Irish pub's next trivia night."

I was only good at country capitals and paranormal trivia. Ask me about the American spiritualist movement or the history of tarot cards and I could write a dissertation. "As long as you can handle the pop culture questions."

He pulled me closer and I burrowed into his warmth. "I've got you covered," he said. "So, what's new at the museum?"

"Aside from the chocolate exhibit? I'm researching starting a subscription box service. You know, like those boxes you can get every month with new dog toys and supplies? But paranormal!"

"A paranormal box?"

"I thought a good name for the subscription might be the Cryptic Crate? Every month, subscribers would get a new set of themed magical items, plus a quick email course or a pamphlet from the museum."

"Sounds like a lot of work."

"Weekdays are slow at the museum. I may as well spend the time writing pamphlets or creating email courses." Though preparing shipments was my least favorite part of the job. My neck tightened. But I had to do *something*. I needed a more consistent income stream. Adding the Gallery had brought in repeat clients, and I was now selling products in addition to tickets, but I could do better. I had to increase sales if I ever wanted to move out of my aunt's garage apartment.

We passed the darkened windows of a Taqueria.

"It's still weird to me to see closed restaurants at this time of night," Jason said.

"What do you mean?"

"In New York, you can get food at all hours." He glanced at me and smiled. "But there are other advantages to small-town life."

"Aw, shucks." I laughed. "You're making this small-town girl blush."

We paused in front of Reign's glass door. Its sign said *Closed* but light streamed from the windows, making trapezoids on the sidewalk.

Jason knocked.

A few moments later, Orson, in a brown apron, jeans, and a T-shirt, opened the door. "Come on in," he said, smiling beneath his beard.

We walked inside. Three other couples stood in nervous pairs beside shelves filled with chocolates. They all wore hair nets.

Orson locked the door behind us, and I flinched. Had he murdered his partner for the money?

"We're all here," Orson said, "so let's get started. You two will need hairnets." He pulled two from the pocket of his apron and handed them to us. "Good thing none of you have beards." He pointed to the white net covering his chin.

Orson led us into the kitchen. "Before we get started, I'd like to give you a brief tour of the factory and an explanation of how we make our chocolate. We won't actually have time tonight to make chocolate from the bean. But we will be pouring molds and making candy, combining Reign chocolate with locally sourced ingredients. That said, I think an understanding of the entire process is useful first." He motioned toward a glass-fronted room at the rear of the kitchen. "We'll start in here."

He opened the door to the room, its other three walls rich, dark wood. To the left, pallets stacked with burlap sacks of cocoa lined the floor. A rectangular metal table stood in the center of the room. Aside from dust, the only thing on the table was a plastic box with a large metal screen on its bottom. I guessed it was a sifter. Against the right wall stood metal racks filled with plastic bins labeled in what looked like code.

I found a spot at the base of the table, beside a garbage bin lined with dusty green plastic. The waste bin was empty except for a fast-food drink container, a straw poking from its lid. Even though garbage bins are for garbage, something about the discarded cup bugged me.

Orson set a tablet computer on the table and played a video of the cocoa harvesting process. He picked up the box sifter. "This is our storage and sorting room. We have to sort the cocoa beans by hand. During harvesting, all sorts of things get through—rocks, screws, bits of plastic, and cracked beans. If a bean is cracked, it will roast more quickly than the others in its batch, so those have to be discarded as well." He glanced toward the plastic garbage bin at the base of the table, beside Jason and me. "I like to sort late at night before going home. I can zone out then and relax."

He cleared his throat. "This room is temperature controlled, because the beans we get from overseas are raw. Once they've been sorted, we roast them." Orson opened the glass door and led us back into the kitchen, to a small orange machine with a funnel at the top. "This is where the real flavor comes in. We develop a roast profile for each batch, with a specific temperature and roasting time. We only use two ingredients in our chocolate—sugar and cocoa—so the roast profile is important."

A mousy woman raised her hand. "You sell chocolates with beans from different countries. Does it matter? Do the beans taste any different?"

He handed each of us a roasted bean to taste.

I cracked it open with my teeth. It was dry and bitter, leeching the moisture from my tongue.

Jason made a face. "The things I do for love."

Love? My heart stopped, then beat double-time. He'd said the word casually. He couldn't have meant it, because we'd only been together a few months. Was I even ready for that kind of commitment?

"Yes," Orson said. "They taste different depending on where they're from and what sort of season they've had. Cocoa beans are a lot like wine, with complex flavors varying on the terroir. That's the amount of rain, the weather, and the location."

He showed us three more machines—a cracker machine, a winnower, and a vibrating machine—and then stopped in front of the melangers. Melted chocolate swirled inside the metal vats, which were roughly the size of tall soup pots. He pointed to the line of red and white tape across the bottom of the floor beside the melangers. "There's expensive chocolate in these, so don't get too close." Orson explained how the melangers worked. "And then the vats tip." He glanced at me, and something seemed to flicker in his eyes. "So we can pour the chocolate out for the next stage, tempering."

Deep metal shelves above the melangers held giant bricks of chocolate in thick, clear plastic bags. "Are those what come out of the melangers?" I asked.

I was trying to sound like I wasn't panicking. Did Jason love me? I liked him. A *lot*. Chemistry? Oh, yeah. But the honeymoon period in a relationship wasn't to be trusted. After it ended, there were always complications.

"Yes," Orson said. "We pour the melted chocolate into this rough block form. Each brick weighs ten pounds, but it's still not finished. We've got three more steps to go."

Jason nudged me. "I know what you're thinking."

I sucked in my breath. "You do?"

"Ten pounds of chocolate. I'd bet you'd like one of

those in your kitchen."

"Heh heh. Yeah. That's what I was thinking." It was a good thing Jason wasn't a mind reader.

Orson finished the tour, then paired us up at long metal tables in the kitchen. Plastic trays lined with wax paper sat on the table in front of us. Along one side of the tray were plastic cups, with small rounds of filling, in two neat columns. A medium-sized bowl covered with a red plastic lid sat beside the tray on a folded towel.

"You can take the lids off," Orson said. "Each bowl contains over two pounds of tempered chocolate, and it will stay liquid as long as you stir it occasionally. Just don't stir in any hardened chocolate at the sides or bottom." He explained about tempering and couverture chocolate, but I only caught every eighth word.

I had to stay cool and stop obsessing over what Jason had said. He hadn't meant it. *Think about something else.*

The image of Atticus's body lying beside the melangers swam into view. My stomach went from butterflies to roiling snakes trying to crawl up my throat. How hot had the chocolate been when it splattered across Atticus? Had it burned him? Had he felt it?

"You okay?" Jason nudged me.

"Sorry." I swallowed my bile. "I guess I'm having a hard time concentrating."

"Orson said he'd give us a recipe handout after the class," Jason whispered. "So you can relax and ponder the murder."

"I was just thinking of ..." I glanced toward the melangers. "I hope he didn't suffer," I said in a low voice.

Jason pulled me close, and I relaxed against his broad chest. "He didn't," he murmured into my hairnet. "It's okay."

But it wasn't. I couldn't get Atticus out of my head.

His partner led us through techniques for dipping the fillings, demonstrating with his own bowl. "Of course, we don't sell nougats and creams," Orson said. "But I wanted you to get a sense of things you could do with our melted chocolate at home." He distributed plastic squeeze bottles filled with chocolate. Soon, we were squirting dollar-sized pools of chocolate onto the wax paper. We dotted the chocolate with organic almonds and dried fruit. My chocolate coins came out lopsided, but Jason managed perfect circles.

"I think my chocolate is defective," I muttered.

"It came out of the same bowl as mine," Jason said.

"I'm talking about the squeeze bottles. Why are your coins perfect?" Actually, all of his chocolates were perfect, while mine had dribs and drabs of chocolate oozing from their bottoms.

"Maybe I'm just that good." His eyes glinted suggestively.

Orson circled around the table toward us.

"Oh, look," I said. "Orson's coming."

Jason turned toward him, and I swapped our trays behind his back.

"How's it going?" Orson asked.

"Great," Jason said. "But Maddie's having a little trouble with …" He turned toward me and glanced down at the trays.

"With what?" Orson asked. "Your chocolates look perfect, Maddie."

"Nothing," I said innocently.

"I've been meaning to stop by your gallery to see your Magic of Chocolate exhibit," the chocolate maker said.

"You should," I said. "We've got a haunted molinillo."

"How is it haunted?" Orson asked.

"I'm still researching that." Or at least, I hoped Herb was. "Where's the ladies' room?"

"Down the hall and on your right," Orson said, moving on to the next couple.

"You know," Jason said, "I *am* a detective. I do notice things like swapped trays."

"Who's *just that good* now?" Grinning, I peeled off my gloves and hustled past the glass-doored storage room and down the hall.

The door to the office yawned open.

I shivered, a chill prickling my spine, and slowed to a halt. Something tugged gently at my gut, drawing me closer to the open door. If I believed in ghosts—and I was halfway there—I'd almost think the spirit of Atticus was urging me on.

My fists clenched. Who was I kidding? It wasn't Atticus calling me into that office; it was my own need to set things right. And there were detectives for that. An excellent one was waiting for me to return to the class.

I glanced over my shoulder. The class was out of sight behind the kitchen's tall rolling racks. And that meant *I* was hidden from view.

To snoop, or not to snoop? That was the question.

I shouldn't.

But there were a lot of things I shouldn't have done, and that had never stopped me before. I thought of Atticus, sprawled on the floor and dripping chocolate. My eyes briefly closed. I slipped inside the office.

The room was spartan. Plastic bins and cardboard file boxes teetered atop metal bookcases. Two simple metal desks faced each other across the linoleum floor. Nameplates proclaimed their owners—Orson Malke and Atticus Reine. A third desk sat wedged into a corner.

I sidled to Atticus's desk and tugged on the top drawer.

Locked. As were all the others.

Rats.

I glanced at the third desk. It also had a nameplate: *Tilde Otterstrom, Accountant.*

Footsteps sounded in the corridor outside. Orson's voice echoed in the hall. "I think I've got one in my office."

My heart seized. There was no way he'd believe I'd gotten lost on the way to the bathroom. I turned right, then left, searching for a place to hide. I grasped the rolling chair, thinking to hide beneath the desk.

"Hey, Orson?" Jason asked. "Have you got a minute?"

"Sure. Is this about Atticus?"

Crap, crap, crap! I edged toward the door and peeked out. Orson's back was to me. Jason's was not, and he was studiously not looking my way. But I knew he knew exactly where I was.

Smothering a curse, I slipped behind Orson and into the hallway. I backed away, into the bathroom.

I washed my hands. They'd somehow become smeared with chocolate in spite of the gloves I'd worn. I adjusted my hairnet (not a flattering look), and walked into the hall.

Jason lounged beside the bathroom door. "I can't take you anywhere," he muttered.

"How did you know I was in the office?"

"The chocolate handprint on the door."

Horrified, I swayed to a halt. I'd left prints?

"Don't worry. They're too smeared for analysis. At least tell me you found a clue that'll break open the case."

"Uh. No."

He smothered a laugh. "Next time, exercise a little restraint, okay? Or at least keep your gloves on."

My gloves had been more chocolate-covered than my hands. I sighed. What had I learned, after all? That Reign had an in-house accountant named Tilde. Which was kind of interesting. I'd have thought a business this size would use a contractor for their accounting. Or maybe Reign was a bigger enterprise than I'd imagined?

"I'm sorry," I whispered, blood pounding in my temples.

"Sorry you did it? Or sorry you got caught?"

Sorry I hadn't found anything. But I forced a smile and kept that to myself.

six

Leo strolled through the museum's front entrance and the doorbell danced on its hook. Textbook under one arm, he stopped in front of the glass counter. His black hair flopped into his eyes. "Am I late?"

"Nope." It was ten in the morning on Friday, and business wouldn't pick up until after lunch. Our sole customers, a middle-aged couple, moved about the Fortune Telling room and exclaimed over the antiques.

"If I gave you the evil eye, it's because I'm antsy," I said. "I need to go to Reign before things get busy." Last night's investigation at the chocolate shop had been a massive fail. My snooping hadn't ruined my evening with Jason, but I was still smarting over getting caught so easily. Master detectives don't leave chocolate fingerprints. Orson would have to notice them eventually. Would he tie them to me? My stomach burned at the thought. "Can you take over? I shouldn't be gone more than thirty minutes."

GD meowed and hopped onto the counter. The ebony cat brushed against the tip jar.

Leo ruffled GD's fur. "No problem. I can handle things here."

I glanced outside. Fog pressed against the windows, coating them in a damp sheen. "Thanks." I slid off the tall chair and grabbed my thick, sand-colored vest off the wall peg by the bookshelf. Shrugging it over my Paranormal Museum hoodie, I bustled onto the brick sidewalk.

The end of the block was obscured by gray fog. I jammed my hands into my vest pockets. The wind shifted, blowing the scent of the dairy pastures into town, turning the fog acrid.

Wrinkling my nose, I strode down the walk, triple checking at corners so I wasn't surprised by a car hidden by the mist. If Orson had figured out what I was up to last night, I was in for an unpleasant welcome at Reign Chocolate. But finding Atticus's body seemed a sign— was I now believing in signs?—that I was meant to be involved in solving his murder. I knew how arrogant that sounded, and I didn't expect to *solve* it solve it. But if I could learn something that would help the police, it would be worth it.

The street seemed strangely lonely for late on Friday morning. Maybe it was the fog or my imagination that set my nerves jangling, but I caught myself shrinking in my jacket and vest, my shoulders hunching.

I passed a well-lit cafe. People lined the long table at the window, their heads bent to computers and phones, isolated even in company.

I shivered and hurried on. Reign was an easy walk, and I needed the exercise. Now that I was over chocolate, maybe I could finally lose those last ten pounds. It had been distressingly easy not to sample the chocolates we'd made last night.

A single set of footsteps echoed behind me.

I glanced over my shoulder. An iron streetlamp pierced the fog.

Tugging my hood over my head, I lengthened my strides. A gust of wind twisted a length of mist into a wraith. It coiled, tentacles of fog flinging outward, reaching for me.

Instinctively, I sheared away. The fog wraith dissipated, and I laughed at myself. But the soft sound came out broken, uneasy.

Behind me, footsteps slapped wetly, like something out of a Lovecraft story.

I needed to stop reading those.

Visions of eldritch gods and tentacular horrors tickled my mind. I swallowed, my heart speeding. *Ridiculous*. It was only a shopper. There was no one better at freaking myself out over nothing than me.

I stopped and turned, waiting for the other pedestrian. I'd prove to myself I was being paranoid.

The footsteps halted.

I widened my eyes, straining to penetrate the fog.

A gust of fog billowed toward me. It curled in on itself, folding at the top as its bottom fringe flowed outward, grasping.

I stood my ground and cocked my head, listening. The damp morning had turned still and silent. For a moment I imagined the town had vanished and I was alone. Then a car rolled past, a gray, indistinct shape, and the spell broke.

"Forget this," I muttered. Mouth dry, I turned and ran.

Now all I could hear were my own footsteps, the pounding of my heart in my ears. Exercise, I needed the exercise. It wasn't as if I was afraid of a footstep. I dodged a mailbox. A van rolled past, a dark rectangle in the fog.

Running is good for you, especially when—

I glanced over my shoulder and collided with something solid.

"Hey!"

"Ooof!" I staggered sideways and pinballed off a cinderblock wall.

"Watch it!" The picketer, Sam, waved his placard at me: *UNFAIR!*

"Sorry." I brushed myself off, hoping the dim light hid the flush I felt rising to my cheeks. "Sorry. I thought someone was … I should have been looking where I was going."

We stared at each other for a full five seconds.

"Weren't you the one who found the body?" he asked.

"Yeah." If someone had been following me, were they waiting to get me alone? "Um, weren't you outside at the time?" Had Sam seen anything? He obviously fit into the disgruntled employee category. But had he been angry enough to kill? I edged away from the man and told myself not to be so paranoid. We were in public, and just because he might have motive didn't make him a killer.

"Right," he said. "*Outside.*"

"Must have been weird," I said, scanning the foggy street and seeing more fog. "You finding out your boss was dead inside Reign the whole time you were out here."

"Yeah. I had no idea. Didn't see a thing."

"How long were you here that day?" I asked and cocked my head, listening. Were those footsteps?

"Since ten that morning."

I stared past him, into the fog. "And no one went in and out the whole time? Not even any customers?"

"Sure, there were customers. I could see them through the window. Atticus was working the counter."

"Do you have any idea when you stopped seeing him

behind the counter?"

Sam shrugged. "A woman went in before you. She waited at the counter five minutes and left in a huff." He glared. "I remembered her because she crossed the picket line. Like you."

I shuffled my feet. "In fairness, it's not really a line. I mean, you need more than one person …"

His nostrils whitened.

"Look," I said, "I had to go inside. I mean, I had an order."

"So?" He brandished the sign. Its wooden handle had a pointy end, ideal for staking vampires or nosy paranormal museum owners. "I had a job, and Orson fired me for no reason!"

"Orson did? Not Atticus?" So much for the picketer's motive to kill Atticus. And since we were alone on the sidewalk, I'd call that a good thing.

His face darkened and he stepped closer. "What did Atticus know about anything? He was just the marketing guy, flitting around with magazine photographers and acting like a hotshot. And he didn't do a damn thing about it when I was fired, even though he knew it was unfair."

Or maybe Sam had a motive after all. I edged away. "Why were you fired?"

"I'm telling you, there was no reason. I came to work on time. I even came to work early, I asked for more responsibility. And because of it, I got fired."

"That's strange. You'd think an employer would want someone like you, someone ambitious."

"Orson said he wanted someone happy with where they were at. Can you believe it?"

What would I do if Leo wanted to be manager? Because there just wasn't a whole lot of growth potential in a paranormal museum. "Maybe he just didn't have a position for you and thought it would be better to let you go now rather than wait for you to quit." It wasn't fair, but I could see the rationale. Still, I'd never do that to Leo. He was like a little brother to me. Leo was also a lot less annoying than my real brother.

"You know, even if I did see who killed Atticus, I wouldn't tell the cops." Sam thrust his sign toward the chocolate shop's glowing windows. "He was weak, and he deserved what he got. If he'd had any guts, he would have stood up for what was right. But no, he did everything Orson said like a little puppy dog. If Orson said I had to go, I was going, even if it was wrong."

"I'm sorry to hear things went down like that," I said tightly. I'd never been a fan of victim blaming. "Did you see Atticus go into the kitchen with anyone that morning?"

"Hey." Sam pointed the sign at me. "Why do you care?"

"I guess because I was the one who found him." I shifted my weight and backed toward the door.

"Wait, are you actually going in there? After everything I told you?"

"Um. Yeah. I need an invoice—"

"But they're crooks!"

I halted. "Crooks?" Was something underhanded happening at Reign?

"They fired me for no reason!"

"Oh." That made them jerks, not crooks. And I suspected there was more to the firing than Sam was saying. "You know what? I'm going to ask them about that."

"You don't need to ask them. I told you what happened."

How was I going to get out of this? "Right. Um … thanks." I turned and darted into the chocolate shop, the bell jingling in my wake. The scent of chocolate coiled, ghostlike, around me.

Orson stood behind the counter in a brown Reign T-shirt, apron, and baseball cap. His net was gone, exposing his thick brown beard. Bleary-eyed, he straightened off the cash register. "Maddie? Here for more chocolate already?"

"Here about that counter position. I talked to my mother last night. She's the president of Ladies Aid. You can expect some phone calls from people looking for work." I glanced through the front window at Sam, pacing the sidewalk and shouting.

Orson sighed. "Did he bother you?"

"No." I hesitated. "He told me you fired him for no reason."

The man bristled. "I fired him because he's aggressive and abrasive, and that's not the kind of counter help we want."

"No," I said, "I guess you wouldn't. Hey, is your accountant in? My invoice was smeared to the point of being unreadable," I lied. My fingers curled. "And since Adele and I are splitting the bill, we both need something for our files. Could I get another copy?"

"Yeah. Tilde's here. I'll—"

A young woman walked into the shop, purse over her arm. She wandered to a display of chocolate bars.

Orson tracked her movements with his gaze.

"If she's in the office, I know where it is," I suggested.

His narrow face creased with relief. "That would be great. Thanks. Just stay out of the kitchen." He pointed to his head. "No net."

I nodded, relieved he hadn't seemed to have

connected me to the chocolate handprint. "Right." I walked around the counter and down the long hallway, past the open kitchen to the office.

The door was closed, the frame free of any handprints, chocolate or otherwise. So someone had seen mine and cleaned it off. Wincing, I knocked.

"Yes?" a woman called out, her voice dull.

I opened the door and leaned in. "Hi, I'm Maddie Kosloski from the Paranormal Museum. Orson told me I could find you here."

The woman looked up from her desk in the corner. She was thirty-something and slender, her brown hair knotted into an elegant bun. She tugged at a wisp of hair dangling beside her earlobe and rose from her chair. Its wheels squeaked against the linoleum floor. She adjusted her blouse, tucked inside her navy pencil skirt. A matching blazer lay slung over the back of her chair.

We clasped hands. I smothered a wince as my bones ground together. She released me.

I let my arm fall to my side, my hand flexing.

"I'm Tilde." She sniffed. Her nose was red, her face blotchy as if she'd been crying. "How can I help you?"

"It's a small thing, really, but since I was so close ... Could I get another copy of our invoice? Somehow, by the time the chocolate reached me, the invoice had gotten smeared, and my accountant can't read the numbers on it." Since I was my own accountant, it was a double lie. I stuffed my hands into my vest pockets.

"That's no problem." She returned behind her desk, the red soles of her pumps flashing, and peered at the computer. "You said you were from the Paranormal Museum?"

"Yes. Though the invoice may be under the Fox and

Fennel. Adele and I went in together on the order."

"To take advantage of the bulk discount, yes. I've got it." She tapped some keys and the printer beside her desk hummed.

"So you're the Reign accountant," I said, louder than I'd intended. There was something familiar about the woman, but what?

"Mmm-hmm."

"I didn't think a business this size would have its own in-house accountant. Does Reign have other shops in California?"

"Not yet," she said. "I'm only part-time with Reign, but they let me use their office."

"Oh?"

"Nepotism." Gracefully, she rose and whisked a sheet of paper from the printer. "My cousin is married—*was* married—to Atticus." The skin bunched around her eyes in a pained expression.

"You're India's cousin?" That explained the sense of familiarity. They had the same heart-shaped face, the same porcelain skin, the same light-brown eyes. She even walked like India, though her movements held a certain coiled tension. "You must have been close to Atticus. I'm so sorry for your loss."

"Thanks." She handed me the warm invoice. "But we never were that kind of family."

"At least you get to work together."

A muscle pulsed in her jaw. "I moved to California recently and thought I'd set up my own practice rather than working for someone else. Atticus thought it best if they didn't do their own bookkeeping. He was marketing. Orson is chocolate making. Neither are— *were*—big on the numbers side."

Neither was I, but I couldn't afford a bookkeeper, not

even part-time. I lived for the day I could offload that chore. Payroll tax forms were the worst. "Have you got a card? I'm not looking for someone now, but I hope to hire a, er, new accountant in the future."

She plucked one off her desk and handed it to me.

"Tilde Otterstrom," I read. "Very Swedish."

"I'm from Kansas. What can I say?"

The door banged open and we both jumped.

Lola, elegant in camel slacks, walnut cable-knit sweater, and matching plaid shawl strode into the room. She stopped short on her four-inch stilettos without even a hint of a wobble, glanced up from her phone's screen, and smiled. "Oh, hello, Maddie. I didn't expect to see you here. Is everything all right?"

"She needed a fresh invoice," Tilde said.

"Mine got smeared," I said.

"Ah." Lola scanned me from my tennis shoes to my hoodie hair, and I suddenly felt underdressed. "I guess a new invoice is the least we can do after what you went through finding Atticus's body."

Tilde's shoulders jerked. "You were the one? Did you see anyone?"

My stomach knotted with suspicion. Funny how everyone was interested in what I'd seen. I grimaced at my rampant paranoia. Tilde's curiosity was natural. The newspapers had printed that Atticus's death had been the result of foul play.

I hesitated, unsure if I should discuss the case. But I wasn't a cop, and I hadn't seen anything but the murdered man. "No. I didn't see anyone." But I'd heard that closing door. Had it been the killer?

"It's strange, though," Lola mused.

"Someone killing Atticus is more than strange," Tilde said sharply. "It's horrible."

"Not that," Lola said, fixing me with her gaze. "That's awful. It's just that before his death, I never saw you in Reign, and now you seem to be here all the time. I heard you attended one of Orson's classes last night."

"Nothing strange about it." I tugged down the hem of my vest. "My, um, friend had ordered tickets weeks ago. And I keep coming back here because of my order."

Lola bowed her head. "Sorry. I guess I'm getting paranoid. With everything that's happened, and everything we need to do now Atticus is gone ..." She fiddled with the brown-and-white plaid shawl over her shoulders, not meeting my gaze, then turned to the accountant. "Are last month's financials done yet?"

Tilde stiffened. "Yes. I gave them to Orson last week."

"You know how my husband is." Lola's smile was wintery. "Can you forward them to my email?"

"Of course," Tilde said.

"Atticus scheduled an interview tomorrow with *Feast California*," Lola said. "I want to make sure I can quote some strong numbers, in case they ask."

"So, they'll be asking about Reign?" Tilde arched a brow.

"What else would they be interviewing me about?" Lola said sharply. "It's a food magazine." Her scarf slipped off one of her shoulders.

Tilde sniffed. "It just seems that most of your interviews are about ... you."

Meow. That seemed a little catty—and bold toward the boss's wife. But maybe as Atticus's cousin-in-law, Tilde felt she could get away with it. Uncomfortable, I shifted my weight.

Lola flushed. "I can't help it if *California Dwellings* was more interested in my home than the chocolate shop. Atticus said it was still publicity for Reign." She turned to me. "It's part of brand building. Atticus believed that we—the people involved in Reign—were the brand, so we have to publicize ourselves and not just the business. It's not something I'm entirely comfortable with, but I'm sure you understand. You're a business owner. You're part of your brand too."

Good Lord, I hoped not. What did that say about the museum's brand? Out of shape? Cheap date? Boring?

"People do business with people," the accountant said as if parroting someone else. She made a face. "Not with businesses."

"That's what Atticus always said." Lola tossed the errant edge of her scarf over her shoulder. The phone in her hand pinged. She looked down and tapped something onto the screen. "I don't know how I can keep up with this social media schedule. Was there anything else we can help you with, Maddie?"

"Um, no. Thanks, Tilde. Nice seeing you, Lola." I backed out of the office and walked through the store and onto the sidewalk outside.

The picketer scowled at me.

I hurried down the street and into the mist.

seven

Pleasantly exhausted from a busy Friday, I swept the museum. The broom shushed across the checkerboard tiles. The rocking chair creaked beneath GD's weight. The cat snuggled into a tighter ball, his head crooking toward the ceiling.

I leaned against the counter and surveyed my realm. As much as I loved a busy and profitable museum, after closing was one of my favorite times, when it was just me and the exhibits.

Something brushed against my leg, and I jumped.

Purring, GD wound around the ankles of my jeans.

"Very funny," I said. "You got me good." How'd he get from the chair to me so quickly?

The phone rang in my hoodie pocket, and I checked the number. Jason.

Grinning like a fool, I answered. "Hi."

"What's going on?"

"I'm closing the museum. You?"

"Just thinking of you."

"Tonight's girls' night, but if you just happened to stop by the microbrewery—"

"I can't. I'm at an accident on Zinfandel Road. A motorcycle and a truck full of artichokes."

My heart stopped. "Leo's—"

"Not involved. Neither is Mason."

My face warmed. Of course it couldn't have been Leo.

He'd only just left and couldn't have gotten as far as Zinfandel Road. "Is anyone badly hurt?"

"Yes. Drive carefully tonight. And avoid Zinfandel Road. I've got to go. I'll talk to you tomorrow."

We said hurried goodbyes and I hung up, saying a silent prayer for the motorcyclist. And then I wondered why a roadside disaster had made Jason think of me.

GD at my heels, I turned off the lights in the Gallery and Fortune Telling rooms, then grabbed the zippered cash envelope off the counter. San Benedetto was a low-crime town, but I always got a little nervous carrying cash to the bank. I wished Leo was with me.

I turned to the bookcase door to leave.

GD sprawled in front of the hidden door. He yawned, showing off his needlelike teeth.

"Really? You're resting right there, right now?"

He rolled onto his back and pawed at the air.

"Come on. Scoot." I reached down and nudged him away.

Quick as a wink, he whipped around and bit my hand.

"GD!" I rubbed my palm. The cat hadn't broken skin. He never did. And he never bit customers—only me, the hand that fed him.

He meowed and raised himself on his hind legs, his forelegs pawing their way up my jeans.

Some cats climb all over people. GD was not one of those cats.

"What's wrong with you?" Scowling, I pressed the special book spine. The bookcase snicked open, revealing Adele's darkened tearoom and our shared hallway that led to the alley.

GD howled, an unearthly wail that prickled my scalp.

I shut the bookcase and double checked his food and water bowls. Both were full. "I don't get it. What's the problem?"

He hissed, and I half-turned.

In front of the bookcase, GD had gone full Halloween cat: back arched, fur standing on end.

Pulse beating erratically, I looked over my shoulder.

No apparition floated behind me.

"If it's a ghost that's sending you into a tailspin …" I paused to enjoy my own pun. Cat. Tailspin. Heh heh. "Anyway, tell him or her to go to the light. Now I have to drive to the bank." I strode to the bookcase and gently shoved the cat aside with my foot.

He bit my ankle.

"Ow!" Hopping on one foot, I pushed open the bookcase and slipped into the tearoom, gloomy in the darkness. I shut the door in front of GD, his fur bristling.

In the dark, it was impossible to see if the cat had broken my skin. I hurried down the tearoom's long hallway and pushed open the heavy alley door.

My pickup waited in the fog-shrouded alley. A light slanted from above, illuminating the beads of moisture on the vintage truck's windows. I glanced at the lit windows above the motorcycle shop next door.

Mason's apartment.

Memories arose, unbidden, of the time I'd spent with him there. Guiltily I shoved them aside. I was over Mason and happy with Jason. But Mason and I had had good times. It had been that darn post-honeymoon phase that had done us in. I lifted the hem of my jeans and examined my unblemished ankle.

That, and—

A car's headlights flicked on at the end of the alley. The car rolled slowly toward me, waiting for me to cross to my truck.

Releasing my hem, I waved to the car and

maneuvered around a garbage bin. I strode toward my red pickup.

The car's engine roared.

I stared, disbelieving.

The car bulleted toward me.

I gasped and dropped the cash bag. Leapt forward, one foot landing on top of my driver's-side tire. I launched myself flat onto the hood of the pickup.

A crash.

The truck lurched.

I slid sideways, halfway down the hood. I clawed frantically at the slick metal.

A screech. A bang.

Another earsplitting crash, and the car's taillights disappeared around the corner.

I half rolled, half fell off the hood and sat, panting, on the damp pavement. *Damn. Damn, damn, damn.* I rubbed my hip. It hurt. A lot.

Something metallic rattled.

A window scraped open above me. Mason leaned out, his blond hair shaggy and unbound. "What the ... Maddie? You okay?"

"I'm fine," I croaked.

But he'd closed the window before I could finish.

Grasping the cold front bumper, I levered myself to standing and retrieved the cash bag. I swayed, adrenaline clotting my system. How had the driver not seen me? I rubbed my palms, grimy and damp, on the thighs of my jeans.

A door slammed open and Mason jogged into the alley. "Maddie! What happened?"

"Someone was driving too fast," I stammered. But I'd *thought* they'd seen me. I'd assumed the person was driving slowly to let me cross to my pickup. I'd even waved to the driver. Had the person not noticed? Or had the near miss been something more sinister?

I studied my pickup. A brownish streak scuffed its side. At least old trucks are sturdy, especially versus lightweight modern cars with plastic bumpers and fiberglass sides.

Mason swore. "The guy had to know he hit your pickup." His brows slashed downward. "I saw the car. A 2016 Ford Mustang, copper colored."

"You know the year?" I laughed shakily. "Whoever it was, they picked the wrong alley for a hit-and-run."

"I couldn't read the plate," he said darkly. "But maybe Slate can help you track the guy down."

"Did you see the driver?"

"No. Too dark. Oh." He stooped and picked my rear fender off the ground. "That's gotta hurt."

I groaned. "I thought I'd gotten off easy." I'd inherited the pickup from my dad, and the sight of the vintage bumper in Mason's hands wrenched my gut.

"Looks like the dumpster didn't escape this idiot either." He examined a long scrape along its green side. "This guy was out of control. Probably drunk."

"Probably," I said faintly.

"I can put your bumper back on, if you want."

That would save me time. Mason rebuilt bikes, but he'd helped me out with my old truck before. And since we were romantically over each other, the favor wouldn't be awkward. Nope, not at all. "Um, thanks. That would be great."

"Want me to keep the bumper for now?"

"I guess so. I can't do much with it."

"All right." He braced the bumper against one brawny shoulder.

"Mason?" His girlfriend Belle leaned out the window

above us, her long hair dangling.

"I'll be up in a sec," he shouted to her. He met my gaze. "Well. I'd better ..."

"Yeah." I backed to the pickup. "Me too. I've got to drop off this deposit."

He hiked up the concrete steps to his apartment.

I drove to the bank and dropped the cash bag in the night deposit bin. In the bank's parking lot, I studied my phone. Jason would want to know about the hit-and-run, but it wasn't an emergency. I hadn't been hurt, and the driver was long gone. And Jason was probably still at the accident scene, dealing with real trauma. Biting my lip, I settled for sending him a text, asking him to call when he could.

I checked my appearance in the side-view mirror. My hair stuck out from my ponytail in predictable places. I smoothed it behind my ear, grabbed my purse, and strolled across the street to the Bell and Brew.

Pausing beside the hostess stand, I scanned the restaurant: the wooden tables, the red-leather booths. Light glinted off the microbrewery's metal-tiled ceiling.

Harper signaled to me from a booth opposite a pair of giant copper beer vats. Adele sat in the seat across from her.

I waved and hurried over. Ducking beneath a stained-glass lamp, I slid into their booth.

Adele glanced up, then returned to frowning over another wedding to-do list.

Harper eyed me. "What happened? Did your mother find out you were investigating? Because you look like you're on the run."

"No. What ... ?" I looked down. My hoodie was askew, the hood wrapped around my neck. I hadn't noticed that detail in the car mirror. Even without the hoodie issue, I looked underdressed compared to Harper in her chocolate-colored turtleneck, and Adele in a sea-green silk blouse. "Someone nearly ran me down in the alley behind the museum," I said. "I had to jump on top of my truck."

"People can be so inconsiderate." Adele thumbed through a sheaf of papers and didn't look up.

"Are you all right?" Harper asked me.

"Fine," I said. "The car scraped my pickup, took off the bumper, hit a garbage bin, and drove off."

"Unbelievable," Adele muttered.

"Mason got the make and model—"

"Mason?" Harper asked.

"He was upstairs and saw it happen from his rear window."

"Is this an Alfred Hitchcock film?" Harper asked, arch. "Why's he ogling you through his rear window?"

"Um, I don't—That's not the point. Someone nearly killed me."

"It's highway robbery!" Adele glared.

"No," I said. "It was only a hit-and-run. My cash bag wasn't stolen."

"What are you talking about?" Adele thrust a paper menu into my hands. "Put the word 'wedding' in front of the word 'party' and the prices triple!"

Harper rolled her eyes.

"I'm talking about my near-death by Ford Mustang." Jaw tight, I explained again about the hit-and-run. "The more I think about it, the more I think the driver had to have seen me. It was like he accelerated intentionally," I concluded.

"He?" Harper asked.

"Or she. I couldn't see past the headlights."

"Why would someone intentionally target you?"

Adele asked.

"Because ..." I fumbled. What *had* I done to put myself in the crosshairs? "Well, there's the murder at Reign. I was the one who found Atticus."

"So?" Harper said. "You didn't see the killer, did you? And you already told everything you know to the police. Even if the killer knew you were the one who found the body, why come after you?"

Good question. Maybe the hit-and-run *had* just been a case of bad driving. A reckless, panicked teenager? I'd already imagined being followed by a phantom in the mist. Maybe my imagination was getting the better of me again?

My legs shifted, restless.

Or maybe it wasn't.

eight

"Good morning." Jason leaned across the glass counter and brushed a kiss across my cheek. My skin tingled at the contact. Damn, he smelled good—of soap and Alpine forests.

Watery sunlight struggled through the museum's front windows. A sullen gray blanket of fog shrouded the low rooftops across the street. The wall heaters rattled, and a dehumidifier hummed behind the counter.

"I'm sorry I couldn't call you last night," he said. "I ended up working past midnight." He wore his usual work uniform—a navy suit and plain white shirt—and he looked sexy as all get-out.

I closed the computer window on Lola's social media accounts. She and Atticus had known how to work their online marketing. I could learn a thing or two from her. "It's fine. You were busy." Besides, Jason and I had a standing date for tonight, Saturday, when we both got to decompress. "Got any fun plans for the day?"

"Solving a murder. Shopping for a new laptop. Planting tomatoes."

"Tomatoes?" I goggled at him. "You garden?"

"I'm a homeowner. You give the weeds an inch, they'll run all over you."

"You're making me feel better about renting."

"Come on," he scoffed. "I saw you white-washing your aunt's fence last month."

"Yeah, I'm a real Tom Sawyer. Or was it Huck Finn?"

"Sawyer. And he tricked his way out of the job."

"Damn. I've given the game away. I was going to trick you into it next time."

"Just say the word and I'll be there. Men exist to do the grubby manual labor women shouldn't have to."

I laughed. "That's exactly the sort of retrograde, sexist attitude I can get behind."

Bracing my hand on his broad shoulder, I kissed him again just because I could. His cheek was rough against mine, and I smiled.

GD sprang to the counter and rubbed against Jason's suit jacket. But any hairs the cat might have been trying to mark him with were hidden by the jacket's dark navy threads.

I frowned at the cat. Last night it had seemed like he'd tried to stop me from going outside, almost as if he'd known there was danger in the alley. But that would imply GD cared about my safety, and that was about as likely as the cat having psychic powers.

I drew a breath to tell Jason about the hit-and-run driver.

"I'm sorry," he said, stroking the cat, "but I won't be able to make our date tonight."

GD purred.

"Oh." Disappointed, I straightened. "Work?"

"The Malkes have organized a candlelight vigil for Atticus. The chief wants an extra police presence."

"Orson and Lola are throwing a vigil? Does the chief think there'll be trouble?"

"Whenever a crowd gathers, there's an opportunity for problems."

"Jason, about last night—"

"I'm really sorry, but there was no way I could have gotten away. Besides, I thought girls' night was sacred."

"It is, but that's—"

"How's your haunted molinillo research?" he asked, in an artful attempt at diverting me.

"Umm … Herb's in charge of that. He'd look into it." As the dealer, Herb was my best source. For now.

Jason relaxed against the counter. "How much did he want?"

"For the research? Nothing." I frowned. Jason was obviously relieved I'd gone along with his change of subject. It was kind of irritating. Maybe separating detective and personal life wasn't as simple for me as I'd thought.

"Be careful," he said. "You get what you pay for."

"Meaning Herb won't come through?" I pulled my phone from the pocket of my hoodie. "Want to make a bet?"

"Hmm, what do you have that I want … ?" He gazed thoughtfully at the ceiling.

"My rapier-sharp wit? My all-American good looks? My totally random knowledge of the weird and occult? Don't the police sometimes use outside advisors for stuff like that?"

Jason grinned. "Forget about it. I'm not using you as a police consultant. Besides, we don't have any occult cases."

"Phooey. I'll just have to settle for knowing I'm right about Herb."

He quirked a brow.

"Challenge accepted." I called the paranormal collector. Herb answered on the seventh ring, just as I was starting to think he was avoiding me.

"Maddie? I have that information we discussed," the paranormal collector whispered. "Have you got a pencil? I really don't have time to fiddle-faddle around. Not with—ow!"

"Um, are you all right?" I asked.

"Yes, I—Ooof! Blast it!"

Bemused, I rubbed my chin. "What's going on?"

"A simple home exorcism. The poltergeists aren't behaving the way they—Stop that!" There was a crash. "I'm on the phone!"

There was a long silence.

Jason drummed his fingers on the counter.

"Herb?" I said.

"You already have the seller's name on the receipt, but here's her phone number." He rattled off a string of digits.

"I thought the original owner was from Mexico," I said.

"The original owner, not the woman I bought it from. I'm afraid you'll have to take it from here."

"Sure, I can do that." The timing was bad, but I really did enjoy researching the objects in the museum. "But, Herb—"

"This is simply outrageous," he said in a muffled voice. "You can't have used the right ritual. I told you we shouldn't have used Latin. If we can't control a simple poltergeist—" The phone went dead.

"Trouble?" Jason said.

I hung up the Bakelite wall phone. "Um ... Just a poltergeist problem, which neither of us believe in, so I guess there's no problem at all." Did I even *want* to know what was going on with Herb?

No, I did not. "Unless you really do want to start an occult police consultancy," I said. "You've helped me often enough researching objects in the museum." Had those moments been diversions as well, keeping me from murder investigations? If so, I got it. I really did. I wasn't a cop, and there were good reasons why civilians shouldn't get involved in murders.

"I'll leave the ghost-busting to you," he said.

"You say that, and yet you keep sticking your nose into my artifact investigations."

"Sticking my nose into someone else's business? Who could I possibly have picked up that habit from?"

"Herb gave me a number for the molinillo seller," I said hastily. I pulled a three-ringed binder from beneath the old-fashioned cash register and thumbed through its pages. "Got it." I smoothed the molinillo receipt with my palm.

"You going to call the seller?" Jason asked.

I glanced around the museum. It was only nine thirty, and two lonely customers roamed the museum. "Why?" I teased. "I didn't think you were that interested in the molinillo. The way you're acting, I might think you enjoyed investigating haunted objects."

"Investigating the past makes a nice break from police work." A shadow crossed his face.

I laid a hand on his, atop the glass counter. "Was the accident that bad?"

He gusted a breath. "It was a motorcycle and an artichoke truck. The biker didn't make it."

My lips compressed. It was awful, but a part of me could only feel relief that Leo hadn't been involved. "Let's see what Susan Jennings can tell us." I dialed, and to my surprise, I didn't get voicemail.

"This is Susan."

I straightened off the counter. "Hi, this is Maddie Kosloski from the San Benedetto Paranormal Museum. I bought a haunted molinillo that I believe once belonged to you?"

She chuckled, her voice rich as melted caramel. "So

you're the sucker who bought it."

"Sucker? You mean it's not haunted?" I asked, alarmed.

"I mean I don't believe in ghosts, and that thing *is* haunted."

Okay. I blew out my cheeks. "Do you mind if I put you on speaker so my associate can hear?"

"Go ahead."

Associate? Jason mouthed.

I set the phone on the counter and clicked the speaker button. "Why do you think the molinillo is haunted?"

"First," she said, "because the guy in Oaxaca who sold it to me told me so. And second, because it rattled every time my son told a lie. He's a teenager. Do you have any idea how often that thing was going off? Believe me, Rick wanted it out of the house even more than I did. It would have been funny if it wasn't so creepy."

"What exactly did the seller from Oaxaca tell you about the molinillo?" I asked.

"Only that it was haunted by a sad woman's ghost and rattled whenever a lie was told."

"Can you tell me the name of the shop you bought it from?" I asked.

"I got it on a trip to Mexico two years ago. So, no. Sorry, I can't remember and didn't bother keeping a receipt. But the store was off that famous pedestrian street, with the cobblestones and the colorful buildings."

"The Andador?" Jason asked.

"That's my colleague," I said hastily.

"Yes," she said, "that's what the street was called. You've been to Oaxaca?"

"Once," he said.

"The shop was a hole-in-the-wall in this sweet little plaza near the Santo Domingo church. It sold Mexican hot chocolate tablets and tubs of mole. And now I'm getting hungry," she muttered.

"Thanks," Jason said. "That's helpful."

Was it? Because I didn't speak much Spanish and had never done an international investigation before.

"You're welcome," she said. "If I think of the shop's name, I'll let you know. But don't hold your breath." She hung up.

"Do you think a hole-in-the-wall would have a website?" I asked, glum.

GD pawed my hand. His claws were not extended, which was unusually considerate for the cat.

"Doesn't matter," Jason said. "I know that plaza. I'd be surprised if there's more than one shop selling chocolate there. And if there are more, we can ask them all."

"We can? Do you speak Spanish?"

"We can—"

The front door jolted open, and a woman in a scarlet Victorian-era gown with a shiny black corset on the outside staggered into the museum. She carried a large cardboard box in one arm and a coffee urn in the other. A pocket watch dangled from a hook on her corset. Her miniature top hat canted at a jaunty angle over her chestnut hair, which was pinned into a neat bun.

Jason leapt to relieve her of the box. Ceramics rattled inside.

She brushed the thick bangs from her eyes and blew out her breath. "I made it! Am I late? I'm not late, am I?"

I hadn't known my chocolate scryer would be wearing a steampunk costume, but ... she looked fabulous. I grinned. "No, you're right on time." I hurried around the counter. "Jason, this is Ursula Morgan, our chocolate fortune-teller."

"That's my alias." She winked. "Can't have the police on my tail."

"She's joking," I said quickly. I hoped she was joking. After everything Herb had put me through over the past year, I took nothing for granted. "Jason's a detective with the San Benedetto PD. Let me get you set up."

Jason trailed us into the Gallery. We placed the coffee urn on the square table against the wall near the fortune-telling canopy.

"Do you mind if I make a few calls?" he asked.

"No," I said, adjusting the canopy. "Go ahead." Fortune-telling by hot chocolate! I might not have been able to compete with the wineries, but I was excited about this idea. I half hoped to get a reading myself. If it involved chocolate, my fortune couldn't be bad.

My stomach lurched, and I sobered. My recent history with chocolate hadn't exactly been good.

The fortune-teller rummaged in her cardboard box. She withdrew a stack of wide white mugs and a box of hot cocoa packets. Ursula arranged the packets and bowls, along with a set of saucers, beside the urn.

"All right," she said, "here are the rules set by the state of California. I cannot pour the water, I cannot open the hot chocolate packets, I cannot stir the hot cocoa. Whoever I'll be reading for will need to do that themselves, so we don't violate any food service rules." She smoothed her skirt, touched her chestnut hair, and adjusted the angle of her hat.

"I'm glad you know the laws," I said, "because I don't." And I preferred not to get busted for serving hot chocolate without a license. Detective Laurel Hammer would be only too happy to haul me in.

We talked marketing, and Ursula promised to pitch the chocolate and tarot decks. Fortunately she had her own copy of the chocolate deck, so every time she used it for a reading, she'd be promoting sales.

I suppressed a cackle of Scrooge-like delight. Cackles aren't sexy, and Jason still leaned against the counter, talking into his phone.

Mason walked into the museum. At the sight of the detective, he stopped in his tracks and glanced my way.

Jason pocketed his phone.

I settled Ursula in the comfy chair beneath the star-spangled canopy. Two customers wandered into the Gallery. Their eyes widened at the sight of the fortune-teller.

Ursula snapped a picture of the setup and smiled. "For social media. You know how it is."

"Right." I should post some photos too. "I'll grab some shots of you telling fortunes later. And good luck," I whispered. She was charging for readings and giving me a ten percent cut. I probably could have gotten more, but I was just happy to have her in the museum.

She settled into her chair and the customers sidled toward her.

I hurried into the main room. "Hi, Mason. What—"

Jason crossed his arms, rumpling his suit jacket. "Mason was just telling me about the hit-and-run last night." A muscle pulsed in his jaw.

I stiffened, my body going hot with discomfort. Dammit, I should have told Jason right away. "He got a better look at the car than I did." I turned to my neighbor. "What brings you to the museum?"

"This wine and chocolate thing. Belle—You're creative. I thought I should do something too and was looking for inspiration. Got any ideas?"

There was a rattle from the Gallery, and I glanced over my shoulder. The male half of the tourist couple adjusted the bowl that held the molinillo.

"But this looks like a bad time," my ex continued. "I didn't get a license plate, Slate, but if you need anything else—"

"Not right now," Jason said, brusque. "But thanks."

Mason swiveled on his heel and strode out the door.

"Why didn't you tell me?" my boyfriend demanded.

"I'd planned to, but Mason beat me to it," I said. "Since it happened last night, it didn't seem that urgent. The emergency's over."

Jason's dark brow creased. "What happened, exactly? Give me the details."

I explained about the near-miss.

"You could have called me last night," he insisted, his firm mouth pressing into a slash.

My stomach tightened. "I wasn't hurt, and it was late, and you were at the accident scene. It didn't seem like there was much to be done. Mason caught the make and model of the car, though—a 2016 Ford Mustang, copper colored."

Jason's expression stilled. He rubbed his jaw.

"What?"

"Atticus had a 2016 Ford Mustang," he said neutrally. "A shiny brown. It was parked behind the chocolate shop when he died."

We stared at each other.

"I'm pretty sure Atticus wasn't driving last night," I said.

Unless ghosts really *did* exist. Heh heh.

nine

My last customers strolled from the museum, bags of chocolate and tarot cards in hand.

Locking the door behind them, I flipped the sign in the window to *Closed.*

Ursula emerged from the Gallery, her scarlet gown trailing on the checkerboard floor. She dropped her receipt book on the counter. "Wow. Was that the last of the customers?"

"We're clear," I said. "We just closed." Beat, I sagged against the counter and rubbed the back of my aching neck. I'd somehow wrenched it in my wild dive on top of my pickup.

The bookcase swung open and Leo backed into the museum, carrying a cardboard box. Inside, the chocolate scrying bowls and plates clinked.

GD looked up from his spot on the rocking chair. His ears swiveled toward Leo.

"This batch is clean." Leo set the box on the table. He reached overhead, yawning, his black Paranormal Museum tee rising up to expose his flat stomach. "Another day of fun and profit."

"And magic!" Ursula said.

"It *was* fun." Even if it hurt to turn my head. The day had been busier than usual thanks to Wine and Chocolate Days. Maybe it was the chocolate buzz, but there'd been a whimsical energy in the air. Even GD had been mellow, letting me pet him without biting me in retaliation. "Everyone was talking about your fortunes, Ursula."

She raised her slim hand over her mouth, covering a yawn. "Good things, I hope."

"You were a hit," Leo said.

"I don't think I've ever read so many fortunes in one day," she said. "I'm exhausted."

"You're not too tired to come back tomorrow, I hope?" I asked, anxious.

She grinned. "Are you kidding? I'll be back. Business was terrific today." She handed me her receipt book.

I flipped through the pink pages and whistled. "I didn't think you'd get this much traffic. I mean, people who come into a paranormal museum are usually in the mood for stuff like this, but this is amazing."

"The chocolate scrying was more popular than the tarot cards. I think people just liked the idea of drinking hot chocolate while they got their fortunes told. And who can blame them on a day like this?" She glanced at the window. Behind it, streetlamps glowed on the sidewalk, their light streaking the damp glass. The sun had set, fog deepening the twilight to the color of slate.

"Since I'm already set up," she said, "is it okay if I arrive tomorrow a little later? Say at ten?"

"That's perfect," I said. "We probably won't get busy until after eleven, but people do show up at opening. Tourists get to San Benedetto sooner than they planned, when it's too early for wine tasting. Then they find their way here to kill time."

Ursula braced her hands on her lower back and stretched. "Maybe I'll finally get a chance to explore your museum."

"You can look around now if you like," I said. "I've got to do some cleaning before we lock up."

"Brilliant!" She clapped her beringed hands together and wandered into the Fortune Telling Room.

Leo angled his head toward the broom, half-hidden behind his motorcycle jacket hanging from a wall peg. "Do you want me to ..."

"You can take off," I said. Even though I paid Leo a fair wage, I always felt a teensy bit guilty about having him work what was essentially a dead-end job. Or maybe I was just afraid he'd quit, so I never pushed too hard. Some day he would go. He was destined for more than taking tickets in a paranormal museum.

"Thanks, boss." He grabbed his jacket off the peg and hustled out the front door.

I locked it behind him and collected the remainder of the cocoa-smeared bowls and plates from the Gallery. Balancing the box of dinnerware on one hip, I pushed the hidden latch on the bookcase, and it swung open.

A faint light gleamed in the closed tearoom. Behind the counter, neat rows of brushed-nickel tea canisters glinted dully on the shelves.

Shadows shrouded the tables. Out of the corner of my eye, one of the tablecloths rustled, as if stirred by a spectral breeze. I whipped my head toward the movement, and pain sparked up my spine. Rubbing my neck, I watched the table.

Nothing moved. Of course. Because, paranoia!

The kitchen door, off the hallway to the alley, stood ajar. A sliver of light knifed through the opening and along the bamboo floor.

"Adele?" I called, sidestepping into the hallway. The bookcase door swung shut behind me. I shuffled deeper into the gloom, toward the kitchen. My flesh pebbled. "Hello?"

"In here!" Adele said.

Relieved, I edged the kitchen door open with my hip.

Adele stood at a long metal table in the center of the kitchen, frowning at one of her interminable wedding lists. She made a note with a pencil. "More bowls to wash?" she asked without looking up.

"Yeah. Thanks for letting us use your sink."

"I *should* complain. You're probably cutting into my business by giving out free hot chocolate."

"It's not exactly free," I said. "They have to pay for the reading." And I knew for a fact Adele's business had been booming, because I hadn't been able to find a seat or even beg for a to-go sandwich at lunch.

"I suppose you're going to the vigil at the park tonight?" she asked.

"Yes, I was planning on it." I was glad the town was coming together for the vigil, and I wanted to be a part of it. But I had a more mercenary reason as well. They say a murderer can't resist coming to his victim's funeral, and I thought the same might be true for candlelit vigils.

"I thought as much," she said. "I'm coming with you."

"You are?"

"We can hardly let you go alone after that hit-and-run. The killer might be at the park." Adele's face scrunched. "Pug would love it. You know how he adores people. But I can't bring him. His cold has turned into a respiratory infection, and he needs to rest. My mother agreed to watch him tonight."

"Is it serious?" I asked.

She blinked rapidly. "The vet says as long as he eats well and gets lots of rest, he'll be fine. And I can't not go to the vigil. I have a policy of attending all my suppliers' funerals."

Adele had more etiquette in her little finger than I had

in my entire body, but that sounded a little weird.

"Er, do many of your suppliers die?"

She looked up from her list and shot me a severe look. "Everyone dies. Atticus is the second supplier I've lost, but he's the first I've lost to murder—that I know of, at least. At any rate, funerals and vigils are for the benefit of the survivors, not the dead. Atticus's friends and widow need to know they have the support of the community." She smiled, sharklike. "And along the way, we can talk about your job managing the social coverage."

I sucked in a quick breath. "My ... what?"

"Social coverage. You know, taking candid snapshots and posting them at the wedding."

Beads of sweat broke out on my forehead. I wasn't a professional photographer. Sure, I took photos for museum events and exhibits, but that was different. I was my only critic. Adele would expect perfection.

She jammed her hands on her hips. "You forgot, didn't you?"

"No, of course not!" I swear this was the first time I'd heard about having social media responsibilities for the wedding. "It's just ... Why me?"

"All you need to do is remember the hashtag."

"There's a wedding hashtag?" Please, let it not be Nakakraut. Or Finkielmoto.

"I told you this! Hashtag, DAOMG."

I stared at her blankly.

"DAOMG! Dieter and Adele, OMG!"

"Right, right. DAOMG. Easy-peasy." I was never going to remember that hashtag. Escaping her glare, I bustled to the sink and got busy washing cups.

When I returned to the museum, Ursula swished from the Fortune Telling Room, a blissful smile on her face. "I never thought I'd get to sit inside an actual spirit cabinet. You have an amazing collection! And all those old tarot cards! I love the way the colors have faded and softened. Or were they originally printed that way?"

"No, they've faded."

She checked the pocket watch dangling from a hook on her corset. "I should get going. See you tomorrow at ten!"

"Till then." I let her out and finished tidying the museum.

Adele slipped through the bookcase, and together we walked through the fog to the park. We joined a trickle of people arriving in twos and threes. The trickle became a river and then a lake, people massing in the park. Sparks of light flowed through the darkness, and I realized I was seeing candles being lit, the flame passing from person to person.

My heart swelled. I'd spent most of my adult life living overseas, moving from country to country, before returning to my hometown. During the process, I'd lost my sense of community. Being a part of one again made me realize how important it was to me.

I scanned the crowd, hoping to see Jason. But if he was there, he was hidden in the sea of people.

A man slipped behind the gazebo, his movements furtive.

Breath quickening, I stood on my toes for a better view, my tennis shoes sinking into the soft lawn. The man had looked like Sam, that picketer from Reign.

"What?" Adele asked.

Brow wrinkling, I stared at the gazebo. The man's figure shifted between the wooden slats. It *was* Sam. He hadn't sounded like he had much love for Atticus, but maybe he was bigger than his anger.

"What?" she repeated.

"Huh? Oh. Nothing. I didn't say anything."

"You had that *look*."

"What look?"

The sleeves of our jackets brushed other sleeves in the crush of people. Someone handed Adele and me candles. We lit them off the flames of the candles beside us.

Too close beside us.

I pulled my hair forward so that it wouldn't accidentally catch fire. For no good reason, crowds made me a little nervous. Even though this one was calm and friendly, I had to force my muscles to relax.

I scanned the park for my community-minded mother. This was just the sort of thing she'd come to, but I couldn't find her in the crowd.

Someone jostled me from behind and murmured an apology before I could turn. I did a quick hair check to verify it was not in flames and returned to people watching.

Orson and his wife, Lola, stood bundled in long coats at the top of the gazebo steps. Lola rested her hands against her husband's chest and lowered her head. The widow, India, stood a step lower, huddled in a colorful Indian blanket coat.

Adele turned her candle in quick, nervous rotations between her fingers. "There must be three hundred people here."

"At least." I adjusted the cardboard circle at the base of the candle that kept the wax from dripping on my fingers.

Reign's accountant, Tilde, stood at the base of the gazebo steps, a navy knit cap pulled over her sleek hair. She looked away, toward a set of speakers propped on a picnic table. I wondered at the relations between the four—Tilde and Lola, Tilde and her cousin India, the three women and Orson. The odds were that someone close to Atticus had killed him. I shivered. Was I looking at a killer?

"Actually," I said, "it's probably closer to five hundred people."

"I've invited five hundred to the wedding," Adele whispered. "It's so many people."

"You could always elope," I joked.

"Are you crazy?" She rocked in place. "Do you have any idea how much money we've spent? My parents would be furious. Plus, I've wanted to get married in that vineyard since I was eight. I can't elope!"

"I was kidding," I said. "You're super organized. I'm sure things will work out."

She groaned. "You make it sound like it's easy. All I do when I'm not working—and sometimes when I am—is plan this wedding."

"Harper and I can help."

"You *are* helping. You and Harper have been wonderful in spite of all my craziness. But there's only so much you can do. Dieter and I still have to make the decisions. And Harper ..." She sighed.

"What?"

"She's been distracted lately. Have you noticed?"

I clasped my hands together on the base of the tiny candle. I *had* noticed.

"Hey, beautiful." Dieter, in a lightweight blue jacket and jeans, jogged to a stop next to Adele. Grasping her around the waist with one arm, he gave her a swift kiss. In his free hand, he held a half-dozen plastic zip-ties.

Adele's shoulders relaxed and she smiled, rumpling his shaggy hair. "You made it."

"Sure," he said, his bronzed face creasing into a grin.

"I wasn't going to leave my girl alone. Though it wasn't easy finding you in this crowd. Besides, they wanted my help setting up some quick fences." He brandished the zip-ties. "Check it out. One of the guys showed me how to break out of these. Tie me up."

He handed me a zip-tie and turned around, his hands behind his back. "Zip me, Mad Dog."

Uncertain, I glanced at Adele.

She sighed and nodded.

I wrapped a zip-tie around his wrists and pulled it closed.

"Tighter," Dieter said.

This could not end well. "If you say so." I tightened the plastic band.

"Watch." He bent double and raised his arms high behind him. "One, two, three." He slammed his wrists onto his lower back.

Nothing happened.

"One more time." He brought his wrists down hard on his low back again and grunted. "It worked for the other guy."

Adele and I shared a look and burst out laughing.

He straightened, his face scrunching. "What's so funny?" His shoulders pulled back and he wriggled, his neck angling one way, then another. "Maybe they're twisted the wrong way."

"Maddie?" Belle Rodale, Mason's girlfriend, appeared beside Dieter. She tossed her long auburn hair over one shoulder and placed her hand atop the head of the blond boy beside her—their son, Jordan.

"Hi, Belle." I shifted my weight. Belle and I had never had a bad relationship, but I felt awkward in her presence. Mason had been her boyfriend first, then mine, and then hers again when he'd discovered they had a son together. It had been the ultimate post-honeymoon-phase complication.

Dieter grimaced and bent over, thunking his wrists on his backside.

"What's he doing?" Jordan pointed at Dieter, who was now pretzeled in half.

"Escaping from zip-ties," Adele said, and her lips pursed.

"I've almost got it," Dieter said.

Holding three candles, Mason emerged from the crowd. "Got some." At the sight of me, his eyes widened. His gaze darted to Belle, to me, to Belle again. "Hi, Maddie. I guess I should have figured you'd be here."

Belle's brow furrowed. "Were you friends with the Reines? I'm sorry, I didn't know."

"No," I said, "not really. But Adele and I bought chocolate from Reign for our businesses. You?"

"Atticus was a rider," she said. "Mason knew him." She rubbed her arms beneath her puffy turquoise jacket. "I can't believe something like this could happen. This place is getting as dangerous as Sacramento."

Mason smiled. "Sacramento's still a safe town, and so is San Benedetto." He reached out as if to put an arm around her. But at the last minute he dropped his broad hand onto her shoulder.

"Was Atticus in your motorcycle club?" I asked him.

"No," Mason said. "He wasn't much of a joiner. He said he preferred to ride with his wife. He had a silver Harley, a classic from the sixties. It was a real beauty."

Bent double, Dieter struck his bound wrists against his butt.

"I don't suppose he said anything to you about being worried," I said, "or—"

Dieter staggered sideways, knocking me into Belle.

I jerked my candle away before it could torch her long hair, but the flame had gone out. "Sorry," I muttered, then glared at Dieter.

"Is a zip-tie the modern version of the ball and chain?" Mason joked.

Belle's eyes narrowed. "That's not funny."

"They're cutting off my circulation." Dieter panted. "They're supposed to break."

"Here." Mason unclipped a pocketknife from his belt and sliced through the plastic tie.

Rubbing his wrists, Dieter heaved a sigh. "You're a lifesaver."

Adele's lips quirked. "Promise me you won't try anything like that at our wedding."

"Thank you all for coming." Lola's voice rose above the crowd. She held an oversized cordless microphone in her hands. "We're here to honor a passionate man, a visionary, Atticus Reine. But first we'd like to thank everyone in this unique, loving community. You've helped us in so many ways over the past few days. Your thoughtful gestures, your conversation, and your hugs have kept our family at Reign strong during this time of grief."

A loud bang cracked the air.

The crowd shifted, pressing me sideways.

I looked around for the source of the noise.

Another bang, a shriek, screams.

Someone shoved me from behind, and I stumbled. And then people were running, bodies tangling.

More bangs in quick succession. People stormed past, jostling us from every angle.

My feet were swept from beneath me. I landed hard on the damp grass and gasped, the air driven from my lungs. Someone stepped on my hand. I yowled in pain.

Get up, get up. I had to get up or get trampled. Limbs shaking, I scrambled forward, rising, and got knocked flat.

Someone stepped on my calf, and I cried out again, pain blazing from my toes to my knee.

"Maddie!" Mason waded through the crowd and hauled me to my feet. "This way."

He half-carried, half-pushed me through the crowd to a cluster of oak trees by the creek. Belle, Jordan, Adele, and Dieter huddled together.

"You're hurt," Adele said, her brown eyes wide. "You're covered in mud."

My leg and hand and side ached. Mud streaked the knees of my jeans. "Just some bruises." I took a step and winced. "I think I'm okay."

"Maddie!" Jason hurried toward us. Lines of tension released in his handsome face. He grasped my shoulders and pulled me to him. "Thank God."

I pressed against the corded muscles of his chest, a sense of security descending like a warm blanket at his touch. "What's going on?"

"Some idiot set off firecrackers by the loudspeakers," he said. "It's only firecrackers," he bellowed. "Wait here," he told us. "I need to check on the injured."

The park had cleared. A few people lay moaning on the muddy lawn. Uniformed police officers hurried toward them.

"I'll help." Mason jogged after him. "I have medic training."

"Who would have done such a thing?" Adele wiped her eyes, and I realized she'd been crying. "I thought ... When we couldn't find you ..."

Dieter wrapped an arm over her shoulders. "It was probably just kids."

"At a vigil!" She gulped. "How stupid could they be? Someone could have been killed."

I gazed across the park, and my heart squeezed. First a murder and now this mayhem. What was happening to my hometown?

ten

Sunday passed, Ursula reading chocolate dregs and tarot cards, filling the museum to the top of its black-crown molding with customers. The museum was closed on Mondays, a day I'd normally spend taking inventory or doing marketing. But I was too restless to do that kind of work today. I was still trying to make sense of the stampede at the vigil.

Sun sparkled off the Formica counters in my fifties-era kitchen as I poured over the newspaper article, looking for clues.

The firecrackers had been set off behind the picnic table where the stereo speakers had been placed. At the edge of the crowd and just above the embankment to the creek, the table and speakers had provided a good hiding spot for the prankster.

But *had* it been a prankster? I bounced my heel on the base rung of my chair. Or were the firecrackers somehow connected to Atticus's murder? Sam had been lurking by the gazebo. Maybe he hadn't been willing to let bygones be bygones after all.

I rubbed the back of my hand and smoothed the paper on the kitchen table. My hand and calf ached from getting stepped on. And my neck still hadn't recovered from whatever I'd done to it. But I was okay, and no one had been seriously injured at the park. It could have been so much worse.

My cell phone rang. Distracted by the streaks of black newspaper ink on my fingers, I answered without checking the caller ID. "Hello?"

"Madelyn, this is your mother. Is it true you were at the vigil Saturday night?"

"Yeah, but I'm okay." I rubbed my palms clean on the thighs of my jeans. I was a little surprised my mother hadn't been at the park herself. As president of the Ladies Aid society, she was ubiquitous at public events. But I was glad she'd passed on this one.

"And you were the one who discovered Mr. Reine's body?"

I winced. "Where did you hear that?"

"So, it's true!"

"Well, yes, but—"

"This is all my fault."

I leaned back in my kitchen chair. It wobbled alarmingly. "Your fault? Why? Do you know something about Reign Chocolate?"

"Not really. If you must know, they've been rather standoffish when it comes to community events."

"That surprises me. They advertise that they source their ingredients locally. Except for the cocoa beans."

"That's not the same as—You *are* investigating this, aren't you?"

"I wouldn't say *investigating*." I rose and set my lunch plate in the sink. "But I did find Atticus's body, and—"

"I know I've encouraged you in the past—you were so lost when you returned to California—but I was wrong. You need to leave this to Jason. He's such a lovely man. I was thinking of inviting him over to dinner. Do you think it's too soon?"

"No, it's—wait. What? You were wrong?" My mother was never wrong. Or at least she never admitted it.

"It's bad enough that your brother works in those awful countries. Every day I check the news to see if someone's tried to blow up his embassy. My heart can't take worrying about you being in jeopardy too."

I leaned one hip against the counter. "Mom—"

"No, I mean it. I realize forbidding you will only encourage you to do it anyway. I simply want you to think about the risks. I'd like to have grandchildren someday, and since your brother and sister show no sign of procreating, that leaves you. You could have been killed at that vigil."

I squirmed. "It was just some stupid kids with firecrackers." My mom had been casting long, weepy, and creepy gazes my way ever since we'd gotten into a dangerous situation last winter. I hoped she got over it soon.

"How are things going with Jason, by the way?" she asked.

My face heated. It hadn't taken long for her to cycle back from procreation to my boyfriend. "I'm not talking about my love life with you."

"I don't see why not," she said. "It's a perfectly innocent question. Now, he doesn't have any children from his prior marriage, does he?"

"Mom!" This was getting way too personal, and no, he didn't.

"What?"

I drew a deep breath and crossed my ink-stained fingers. "I'm not investigating. I'm just keeping my ear to the ground, like anyone would. I know I'm no private detective."

"You *could* be a detective, don't get me wrong. You're quite clever. I'd just prefer you to stay alive. Jason too, of course, but that's different. He's a professional, and he's armed."

I almost asked her about any gossip she'd heard on the gang at Reign, but then I remembered I wasn't investigating. "Well, I'm okay. Thanks for calling."

"Have you spoken with Harper lately?"

"Harper?" I asked, surprised. "We met for girls' night on Friday. Why?"

"Oh, no reason. Just curious. Let me know about that dinner with Jason. Bye!"

"Bye." Perplexed and a little deflated, I stared at the phone. My mother usually had her finger on the pulse of all the local gossip. Too bad I couldn't pick her brain without admitting I was investigating. What I needed was an alternate source.

I escaped to my laptop and the wide, wonderful world of social media. Lola Malke was plastered all over the Internet. She had social accounts on every platform I knew about, and probably some I didn't.

She'd posted photos of the vigil—pre-riot—and I scanned them for clues. There were lots of artful shots of candlelit faces and close-ups of somber mourners, but none of Orson.

My mouth twisted. Leaving her husband out of the shots seemed kind of weird. If she was keeping up the social media for business purposes, Orson, as the last surviving chocolate maker, should be featured.

I scanned through several vigil pics of India, her expression bleak. If India was faking her mourning, she was a damned good actress.

Something rapped the kitchen window, and I looked up, startled. A small brown bird pecked the glass, cocked its head, and flew off. Lost in thought, I stared past the blue curtains.

I recalled myself and checked the social media

accounts of my other suspects. Reign Chocolate's accounts hadn't been updated since Atticus's death, and there were no clues as to his murder on the site that I could find.

For the heck of it, I checked up on my friends. Adele's accounts were filled with the usual tea and scone recipes and tasteful photos of tea sets and flowers.

Harper … My brows lifted. Harper had gotten active lately on social media, posting pictures of clients and charity work she was involved in. I whistled. She was involved in a lot of charity work. Good for her. She'd been private in the past, for fear that her interest in Italian witchcraft would be discovered. I was a little surprised to see her stepping out online now. I bit the inside of my cheek. Had I imagined a change in her? If something was up, she'd tell me. Right?

I should post more about the museum. Maybe I should get myself online more? After all, it was only an online persona. It wasn't real.

I looked out the kitchen window again. The fog had cleared, and blue sky framed my aunt's two-story house next door. Vineyards and orchards stretched as far as the eye can see, which was pretty far. San Benedetto was so flat, you could watch your dog run away for a week.

Good thing I owned a cat, then, though GD would take issue at being labeled a possession. In his opinion, I was staff.

I sighed. Enough messing around online. It wasn't getting me anywhere, and it was high time I got out of my apartment. Reign was an associate member of the Wine and Visitors Bureau, like my museum. Maybe the woman who ran the bureau had some intel on the chocolate company.

Grabbing my purse and a lightweight blue jacket, I

walked downstairs to my truck and drove into town.

The Wine and Visitors Bureau was in a gabled building on the outskirts of downtown. Vines, just starting to bud, climbed its brick walls. I parked in the lot beside the educational vineyard.

Like my museum, the Visitors Bureau was closed Mondays. But I knew Penny would be in her office. I walked to the side door and gave it an experimental tug. It creaked open, and Penny plowed into me.

"Oooof!"

We bounced off each other.

"Sorry," we said in unison.

She touched her curly gray hair and brushed the ample frontage of her black cardigan. It was embroidered with tiny bunches of grapes and wine bottles. "Hello, Maddie. I hear your chocolate exhibit is not to be missed. Something about a fortune-teller?"

"I'm glad to know you heard about it." I rubbed the back of my neck. "She'll be at the museum every weekend this month."

Penny's brow furrowed. "Weekends are my busiest time, but I wonder if I can escape for a chocolate reading? And speaking of escapes, no offense, but I'm in something of a hurry." Her gaze traveled from my head to my toes, taking in my neat white blouse, jeans, and open-toed black shoes. "Unless you want to be my plus-one and come to lunch with me? I really don't enjoy these things. I'm just not the networking type."

"What things?"

"Lola Malke is having a tea at her house. If she had any public spirit, she would have held it at the Fox and Fennel." She sniffed. "Unless Adele is catering it at Lola's and I hadn't heard?"

"I don't think so." Surely Adele would have

mentioned that.

"Too bad. So, would you like to be my plus-one?"

My cheese sandwich hadn't exactly been filling ... "Sure. I'd love to come."

"I'll drive."

We piled into her Honda. Cardboard boxes jammed the rear seat, forcing my passenger seat forward. I hunched, uncomfortable, my knees scraping the glove compartment.

We roared onto the road, and I hastily buckled my seat belt.

"Sorry about the boxes," Penny said. "I hope you can fit all right." She zipped out to pass an asparagus truck and I smothered a yelp.

A yellow VW bug roared toward us. Horn bleating, Penny swerved back into our lane.

I caught a glimpse of the VW's driver, Herb, shaking his fist as we flashed past.

"I'm glad you stopped by the Visitors Bureau," she said.

I gulped. "Oh?"

Her hands clenched the wheel. "It's this murder. It brings back such terrible memories."

Of a body Penny had discovered. I bit my bottom lip. I'd been there too when she'd found that body. It hadn't been a good day.

Her voice quavered. "Perhaps I'm being silly in my old age. San Benedetto always seemed like such a safe and quiet place. Now ... I'm not so sure. This has to stop, Maddie."

Guilt twisted inside me. But I wasn't responsible for what had happened at Reign. So why was my heart pounding, sweat beading my hairline? Was it remorse, or fear of becoming roadkill?

"You heard I discovered Atticus's body?" I asked.

"I had not heard that. Does your mother know you're looking into this?"

"Who says I am?"

Penny shot me a look. "Because you're always in the thick of it, aren't you?"

I slumped in my seat. "I'd rather she didn't know. She'll just worry."

"You can't blame her for that."

"No." I sighed. "I guess I can't."

"But I confess, I'm glad you're taking an interest. You were so decisive when ..." She swallowed.

When she'd found that body. I'd felt more panicked than decisive that day, but I was glad she thought so.

Penny cleared her throat. "Of course, we have a wonderful police force."

"Of course," I said quickly.

"But there's nothing like small town gossip, is there? So let's see if I can clear anything up." She tapped her chin with one pudgy finger. "Some people think our new chocolatiers are a little too chic for San Benedetto, but I'm thrilled they're here. As much as I love our, shall we say, natural farm atmosphere, we can use a little modernization."

"I've heard the grumbles too," I admitted. "Mainly about how expensive their chocolate is. But I don't think it makes a motive for murder."

"Certainly not!" The Honda drifted left and Penny bumped along the yellow median. "But those chocolate makers ..." She crimped her lips together.

My hand tightened on the car's grab bar. "What about them?" I squeaked.

"Oh, it's probably nothing."

"Penny ..."

"I did hear they were tardy with some of their payments to one of the farmers," she said rapidly. "He's a bit of a crank, though. Frankly, I'm only surprised he didn't demand payment up front."

I studied her profile. Why did I get the feeling that this wasn't what she'd initially been about to say? "Which farmer?" I asked.

"Oh, I can't remember. Not a vintner."

"You remembered he was a crank."

She turned down a long driveway. "He's eighty-five. Trust me, he's no killer."

"Maybe not, but you should tell the police."

"Hmph."

Trellised grapevines lined the yard in front of a two-story Victorian. The house gleamed white, its red-tile roof a counterpoint to the cloudless sky. A timber-frame extension with a vaulted ceiling and lots of windows had been added to the front of the house. The extension's double doors were thrown open to reveal a dining area. Women mingled inside, and also in the small vineyard.

Penny parked behind a row of cars, and we crunched down the gravel path to the gathering.

Lola, in black leggings, knee-high suede boots, and a loose camel-colored turtleneck, emerged from the dining area. She snapped a picture of a trio of women with her phone, then glanced toward us and waved. "Penny, hello!"

"Hello, Lola. Maddie is my plus-one," Penny replied, motioning to me. "She runs the Paranormal Museum."

"Of course, we know each other." Lola smiled warmly. "I'm glad you came. I should have thought to invite you, since you're an associate member of the Visitors Bureau, like us. Here." She squeezed between Penny and me and snapped a selfie. She glanced at the screen. "Cute!"

"I'm very sorry for your loss," Penny said stiffly. "What happened at the vigil was inexcusable."

"Ah." Lola released us. "I guess this event seems a little disrespectful, all things considered. But Atticus and I had planned this networking tea for weeks."

"You and Atticus?" I asked.

"I helped him with marketing," she said. "Well, I have to support Orson any way I can. So, it didn't seem right to cancel today's event. And since we're going forward with the tea …" She brandished her phone. "What's the point of having an event if you don't post photos, right?"

"That's an extension, isn't it?" I nodded toward the dining area jutting from the front of the Victorian.

"It is." Lola beamed. "We wanted more space, especially for the kitchen and dining room, but we wanted to keep the Victorian feel. The renovation was featured in *California Dwellings*."

"How did your interview go with *Feast California*?" I asked.

She sighed. "It was fun, in spite of the circumstances. They brought a photographer, and I think we may go on the cover." She leaned closer. "That's another reason I planned this tea for today. We had to rake the gravel before the magazine photo shoot, and I thought I'd take advantage of how nice everything looks."

Penny edged toward the open doors to the dining area and the rough wooden dining table inside.

"Do the police have any idea who set off the firecrackers?" I asked Lola in a low voice.

"None. Or if they do, they're not telling me." Lola's expression darkened. "I told them who to look at, but I don't think they believed me."

My breath hitched. "You know who was

responsible?"

Lola glanced around at the milling women. None were close enough to overhear. "You probably noticed the other day how oddly Tilde was behaving."

"You think Tilde set off the firecrackers?"

"She walked away from the gazebo right before the firecrackers went off. I was taking pictures." She scanned through her photos. "Look." She handed me the phone. On its screen was a blurry shot of Tilde, walking past the picnic table with its sound equipment.

"Would you email me that?" I asked. That photo was going straight to Jason.

"Sure. What's your addy?"

I gave her the museum's address, and she typed it in with her thumbs.

"But why would Tilde disrupt the vigil?" I asked.

"She was practically stalking Atticus," Lola said, not looking up from her phone. "Tilde's horribly jealous of whatever her cousin India has—including her husband."

Now that was interesting. Could Atticus's murder have been a crime of passion? "Can I use your bathroom?" I asked.

"Of course." She gave me directions to the downstairs bath.

Careful to wipe my feet on the mat, I walked inside the Victorian. Lola and Orson must have knocked out some of the interior walls too, because the living room was open and spacious. I found the guest bathroom easily, beside the stairs.

No one was around, the soft chatter coming from the dining area now hidden around a corner. Lola and Orson were suspects. I might not get this chance again. Heart pounding, I tiptoed up the stairs to a long hallway and tried a door.

Locked.

Rats. My gaze darted up and down the hallway.

I wasn't sure what I was looking for, but I tried another door. It opened onto the master bedroom. White walls. A gray carpet. Antique furniture painted in pinks, deep blues, and grays.

A door stood open in the opposite wall. It was probably the master bath and not the office I'd hoped for, but I tiptoed toward it anyway, glancing at the bureau as I passed. I didn't see any incriminating evidence.

A board creaked in the hallway.

I froze, breath stopped in my chest.

I stood like that, taking shallow, quiet breaths for I don't know how long. But I must have imagined the noise. It didn't repeat itself, and no one strode inside shouting *j'accuse!*

The door did indeed lead to a bathroom, and I paused in the entry. There was a fireplace besides the giant clawfoot bathtub. Stifling a sigh of envy, I went to the mirrored medicine cabinets and opened them. They were filled with expensive-looking indigo bottles of organic tinctures and lotions. I plucked an orange plastic pill bottle from a shelf. Lola had a prescription for valium.

Ugh. Now I felt like the worst kind of snoop.

Pulse racing, I returned downstairs without being spotted and rejoined the garden party.

"Find it all right?" Lola asked.

"Maddie?" My mother stood before us, the sunlight glinting off the silver threads in her hair. She wore crisp white slacks and a blue denim shirt tucked beneath a belt studded with turquoise. Her jaw hung open. It snapped shut.

I flinched.

"How unexpected," my mother said in a strangled

voice. "I was hoping to talk to you, dear. Hello, Lola. Would you excuse us for a moment?" She grasped my elbow and steered me toward a peach tree. "What are you doing here?" she hissed, her blue eyes snapping with annoyance.

My spine stiffened. "Penny invited me."

"I'll just bet she did." My mother's face pinched. "You have no business investigating that man's murder."

"We were just talking—"

"You were interrogating."

"Actually, Lola was doing most of the talking."

She angled her head, her squash-blossom earrings dancing. "You said you wouldn't."

"I said I *wasn't*." And I hadn't been, at the time. "Honestly, we were just talking."

"There's no *just talking* with you when murder's involved."

"Lola told me that Tilde, India's cousin, was obsessed with Atticus. Do you think it could be true?"

My mother's eyes narrowed. "Don't even try to make me an accessory to whatever it is you're doing."

"Hi, Fran." Penny, holding a plate full of finger sandwiches, waddled up to us. "What's new at Ladies Aid?"

My mother rattled off their latest list of fundraisers. "Can I count on you?" she asked Penny, but she stared hard at me.

"All excellent causes," Penny said. "Of course I'm in. Maddie? What about you?"

"I'm in too," I said, my stomach sinking. If I knew my mother, I was in up to my neck. I edged away. "Well, I'll see you later."

"Oh, no, Maddie." My mother's smile didn't touch her eyes. "I'm not done with you yet."

eleven

I sat behind the museum counter and checked our online sales. Outside, the streetlamps flickered on in anticipation of the coming darkness. Twilight had fallen, the sky turning the color of a bruise. After my mom's chewing out, *I* felt a little bruised. The woman was giving me mental whiplash.

When I'd first started sticking my nose into other people's murders, she'd warned me off. Then she'd gone all in, urging me on. Now she was warning me off again? I wished she would make up her mind.

I examined a fresh bandage around my thumb—a casualty of packaging ghost-hunting equipment for shipment. Cardboard paper cuts were the worst. Maybe starting up a subscription box service *wasn't* the best idea. It would mean more packing and mailing.

GD hopped onto the glass counter. He stretched gracefully across it, his ebony tail lashing the keyboard.

"The joke's on you," I said. "I'm not using the computer."

I was still wrestling with the need to make more money. Lola had a gorgeous house. I had a rented garage apartment. Harper was making money hand over fist as a financial advisor. And Adele's tearoom had to be more profitable than my museum.

GD lightly bit my hand.

I scowled at the cat. "Stop that."

Sure the museum was over-the-top fun, but I was a

grown woman. How was I ever going to retire at this rate? Another idea for bringing in income had occurred to me: maybe I should offer an online class on ghost hunting? I could partner up with the ghost hunters who staked out my museum every month ... Or I could get going on that subscription service, though I didn't really want to. I taped the last of the packages. My problem was I had too many ideas.

Take the murder. Orson could have killed Atticus for the buy-sell insurance. Of course, the insurance money would enable Orson to buy India's share of the business. That half million paid to India, in turn, gave her motive.

My mouth pressed flat. And what was up with the tension between Tilde and Lola? Tilde was India's cousin. If Tilde wanted to keep her job, it didn't pay to give attitude to the owner's wife. And if Orson was going to buy India out, Tilde's nepotism angle would vanish.

And then there was Sam, the employee they'd fired. Revenge was an incentive for murder, and he'd been nearby when Atticus had died and when those firecrackers had gone off. But I was pretty sure he'd been outside the chocolate shop when I heard that door close, and the closing door had to have been the killer leaving, didn't it? Which meant he hadn't killed Atticus. And he might be willing to share gossip about his ex-employers.

I needed to talk to Sam.

Unfortunately, I didn't know his last name or where to find him. "Maybe he's at the chocolate shop," I told GD.

The cat sneezed.

"It doesn't hurt to look," I said, defensive. Besides, I could use the exercise. I'd eaten a little too well at Lola's lunchtime tea, and my jeans felt snugger than usual.

I locked the cat inside the museum and pocketed the

key.

GD stared sullenly through the window, as if peeved I'd abandoned him. It's not as if he enjoyed my company. To GD, I was merely a kibble delivery system.

Someone shrieked behind me.

I whipped around, heart thudding.

A crow shot from a denuded plum tree and into the darkening sky.

I swore, pressing my hand to my thumping heart, and looked up and down the street. A bird. It had only been a bird, and my face heated with embarrassment. At least no one had seen my mini freak-out. The wide street was deserted. The few lit shop windows only served to highlight all the blackened windows up and down the street.

My low heels clacked on the brick sidewalk and I shrugged out of my jacket. The sun was a dying hint upon the horizon, and there was something oppressive about the evening air.

Footsteps pattered behind me. Tensing, I glanced over my shoulder.

A woman with a toddler clasped to her chest hurried past.

I blew out my breath. *Calm down.* Nothing bad was going to happen walking down Main Street.

Unless I'd just jinxed myself by thinking that.

Lights flowed from the windows of Reign, and I hurried toward them. Sam wasn't pacing the sidewalk, and I almost felt relieved. But it meant I'd have to track him down some other way.

The chocolate shop was still open. I figured I might as well check out what was happening inside, even if the smell of cocoa now made my stomach queasy.

I pushed open the door and nearly bumped a

customer standing in line. I edged inside. Customers milled in front of the polished driftwood displays of chocolate. They lined up at the counters, nibbled from sample trays.

Behind the counter, Tilde and Orson worked two cash registers.

The accountant looked flustered. A brown apron hung askew over her business-like blouse. Strands of dark hair escaped her bun.

Orson's smile seemed harried but genuine beneath his beard. Behind the register, he was beard-net free.

Tilde turned too quickly, bumping into him.

He grinned, steadying her, then turned to chat with a customer.

Scowling, Tilde banged out an order on her cash register and handed a brown bag to a waiting customer.

I grabbed a chocolate bar off the shelf and got in line. They were doing amazing business for a Monday evening. I guessed from Tilde's presence that they hadn't hired new counter help yet. Working the cash register couldn't be a part of her job description, but she was doing it anyway. She might be grumpy, but she was willing to pitch in. It made me like her more.

"Maddie?"

I turned.

Belle stood in line behind me.

"Oh," I said, "hi! Satisfying a chocolate craving?" Belle was tall and slender. I had none of those attributes, and jealousy pinged through me. I needed to either get over my insecurities or get off my duff and lose weight.

"Something like that." She shifted, crossing her arms over her denim blouse. "Even though I moved to Sacramento, I still have a few clients here in San Benedetto. The salon lets me rent a chair."

"Great." *Great, great, great.* The salon had to be closed by now. She was really hanging around to see Mason, which was normal given their relationship. Why not admit it?

"Have you seen Mason?" she asked.

I started. "Not today. Why?"

She opened her mouth as if to speak, then closed it. Her pale brow furrowed. "No reason. So how are things with you and the detective?"

"Great. He took me on a date to a chocolate class." I motioned toward the counter.

She blinked. "Before or after the murder?"

"Um. After."

"Tell me he wasn't ..." She lowered her voice. "Detecting on a date."

I grimaced. I'd been the guilty party on that score. "He booked the class six weeks ago. It was just one of those things."

"And you?" Belle asked beneath the murmur of the crowd. "Is your being here now just one of those things?"

"Not entirely," I admitted.

"If you're here to interrogate someone, I don't think you'll have much luck. They look way too busy to talk."

Tilde passed a paper bag over the wooden counter to a customer, and the line edged forward.

"I'm sure you're right," I said. "But here I am. I don't suppose you've heard any murder gossip at the salon?"

"Do you really think all hair stylists gossip with their customers?" she asked shortly.

"No, I—uh—" Why was I always sticking my foot in my mouth around Mason's girlfriend?

"Well, they don't. Just me." Belle broke into a grin. "I did hear that Tilde has a shoe habit, if it matters."

My shoulders relaxed. "Shoes?"

"Manolo Blahnik, Miu, Louboutin, Jimmy Choo ... I guess you haven't been looking at her feet."

We edged closer to the counter.

"No," I said. "And I figured you for more of a hair person."

"Hair's a professional interest. Shoes are for fun." She hitched up the hem of her jeans to display a sequined pump. "I can only dream of the shoes she wears."

We moved forward in line.

"I did notice she was wearing those pumps with the red soles." I wasn't a total fashion ignoramus, even if I did tend to wear Paranormal Museum T-shirts a lot. But that was advertising.

Belle sighed. "Christian Louboutin. Elegant and sexy all at the same time."

"How expensive are those heels?"

"It depends on the style. Six hundred, two thousand, more?"

Two thousand dollars for a pair of shoes? I lowered my head, studying Tilde behind the register. How could a self-employed accountant afford that? Maybe I *had* gone into the wrong business.

The person at the counter took their bag and left.

Excusing myself to Belle, I stepped up to Tilde's register and handed her the chocolate bar. "Hi, Tilde. Nice to see you again."

"That will be eight dollars."

I bit back a grimace and fumbled with my wallet.

"Things have gotten busy at Reign." I thumbed through my bills in search of something larger than a one.

Her brows slashed downward. "Ghouls. It must be true that no publicity is bad publicity, because since

Atticus's murder made the national news—"

"National?" I blurted.

"He's a name." Tilde said the last word as if it tasted bitter on her tongue. "Lola probably sent out a press release."

"Tilde!" Orson bustled over to us. "Are you doing okay here?" He shot me a glance.

"Fine," she said.

"Because we're a little short-staffed tonight," he said.

"No luck on finding a new counter person?" I asked.

"Actually," he said, "thanks to your mother, we did find someone. But she can't start until tomorrow. Are you just getting the chocolate bar?" He snatched it up and walked to his register. "Eight dollars."

I handed him the bills. "Have the police—"

"No. And I really can't talk about it now."

My face warmed. Belle was right. This was a terrible environment for an interrogation.

I bought the bar. Looking for Belle, I hustled from the shop. When we weren't being stiff with each other, she was fun to talk to. Maybe I could invite her to lunch, or at least exchange numbers.

But I didn't see her on the sidewalk, and I felt … relieved.

twelve

"Hola." Twisting the cord around my finger, I pressed the wall phone's receiver tighter to my ear. "*Me llamo ... Habla Ingles?*"

"A traditional Japanese wedding, can you believe it?" Adele paced, her pink heels silent on the museum's checkerboard tiles, an elegant white mug in her hand. Beneath her Fox and Fennel apron, she wore a slim, pink pencil skirt and white blouse.

Oblivious to GD's glares from the haunted rocking chair, Pug whuffed in his bed beside the counter. Adele hadn't wanted to leave him at home, but she couldn't bring a sick dog into her tearoom. The museum was now the designated kennel.

A man's voice crackled over the phone line. "Yes, yes! How can I help you?"

I relaxed. Jason had come through with the name of the shop owner at the right chocolate shop in Oaxaca. I'd been planning to spend my day on this, since the museum was closed on Tuesday, but Adele had other ideas.

"Have you seen the hats they wear?" Adele picked up the bronze skull and set it back on its pedestal. "Can you imagine wearing one of those in the June heat?"

"Hi, I'm Maddie Kosloski from the San Benedetto ..." I hesitated. If I said I was from a paranormal museum, the man might think I was a crackpot. "San Benedetto. I'm trying to reach Mr. Moreno."

GD dropped from the chair and stalked toward the pug.

"Yes, this is Pablo Moreno."

Adele rubbed a pink lipstick stain from the mug. "My mother says I need to be more accommodating, but she's just afraid of *her* mother. And it's my wedding, isn't it?"

"I recently purchased a haunted molinillo," I said. "I was told it once belonged to you, and wondered if I could ask you a few questions about it?"

"The Santa Muerte molinillo?" he asked.

"Santa ... Saint Death?" My voice cracked on the final syllable.

GD leapt onto the counter, his ears pricked with interest. For the cat, murder apparently took precedence over dogs. Pug, expression plaintive, looked up at him.

"What does Santa Muerte have to do with the molinillo?" I asked.

"The woman who owned it was a devotee of the Saint."

Great. A devotee to Saint Death, whoever that was. But you never knew. Saint Death could be totally innocent and have absolutely nothing to do with necromancy. Nothing at all. "I don't know much about Santa Muerte," I said cautiously. "What does being a devotee to her mean?"

"In that lady's case, it means she was in trouble and needed the Saint's protection. But the Saint could not help her. She died of a broken heart."

Romantic, but vague. "I'm sorry to hear of her passing. Was the lady a friend of yours?"

"I knew her sister. She gave me the molinillo after the funeral. She said it was bad luck."

"And those stiff robes," Adele said, brandishing her mug and managing to spill not a drop. "They're totally unflattering to my figure."

"What was her name?" I asked Mr. Moreno. "The owner of the molinillo, I mean. Not her sister."

"Felicitas Ocasio."

I made a note on a yellow notepad. "And the molinillo became haunted after she died?"

"That is what her sister told me." He coughed. "The molinillo was very—how do you say? Annoying."

"It's enough to make anyone crazy," Adele said. "I can't make *everyone* happy."

"Why annoying?" I asked.

"Wouldn't *you* be annoyed?" Adele slammed the mug on the counter.

The cat started, green eyes wide, fur bristling. Pug sneezed.

"I have a busy shop," Mr. Moreno said. "The molinillo would not stop shaking. Customers thought we were having an earthquake."

"So you had it on display?" I frowned at Adele, but she'd turned to the window and was pondering the morning fog.

"I have many molinillos," the chocolate shop owner replied, "but a haunted molinillo was something new, and it is an antique. Special. I thought displaying it would be charming. But when that American woman asked to buy it, I was glad to see it go. I do not believe in ghosts, you understand, but that molinillo is haunted."

I smiled, wry, at the echo of Susan's words. She hadn't believed in ghosts either, and yet … "Is there anything else you can tell me about Felicitas? Was she a professional chocolate maker?"

He barked a laugh. "Her? No. She used the molinillo

like everyone does, for making our famous chocolate drink. She was young. She was beautiful. And she loved the wrong man."

"Why wrong?"

"Because he broke her heart," he repeated.

"When you say she died of a broken heart, do you mean—?"

"A broken heart," he said firmly. "And that is all."

I winced, feeling rebuked. "Is there anything else you can tell me about the molinillo?"

"It shakes when someone lies. But I think you already know this."

"So, if this story of the haunted molinillo is true—"

"It is."

"Maybe I can include fake cherry blossom bouquets." Adele adjusted the *Closed* sign in the window. "Maybe that will satisfy her."

"Then how does the lying fit into it?" I stuffed my finger in one ear. "Did Felicitas's boyfriend lie to her?"

He sighed. "He lied to everyone. I am sorry, I must go. I have a customer."

"Thank you, Mr. Moreno. You've been a big help."

But he'd already hung up.

Thoughtful, I set the old phone on its wall receiver.

At least I had a name. What had really happened between Felicitas and her boyfriend?

GD sniffed the dangling cord, his whiskers twitching, then got bored and hopped to the ground, landing beside Pug in his dog bed.

Pug got to his feet. GD shoved him aside with a well-placed body slam and dropped to the bed. The dog whuffed and snuggled in beside him.

I didn't think I could bring myself to track down her sister and ask. Most of my exhibits were connected to people decades dead. But the people who'd known Felicitas were still alive. Her tragedy was recent and must still be painful for those involved.

I glanced at the notepad on the counter and sighed. Sometimes I wondered if taking over this museum had set cosmic forces in motion. Was Herb right? Was it more than coincidence that I was involved in *two* chocolate-themed cases—murder and molinillo.

"So," I said to Adele, "what are you going to do?"

Adele turned from the window. "I love my grandmother, but I can't turn my wedding plans upside down for her. Can I?" Her expression turned pleading. "She's threatened to curse me."

"Cursing?" I blinked. "Is that a Japanese thing?"

"Don't stereotype. People throw curses around all over the world. It's universal. You own a paranormal museum! You should know this."

"Okay, okay." I raised my hands in a defensive gesture. "Sorry."

"No." Adele blew out her breath. "*I'm* sorry. It's all gotten so complicated. Dieter just wants to have a fun party, but this is our wedding!" She bit her lip. "I love Dieter, but we're so different."

"Different in important ways?" I asked, knowing the answer.

"No. We agree on money and family and the critical things. And when I'm with him, it's as if ... I'm lighter."

I nodded. Adele and Dieter might have had a whirlwind romance, but they'd known each other forever, and Adele was level-headed. This wasn't a post-honeymoon-phase complication. It was pre-wedding stress.

And I wasn't going to be blindsided by a romantic complication with Jason once the scales of desire fell from my eyes. I wasn't sure where things were going with us, but I didn't expect any unpleasant surprises. Jason was an open book. My stomach squirmed. At least, I hoped he was.

"I've known him for so long—I *know* him," Adele said. "He's a good man. I love him."

"And wedding planning is stressful."

"Sometimes I feel like I'm having an out-of-body experience. Some days everything is awful. I look at myself and wonder, how did this happen? And then other days … When Dieter and I came together, it was all so easy. How did I get so lucky with him?"

"Because you and Dieter deserve to be happy."

"And I was so caught up in my problems," Adele said, "I wasn't even listening to your advice. What do you think about the Japanese wedding?"

Oh, jeez. Did I have advice? I fumbled. "I think that everyone involved in your wedding is coming from a place of love."

Adele stared at me. "That's … exactly right. How did you … ?"

"I might have read it in a magazine," I admitted.

She laughed. "All right. You've listened to my rant. You've even taken in my poor dog." She bent to ruffle his tawny fur and pulled a bone-shaped treat from her pocket.

Pug eagerly gobbled it down. The cat sniffed and stalked into the Fortune Telling Room. He and Pug generally got along, so I wasn't worried about keeping an eye on them. But GD did not like watching others eat if he wasn't getting a piece of the action.

"Now what's bothering you?" Adele asked.

"Aside from my molinillo research?" I motioned to the yellow pad on the counter. "Nothing."

"Don't lie to me, Maddie. I saw the look on your face a few minutes ago."

I peered at the computer, open to an invoice. Why was I hiding my relationship worries from Adele? She knew the worst of me, and she was one of my best friends. "I was just wondering—"

Someone rapped on the door. Mason's broad frame filled its window.

Adele looked a question at me, and I nodded.

She unlocked and opened the door. "Hi, Mason. How are things?"

"Hi, Adele, Maddie." A blue T-shirt stretched across his chest. His thick blond hair was tied back in its usual ponytail.

I swayed on my tall chair and hopped off before I fell off. "What brings you to the museum?"

"Um ... Wine and Chocolate Days." He jammed his fingers in the front pockets of his faded jeans.

A semi drove past, rattling the objects on their shelves.

Adele quirked a brow. "Don't tell me you're thinking of getting involved this late in the game. Besides, I wouldn't think motorcycles would have much to do with wine or chocolate."

"Yeah," he said. "They don't. That's the problem. And I don't have Maddie's creative brain."

"Chocolate wrapped in foil to match the chrome?" I suggested. "Chocolate shaped like motorcycles? I dunno. Search the Internet for motorcycles and chocolate. Maybe you'll find something." That advice was even less helpful than what I'd given Adele.

He glanced at Adele. "Thanks. That's exactly what I was looking for."

Something rattled in the Gallery, and I looked out the

window.

Herb's VW Bug drifted past outside.

A chill rippled up my spine. I leaned across the counter and peered into the Gallery. Still and silent, the molinillo sat angled in its ceramic bowl.

"Something wrong?" Mason asked.

"No," I said, uneasy. "I'm fine."

In the Gallery, the molinillo rattled.

thirteen

Wednesday dawned rainy and cold, customers trailing muddy footprints across the museum's black-and-white floors. The heater steamed the windows, fog muffling the museum in a sullen gray blanket.

But at least we had customers—more than usual for a Wednesday thanks to Wine and Chocolate Days. Guests studied the framed photos of murderers on the glossy white walls. Milled between shelves lined with haunted objects. Wandered in and out of the Fortune Telling Room. Told silly lies over the molinillo in the Gallery and laughed, sharing nervous glances.

Leo had left for his statistics class, and I sat alone behind the counter. I handed a middle-aged couple their tickets and brochure, and they wandered into the Gallery.

Shifting on my tall chair, I half-heartedly studied a webpage on how to start a subscription box business. I bit my bottom lip. Did I have the bandwidth to stuff boxes every month? And why had my mom asked the other day whether I'd spoken with Harper? The latter was a small mystery and easily solved. All I had to do was call Harper and find out what was going on.

As if summoned by my thoughts, Harper strolled into the museum. The collar of her long cinnamon-colored coat was turned up against the chill. She tugged her dark hair free from the thick matching scarf wrapped around her neck. "Is Adele around?"

"No. She's probably in the tearoom."

Harper's shoulders relaxed. "Thank God."

"Uh oh. What's happened?"

"You know that wedding checklist of hers?"

I groaned. "How could I forget? Did you know she made me her social media manager?"

Harper burst into laughter. "Oh boy. Hold on." She walked behind the counter and nudged me away from my computer. She opened an Internet site. "You need to read this."

Q: Who should I assign to manage social media coverage during the wedding so I don't have to?

A: Taking candid snapshots is a great job for that awkward friend, who'll either end up a wallflower or fall into the wedding cake if they're not kept busy.

I sputtered. "That's—I am not awkward!"

Harper raised her hands, palms out. "Hey, don't shoot the messenger."

"There's got to be another reason she asked me to take charge of her social media." I blew out a breath. Adele's wedding wasn't about me. I needed to get a grip. "So, what's on your mind?"

"I was supposed to send out the event schedule to the vendors, so they'll have time to give us feedback."

"You didn't forget!?"

"No." She glanced at the bookcase, toward the tearoom hidden behind it. "But I couldn't get in touch with the baker, the woman who was supposed to make the wedding cake."

My scalp prickled. "*Supposed* to?"

"So, I drove to Sacramento yesterday, where the bakery's located."

"And?"

"It's out of business," Harper whispered.

My stomach lurched. "Okay. Okay. Let's not panic. We have three months until the wedding. This isn't a disaster."

"Only two and a half months." She clawed a hand through her hair. "Don't you remember Adele complaining? All the good bakeries need five- or six-months lead time."

I swallowed, bracing my elbows on the counter. "Adele must have had a runner-up on her bakery selection. I'm sure if she explains the emergency, she'll be able to find someone to make the wedding cake."

"I know it will all work out in the end," Harper said. "But how are we going to keep her from having a major freak-out now?"

The bookcase slid open and Adele strolled into the museum. "You wouldn't believe the caterer. I felt like I was on a bad date. He almost laughed at my budget, and acted like my request for a vegan, gluten-free alternative was crazy! But the good news is, I think Pug's getting better. He was coughing much less last night."

Harper and I glanced at each other.

"What's wrong?" Adele braced her hands on her hips, rumpling her Fox and Fennel apron.

Harper shot me a helpless look.

Tell her, I mouthed. Best to get this over with.

Harper bit her bottom lip. "Um, you know that baker in Sacramento you chose for your wedding cake?"

"How could I forget?" Adele said. "They were the only cake samples Dieter really loved. And her designs are gorgeous. Why?"

"I went there this morning," Harper said, "to deliver the event schedule."

"Is there a problem? That's why I wanted the vendors to see the schedule now, so we could work any issues out in advance."

"The bakery's out of business," Harper blurted.

Adele blanched. "What?"

"They're gone," she said. "The building's vacant."

"But …" Her arms dropped to her sides. "They can't be out of business. Maybe they moved," she said, voice reedy.

"I talked to one of her neighbors," Harper said in a rush, "and he told me that they'd gone out of business and sold their equipment. I checked their website, and it still says they're at their old address. There's nothing online about, well, anything. The phone number's not working. I guess it's been disconnected. And no one responds to my emails."

The wall phone rang, and I jerked on my tall chair. "Sorry," I muttered. "I should …" I lunged for the receiver. "Hello, this is Maddie at the Paranormal Museum."

No one answered.

"But I gave her a deposit," Adele whispered.

"Hello?" I asked again, impatient.

Adele, pale and wide-eyed, stared at Harper. Harper knitted her lip.

I didn't know whether to drop the phone and hug them or duck beneath the counter.

"There's a bomb," a mechanical voice rasped.

"Fantastic," I said, and blinked, an icicle piercing my core. "Wait. What?"

The voice was electronic, as if run through one of those voice changing machines. "There's a bomb in your museum."

My mind blanked, unwilling to process the information. But my body got the message, and a cool shiver stiffened my spine. "Who is—"

A dial tone buzzed.

Breathless, I took two tries to hang up the phone. It had to be a crank call. But was it possible? I scanned the museum, the customers milling about.

"What's wrong?" Harper asked.

People had been in and out all day. Someone could have tucked a bomb anywhere. "You need to get out," I blurted. "Now!"

Adele blinked. "Well, that's not very nice. Just because my wedding is blowing up in my face—"

"That was a bomb threat." I hurried around the counter. "Harper, call the police. But make the call outside. Adele, you might want to—"

But she was already moving toward the hidden door. She slipped into the tearoom and pushed the bookcase shut.

Harper hurried outside, her cell phone pressed to one ear.

"Excuse me," I said loudly.

On the haunted rocking chair, GD pricked up his ears.

Guests turned and stared.

"There's been a bomb threat," I said, in what I hoped was a calm and commanding voice. "So, everyone please make your way outside and away from the building."

A cluster of guests turned to each other, consternation on their faces. I hustled past them and into the Fortune Telling Room. Half a dozen people were examining the aged tarot decks, the spirit cabinet, and the vintage spirit table with its crystal ball.

"Hi," I said. "I'm sorry, but there's been a bomb threat. Please walk outside and away from the building."

I rushed back into the main room, where the same guests were still standing around like bumps on logs, waiting to see what would happen next. My neck stiffened. "I'm not kidding, it's a real bomb threat. The police are on their way." I hoped the last bit was true. But they'd take Harper seriously. They had to.

Through the window, I could see people milling on the sidewalk outside. I guessed they were from the Fox and Fennel, because no one was budging from the museum.

I trotted into the Gallery. Four people examined the chocolate bars on the black shelves. I clawed my hair. "Excuse me …"

A portly, middle-aged woman brandished a bar of Reign chocolate from Peru. "I'd like to buy this, please."

I struggled for patience. "I'm sorry, but there's been a bomb threat at the museum. Everyone needs to go outside and move away from the building as quickly as possible."

"But what about the chocolate?" she asked.

"Your ticket is good all day," I ground out. "I'd love it if you came back, and you can buy it then."

A cell phone rang in someone's pocket, and I started.

"I can't come back if the museum's been exploded," she said.

"It's probably just a prank," I said, my voice taut. "But for safety's sake, we all need to move outside."

A woman poked her head inside the Gallery. "I'd like to buy a deck of those chocolate tarot cards."

Seriously? Bomb threat! Odds were it was a fake, but it wasn't the sort of risk worth taking. "Look, if it's a fake threat, then nothing will happen. But if it's real, it's a problem." *Talk about understatement.* "So there's no point to sticking around. We all need to leave. You can buy the same chocolate bars at Reign, just down the street." I grabbed a box of Tarot cards off the shelf.

"And I can sell this to you outside."

"Then why can't you sell me the chocolate outside?" the first woman asked.

My hand clenched on the tarot deck. "Fine. Let's go!"

Adele strode into the Gallery, her heels clacking. "What are you people doing in here? Don't you know there's been a bomb threat?" She clapped her hands. "Out. Everyone out now, please."

The rooms cleared.

"Really, Maddie," my friend scolded as she scooped up GD. "It's probably a hoax, but you need to take these things more seriously. I mean, what were you doing in there? Waiting to see if you got blown up?"

Augh! "I was—forget it." I hustled her out the front door, then returned inside to double check the Fortune Telling Room—empty. I hurried onto the sidewalk. Sirens wailed, growing louder.

"The police are on their way," Harper said, pocketing her phone. "They said to get everyone out and wait across the road."

My reflection wavered in the window of the motorcycle shop next door. "Mason! I've got to tell him about the threat. I'll meet you across the street."

Heart thudding, I darted into the motorcycle shop.

A burly man ran his hand over the polished seat of a sleek bike.

Mason and Belle stood in one corner, tension vibrating through their bodies. She stabbed a finger at his broad chest. Mason hung his head and said something in a low voice.

She shook her head, her loose auburn hair flowing over the shoulders of her motorcycle T-shirt. Her lips pressed into a tight line.

"Mason! Belle!"

They jerked apart, their faces flushing.

"Someone called in a bomb threat to the museum," I said. "The police are on their way. But since you're next door—"

"Got it. We're closed," Mason shouted to his customer. "Bomb threat."

The burly man nodded and shuffled out the door.

Mason grasped both our arms. "Come on. Outside, you two."

"The police said to wait across the street," I said, breathless, as we exited onto the drizzly sidewalk.

Laurel's blue muscle car screeched to a halt beside us. A squad car parked behind hers. As Mason and Belle crossed the road, I felt my muscles release. At least they were safe.

The detective stepped from the sports car and motioned to the two cops emerging from their black-and-white. "You two, set up barricades. You know the drill." She glared at me. "If your cat's in there, it's on its own." She looked as if she enjoyed the idea.

"He's across the street," I said, wiping the damp from my forehead. "With Adele." GD's relationship with Detective Laurel Hammer was as fraught as my own. The detective detested us both.

Laurel shot a startled look at the opposite sidewalk, and her hand drifted to her holster. Her mouth compressed, and she relaxed her arm. "What happened?" she asked.

"Someone called the museum and said there was a bomb inside," I said.

"Did you recognize the voice?" She stared, lips curling, at the museum.

Across the road, Adele's waitresses poured tea into white cups for the crowd huddled beneath shop awnings.

"No," I said. "They used one of those mechanical synthesizer things."

The detective snorted. "They have apps to change voices nowadays. Yeow!" She rocketed into the air and pointed at a nearby plum tree. "You said that cat was across the street."

GD prowled toward us, his head low.

I scooped him up before he could get to Laurel. The cat howled, thrashing in my arms.

"Anyway," I said quickly, "the museum's been cleared, and so have the Fox and Fennel and the motorcycle shop."

She eyed the struggling cat. "Who wants to blow up your museum?"

GD nipped my hand and growled.

"Ow!" I scowled at him. "No one! I mean, I don't know. It's gotta be a hoax, right?"

"Knowing my luck," she mumbled beneath her breath.

"What?"

"Yeah, it's likely a prank. But don't even try to tell me this was random. It's always *your* museum. Arson. Murder. Stampedes. I should have it shut down as a threat to public health."

"It's not—You can't do that, can you?" I hugged GD tighter and he quieted, black ears flicking.

She stepped closer, looked at GD, and retreated a step. "Do you know what happens to bars with customers that always cause trouble?"

Gulp. "No."

From the corner of my eye, I watched cops herd passing pedestrians to the other side of the road. Why were Laurel and I still standing dangerously close to a museum that might explode?

"Have you heard of nuisance laws, Kosloski?"

"We're not a nuisance," I said, shrill. "It's not my fault. I didn't ask for this."

GD meowed an agreement.

A blue Prius swerved into a parking spot on the street. Mike, a wiry young reporter from the *San Benedetto Times*, leapt from the car. He snapped a picture of Laurel and me with his cell phone. "What's going on? Bomb threat?" His Adam's apple bobbed above his thin blue tie.

The detective's steely eyes narrowed. She turned to me. "You called the press? What is this, a publicity stunt?"

I edged sideways. "I didn't call the press. Tell her, Mike."

"Nah," he said, "it was an anonymous tip. The person used one of those voice-changing apps."

Laurel glared at me. "What's that saying of yours? No publicity is bad publicity?"

"It's not my saying." Anxious, my gaze flicked to the brick museum. "I didn't invent it. Look, this is a real bomb threat."

The detective's nostrils flared. "That horror show of yours is a menace to life and limb."

"It's not," I said weakly.

The bomb threat had to be a random prank? Right? My stomach flipped. Or had someone targeted me, my customers, my friends?

fourteen

So, there was no bomb.

But the museum was shut down for the rest of the day while the police and fire departments poked around looking for one. The ticket refunds were a dagger to my shriveled heart, though most of the customers seemed cheerful enough with a bomb threat story to tell.

The authorities finally let Jason and me inside at closing time.

"Oh, Maddie." Hands on his hips, Jason surveyed the museum. Books and curios lay tumbled from shelves and scattered across the checkerboard floor. "I don't like this." Muscles rippled beneath the shoulders of his navy suit jacket and quickened my pulse.

I tore my gaze from him and swallowed. "Me neither. Couldn't your officers have been a *little* neater?" I picked up the bronze skull, which had rolled beneath the antique rocking chair. My forehead scrunched with annoyance. Bronze skulls aren't cheap! Fortunately, it seemed undamaged.

Imperious, GD perched on the counter, his tail wound around his paws.

"I'm talking about the bomb threat," Jason said.

"I know. It's a lot like what happened in the park, isn't it?"

He stared at me.

"A prank that isn't funny," I explained. "It might have been only firecrackers at the vigil, but the stampede caused real harm." I jammed my hands into the pockets of my hoodie. Today's bomb threat might have had the identical effect if people had panicked. Was the same mind at work? And what did it have to do with Atticus's murder, if anything?

"You think the two incidents are connected," he said slowly.

"Well … maybe." Were they? Having an overactive imagination was both blessing and curse. My imagination was great for marketing the museum. But it also led me down dark rabbit holes of imagined future ruin and an impoverished old age. I pushed my hands deeper into my pockets, stretching the black fabric. Was I imagining a connection between the disaster at the vigil and the bomb threat?

Jason rubbed his chin.

"You think I'm crazy," I said.

"No. No, I don't. But we don't have any evidence the firecrackers at the vigil were anything more than a prank. I can't make a case built on speculation. But I don't know why kids would target your museum. The local kids *like* your museum."

We were a special favorite among Goths and teenage boys. "I don't know why someone would do this either, unless it's also somehow connected to the murder. The timing is suspicious."

His brows lowered. "Why would someone threaten your museum over a chocolate maker's murder?"

"Because I was the one who found the body? Maybe the killer thinks I saw something I shouldn't have?"

"Which you didn't."

"No, of course not." My cheeks seemed to tingle. "I told you everything I saw and heard." I hesitated. "But I do have sort of a reputation for, um, getting involved.

And since Atticus's death, I've been, well, seeing more of the suspects than usual."

"Seeing." His gold-flecked eyes narrowed.

Uh oh. "Penny invited me to be her plus-one at Lola's tea on Monday." And I'd forgotten to send him Lola's photo of Tilde at the vigil. My stomach sank.

He grunted. "Don't those sorts of things usually happen on weekends?"

I relaxed a bit. He wasn't going to bust me for interfering, which, let's face it, I just might have deserved. "Not in San Benedetto. Not when most of our business happens on weekends. Monday is a local business owner's only real day off."

"Anything unusual happen at the tea?"

"Not really. Lola told me that Tilde—the accountant—was obsessed with Atticus, who happens to be her cousin-in-law. I think the phrase Lola used was 'practically stalking.' Oh, and my mom wanted to ask if you were free for dinner."

"Hm. Did India know about her cousin and husband?"

"I'm not sure if there was anything to know. Lola said Tilde was obsessed, not that she and Atticus had an affair. She thought Tilde might have set off the firecrackers. She sent me a picture. Here." I grabbed my cell phone and forwarded him the photo.

His phone pinged. He ignored it. "Lola Malke said that?"

"Yes."

"But why tell you? You were snooping, and she knew it, didn't she?"

"It's not like I was searching her closets." I hadn't gotten farther than the master bathroom. "I mean, sure, we were talking about Atticus. I found the man's body.

He was her husband's business partner. His death is front of mind."

Jason glanced toward the wreckage in the Gallery. My neat pyramids of chocolate bars and tarot decks lay in untidy heaps.

"What about the molinillo?" he asked. "Were you able to get in touch with that guy in Oaxaca?"

And the subject was changed. I felt an instant's squeezing disappointment, then shrugged it off.

"Yes," I said casually, "he was a big help. He told me the original owner was a woman named Felicitas Ocasio. She died of a broken heart over some guy. Her sister inherited the molinillo, but the rattling freaked her out. So she sold it to his chocolate shop."

Jason lounged against a freestanding shelf and propped his chin on his broad hand. "A broken heart? You mean a heart attack?"

"I don't think so. If it had been, he would have told me straight out, wouldn't he?" I frowned. Unless Mr. Moreno's command of English wasn't as good as I'd thought. "When I pressed him, he just repeated himself. I don't think he had a high opinion of Felicitas's boyfriend."

"Interesting. Felicitas Ocasio ..." Jason grinned, and I felt my worries melting. "I've got a friend on the Oaxaca police. We can ask if he knows anything about her death." He shrugged out of his suit jacket and dropped it on the counter beside GD. The cat sniffed its navy sleeve.

"Really?" I asked. "That's fantastic! Thank you!"

"So where do I start?" he asked.

"What?"

He rolled up his sleeves. "With the cleanup. You'll be here all night if you're on your own, and since I don't see

Leo anywhere, I'm guessing you are."

"I didn't want to call him in for this. He's studying for an exam."

"Which leaves me. Where do you want me?" He waggled his brows, and I laughed at the double entendre.

I stepped closer and rested my hands on his broad chest. "Right here."

Leo sold a ticket to a woman draped in a scarlet caftan and thick scarves. He handed her a brochure and a tarot card. "Your card of the day."

She glanced at it and smiled. "The Star. My lucky card. Thank you."

Ears twitching, GD watched the transaction from his perch on the counter.

"If you have any questions about the exhibits," I said, "just ask." I leaned on my broom. Jason and I had straightened everything up last night, but I'd saved the real cleaning for this morning.

"Thank you." She wafted past me. "But my spirit guides usually tell me all I need to know." The woman vanished into the Fortune Telling Room.

Leo groaned. "A bomb? I miss all the good stuff. Why didn't you call me yesterday?"

The cat meowed an agreement.

"You were in class," I said. "And there's not much you can do for a bomb threat except leave."

"I wasn't in class all day," he grumped.

"Sorry." *Not sorry.* Why would I bring Leo into a potentially dangerous situation? I adjusted a creepy doll on its pedestal and brushed off my hands on the hips of my jeans. "You could help me with a new project."

He cocked his dark head. "Oh?"

The paranormal box idea seemed too big for me and

Leo. But I had another promotional idea. "What do you think about the museum doing a podcast? You know, we could talk about objects in the museum, weird paranormal stories, take some callers ..."

His brown eyes lit. "Are you kidding? Podcasts are hot right now!"

"The thing is, I'm not sure about the technical side—"

"Hey, I got this. We can do it right here in the museum after hours, when it's quiet. I've got equipment we can use."

The bookcase swung inward, and Adele backed into the museum. She carried a box of Reign chocolate bars. "Can you do me a favor?"

I tugged at the collar of my T-shirt. I owed her about a million after the Fox and Fennel got shut down yesterday. She'd soothed all my guests with free Earl Grey on the sidewalk and hadn't complained about her own loss of business. "Thanks, Leo. Let's talk more about this later." I turned to Adele. "Sure. What's up?"

She set the box on the glass counter. "My parents think they're going to be short on chocolate, and I've got extra bars. Can you take these to Plot 42?"

"When?"

She winced. "Now? I'd go myself, but—"

"It's fine," I said quickly and took the box. The bomb threat had lost me some business, sure. But at least my guests had bought tickets in advance (and I'd promised the tickets were good for a return visit). Adele had to be out a lot more. How many of her guests had left without having had a chance to pay? Plus, her staff earned hourly wages whether she sold tea or not.

I checked my watch. It was nearing noon. "Leo, do you want me to get you a burrito on the way back?"

"Do you have to ask?" He quirked a brow. "Super beef burrito, hot salsa, refried beans."

"Got it. Adele?"

She backed toward the open bookcase. "No thanks. I prefer to keep my stomach lining."

"I'll be back in an hour," I told Leo and hurried to my vintage pickup.

As much as I loved our fifties-era downtown, my muscles relaxed as I escaped through the adobe arch. Rows of twisted vines fanned past the truck windows, the first hints of green sprouts appearing on the vines. Yellow mustard flowers blazed between the rows. Puddles from yesterday's rain glistened in the sunlight.

Cranking down my window, I inhaled the scent of damp earth. I wouldn't want to be a farmer—the work and hours were too hard. But I loved living around farms, cow smell and all.

I turned down the gravel road to Plot 42 and parked behind the weeping willow.

Grabbing the box off the seat, I slid from my pickup and ambled toward the open barn door. Droplets glistened on the orange and yellow mums along the path.

I passed the chalkboard *Open* sign and walked inside the tasting room. Hanging metal lamps blazed cheerfully from the barn's rafters.

The tasting bar was empty. But it was still early for wine tasting, and only a Thursday.

Voices floated from behind the steel wine barrel racks on my left. Adele, Harper, and I had played in this barn, so I didn't think twice about walking behind the wall of barrels. Then I recognized one of the voices—Orson Malke—and stopped short of the narrow corridor.

"... knows about ... affair ..." The word sputtered on the damp air.

"This is awful," India said. "Atticus—"

Her words were lost, too low for me to hear.

I edged closer to the wall of barrels. My foot brushed something metal and it clattered on the concrete floor. I winced.

"Hello?" India asked.

Cursing silently, I backed into the tasting room proper. "Is anyone here?" I called. "Chocolate delivery!"

India hurried around the stacked barrels. "Oh, hi Maddie."

"Adele asked me to bring this chocolate." I shifted the box in my arms. "But I thought I heard Orson here?" I angled my head toward the steel barrels. "Was there a miscommunication? Did he already bring you the chocolate you need? Because if he did, I'll return this to the Fox and Fennel."

Orson emerged from behind the wall of barrels. "No miscommunication." He combed his fingers through his beard. "I was here to check on India. I didn't realize there was a chocolate deficit."

India toyed with her braid, her fingers twitching nervously. "You heard us?"

"Ah ... not really." I walked to the tasting bar and set the box on top.

When I turned, India and Orson faced me. They formed a barricade, their arms crossed over their chests.

I stepped backward and bumped against the bar.

Beneath India's tank, her muscles were taut as barbed wire. "It's not what you think," she blurted.

"India!" Orson half turned, arm outstretched as if to grab her. "We don't know—"

"Orson and I dated before I met Atticus," India said. "But we all parted amicably. We were all okay. They never stopped being best friends. And then Lola ..."

"Found out about the affair?" Wow, I was getting pushy.

India flushed. "There was no affair. Well, I mean—"

"She misspoke," Orson said. "When India and I were first dating, I was dating Lola as well. Lola and I weren't exclusive, but I never told her about India. It wasn't technically an affair."

"There's no sense telling Lola now." India bit her lip. "Nothing happened between us after we were each married. There's nothing between Orson and me now but friendship."

"And there never will be," Orson said stiffly.

Color me suspicious, but if that were true, why had they been discussing it? "Sorry. It's none of my business."

"You don't believe us," India said, her light brown eyes earnest.

"Look," I said, "this is between you two and Lola. And from what you say, it was no big deal. Besides, I can only imagine what you're both going through right now."

She tugged on her braids. "You have no idea. Someone killed my husband, and all I can think is that they're still out there, watching. It's made me paranoid. I even accused—" She glanced at Orson, and he laid a broad hand on her shoulder.

"It's all right," he said. "Lately I feel like I'm being crushed in a melanger myself."

"It's not all right. It wasn't fair of me." India shivered. "I must be going crazy. I even feel like I'm being watched sometimes, watched by someone who—" She swallowed.

"You felt like someone was watching you?" I asked. "When was this?" Maybe I hadn't been paranoid about those phantom footsteps after all.

She laughed harshly. "All the time. Crazy, right? And then I kept thinking of what Atticus said before he died."

Orson made a sound in his throat.

"He was worried about the books," she continued, "but of course they're fine. Tilde said they were fine. She does the books, and Atticus was never a financial guy. Oh, he was great at making deals, but when it came to day-to-day budgeting ..." She smiled wanly at Orson. "You know how he was."

"But the books worried him?" I asked. "How?"

She gestured with one hand. "I don't know. He never said."

Cousin Tilde did the books. Cousin Tilde was in love with Atticus. Cousin Tilde had conveniently disappeared before the firecrackers went off at the vigil. My insides quivered. Was cousin Tilde a killer?

fifteen

Yawning, Leo slouched toward the museum's front door. He shrugged into his black motorcycle jacket. "You sure you don't need me for anything?"

"I'm good here. Thanks for everything today." I slid that day's cash into the zip bag and locked it in the small safe beneath the counter. I was getting excited about the podcast, and Leo had given me some good ideas. We were going to do a test run on Tuesday night.

"Then see ya tomorrow." He sketched a casual wave and vanished onto the darkened sidewalk.

"See you," I called.

The door banged shut. The *Closed* sign slipped sideways in the window.

I adjusted the sign and surveyed my museum.

GD stalked an invisible mouse in the main room. The bronze skull gleamed on its pedestal. Even the creepy dolls looked prim, their singed skirts arranged neatly about their legs.

I'd spent most of the day tidying up, so there wasn't much left to do now. Even better, I'd sold an abundance of chocolate and tarot cards. *Thank you, Wine and Visitors Bureau, for all the tourist promotions.*

The Bakelite wall phone jangled and I nearly jumped out of my shoes. Bomb threats rattling in my skull, I gingerly plucked the receiver from its metal hook. "Hello?"

"Maddie Kosloski?" a woman whispered.

"This is Maddie. How can I help you?"

"It's Tilde, from Reign. Can you come here?"

"To the chocolate shop?" I stilled on the outside, but on the inside, my pulse giddy-upped. "Why? Is something wrong?"

"It's about your invoice," the accountant said. "There was a small problem."

"A problem? Do we owe you more—"

"No, no, nothing like that. Just, please come. As soon as you can." She hung up.

Puzzled, I stared at the receiver, then glanced out the window. The iron streetlamps flickered on. No way was I going to that chocolate shop alone.

I hung up and dialed Jason.

"Hello?" His voice was low and rumbly, and heat spread from my chest.

"Hi. It's Maddie. I'm calling from the museum phone."

"Is your cell phone not working?"

"No, it's fine. I was just near this one."

"Can't stay away from me, can you?"

My cheeks warmed. "No, that's … Well, yes, but that's not why I'm calling."

"Let me guess, the killer tied you up and you just escaped."

"Um, is that sarcasm?" I grinned. I couldn't help myself. "Because if it is, you're not very good at it."

He chuckled. "I'm only giving you a hard time. What's going on?"

"I just got a strange call from Tilde." I wrapped the cord around one finger. "She asked me to come to Reign. Something about an invoice, but she wouldn't explain what. It seemed … weird."

"I'll meet you there in ten minutes."

"Thanks," I said, grateful I didn't have to explain my fears. We said quick goodbyes and hung up.

I checked GD's food and water, then grabbed my purse and strode out the door, locking it behind me.

San Benedetto pretty much rolled up its sidewalks when the sun went down. Aside from a few lit restaurants and bars, the road seemed eerily deserted. Hunching my shoulders, I hurried down the sidewalk.

I didn't trust Tilde. Not after everything I'd learned. But at this point, I wasn't sure what information I *could* trust. Just because Lola told me that Tilde had been stalking Atticus, it didn't make it true. I thought back to the vigil. Had Tilde stepped away from the gazebo so she could set the firecrackers? And if she had, why?

My breath plumed before me. Ribbons of black cloud blotted out the stars. A gibbous moon rose above the squat brick-and-stucco buildings on Main Street.

India and Orson told me their romantic relationship was long over. But was it? And if Lola had found out that they were still an item ...

No. If Lola found out, it wouldn't have been a motive for her to murder Atticus.

But if India and Orson were having an affair, they had reason to kill. A crummy reason, but reason enough.

Someone jerked me backward by the collar.

I gasped, spinning around and raising my fists. Pain lashed my cheek and I gave a low cry.

And stared at a plum tree.

I glared at the swaying branch, low and whip-thin, that had snagged my hoodie. "For Pete's sake." Annoyed and a little embarrassed, I unhooked myself, smoothed the hood over my thick down vest, and continued on.

Atticus's death *could* have been unintentional. People

didn't realize how deadly a hard shove could be. What if there'd been a quarrel, Atticus was pushed, and he fell and cracked his skull?

On that soft rubber mat? No way.

I approached another plum tree and gave it a wide berth.

Okay, he'd hit his head on something else.

On the melanger? That would explain why the vat had tipped, but not the position of Atticus's body.

Or, someone had whacked him in the head with something, and then he'd fallen, grabbing the melanger on the way down ...

A black Mercedes cruised by. It slowed, and my scalp prickled.

I must be going crazy. That was what India had said, and that she'd felt like she was being watched. So did I. Were we both paranoid? Or was it only me?

I picked up the pace and arrived at the chocolate shop as Jason's black SUV parked beside the sidewalk.

He stepped from the car. His muscular shoulders filled his navy suit jacket and my heartbeat quickened. This was the way it was supposed to be—the two of us, working together.

He kissed me lightly on the cheek, then more firmly on the mouth. In spite of my anxiety, I melted into his embrace.

A car honked, roaring past.

We broke apart, breathless.

"What have you gotten yourself into now?" he asked.

"Nothing, I hope. That's why I called you."

"And I appreciate that." He eyed Reign's windows, his brows pulling together. "Tilde asked you to meet her here? The shop is closed."

"No, it's—" I turned. The lights were on inside,

illuminating the mercury cinderblock walls, the counters, the chocolate displays. But a *Closed* sign hung in the front door. "That's strange. I thought Reign closed an hour after the museum on Thursdays." Maybe Tilde wanted to have a private conversation?

Or maybe she was one of those female serial killers and I was her next victim.

Good thing I'd brought someone armed and dangerous. I cut a glance to his hip. Yep. He was armed.

I knocked on the glass door.

No one came to unlock it.

"The office is in the rear of the building," I said uncertainly. "Maybe Tilde can't hear me knocking?"

"Wait here. I'll check the back door." He strode around the corner.

I peered through the glass. Kitchen lights streamed through the narrow window in the cinderblock wall behind the register.

One hand braced on the door's elegant handle, I leaned closer, nose nearly touching the glass.

The hallway lights were on too.

Weird. A chill rippled my spine.

I pressed closer, straining to see deeper into the shop. Tilde was probably in the bathroom.

The door jolted open.

I squeaked and staggered inside, stumbling into a chic display table. The pyramids of chocolate bars shuddered at the impact but didn't fall.

The door had been unlocked this whole time? Wildly, I looked around. "Jas—"

The door clicked shut behind me and I jumped. I worked to slow my breathing and rubbed my damp palms on the thighs of my jeans.

"Jason?"

No response.

Of course he couldn't hear me. He must be at the back door by now.

"Hello?" I called, uneasy. "Tilde?"

The secondhand on the clock above the kitchen window ticked.

"Tilde?"

I strained my ears.

Something creaked.

I started, whirled.

Chocolate bars sat stacked on their shelves. A spiky air plant clung to a bit of driftwood dotted with wrapped chocolate squares.

I blew out my breath. The sound had probably been the building settling.

Yeah, that was it.

"Hello?" I called.

A car drove past outside.

This was ridiculous. I strode down the hallway, pausing to stick my head inside the kitchen. It was empty, the metal racks and counters gleaming. I hurried to the rear door and pushed it open.

Jason stood there, hand raised. He dropped his arm to his side. "How'd you get inside?"

"Turned out the front door was open."

He cursed softly.

"I don't think anyone's here," I said, stepping aside.

He prowled past me, pushed the office door open, and vanished into the room.

Feeling suddenly vulnerable, I hurried after him.

He stood behind Tilde's desk, staring at the floor.

My heart clenched. *No. Oh no.* "Is she—?"

"Go outside," he said sharply.

But he was too late. I couldn't unsee Tilde, lying

beside her desk, blood pooling around a square block of wood centered over her heart.

sixteen

Jason knelt beside the fallen woman and took her pulse. But her eyes were open and dull.

Tilde was dead.

My insides wrenched, and I pressed my hand to my mouth.

One of Tilde's arms was out flung, her hand curled against the wall, pink fingernails pressing into her palm. I stared at the strange square block pinned to her chest. Pinned …

I gasped, reeling into the hallway. She'd been stabbed with a receipt holder. And suddenly, the image of Tilde seemed to merge with that of Atticus's body. *Wrong, wrong, wrong.*

I rubbed my eyes, and the strange double-vision vanished.

Jason pulled his cell phone from his jacket pocket and called it in. He ended the call and looked up at me, still standing horror-stricken in the open doorway. "You should wait outside," he said.

Right. I should because it was a crime scene, and my presence risked messing it up. It was a logical request, and no doubt police procedure, but my throat tightened. I nodded and left the building, to shiver on the front sidewalk.

A gray Mercedes rolled past, the light from its headlamps flattening the street in tones of gray and yellow. It flicked its high beams, temporarily blinding me.

When I'd rubbed the spots from my eyes, a man, his fists jammed into the pockets of his windbreaker, strode toward me.

My breathing grew uneven. I edged against the wall of the chocolate shop to make way.

He passed, head lowered, without acknowledging my presence.

A siren sounded in the distance, and I pressed myself closer to the wall. First Atticus, now Tilde. The accountant must have known something, seen something...

But why had I seen Atticus when I'd looked at Tilde's corpse? There must be some connection, something more than the coincidence—no, it couldn't be coincidence—of them both being killed in Reign.

I straightened off the wall. I had to return to the chocolate shop and figure this out.

Turning, I reached for the door handle.

A blue sports car screeched to a stop behind me and my shoulders tightened.

"Kosloski!" Laurel slammed the muscle car's door. "Where's Slate?"

"He's inside, in the office. But—"

"Stay here."

She stormed into the chocolate shop.

Folding my arms, I cooled my heels on the sidewalk, and more law enforcement personnel arrived. One cop tried to shoo me off, but I explained I was with Jason, and he let me stay.

All right. I'd just figure out what was bothering me about the murder scene—aside from the murder—without going inside. I shuddered, remembering Tilde's supine form. Come to think of it, I would *rather* stay outside.

The gibbous moon rose higher above Main Street's single-story buildings. I hugged my arms tighter and leaned against the wall, trying to make myself inconspicuous.

The phone in my pocket rang, and I jerked away from the cold brick. I fumbled the phone and saw it was Harper.

"Harper! Thank God you called."

"Why? What's wrong?"

I slithered away from the door, away from the cops flowing in and out of the shop, away from the corpse cooling in the building behind me. "There's been another murder," I said in a low voice. "Tilde. But don't tell anyone. It's just happened. No one at Reign knows yet." *Except for the killer.*

"What happened? Where are you?"

"At the chocolate shop."

Harper groaned. "Tell me you didn't discover the body. You know how the police feel about that."

"I was with Jason. I probably shouldn't be telling you anything right now, but …" But I was standing on a dark and lonely street, and my adrenaline was ebbing, leaving me shaky.

"Do you want me to come over there?"

"No," I said quickly. Jason definitely wouldn't appreciate bystanders. "I only …" I cleared my throat. "It's good to hear a friendly voice. Why were you calling?"

"What? Oh. I just wanted to see what you were up to."

"Standing on a sidewalk, hoping this doesn't mean another interrogation at the police station," I said. But something in Harper's voice had rung false.

"Surely that won't happen, since you and Jason found the body together?"

"I guess," I said uncertainly. "I hope so."

Jason and Laurel walked outside. He scanned the sidewalk.

I raised a hand and caught his eye. "I need to go. I'll talk to you later."

"Sure. Call me if you can."

We hung up and I pocketed my phone, hurrying over. "Jason—"

Laurel's lips peeled back in a snarl. "I'll take her statement."

Jason nodded, expression impassive. "Sure. Maddie, we'll talk later." He returned inside the chocolate shop.

The glass door banged shut.

"Is everything all right?" I asked Laurel.

"A woman's been killed, nitwit. Of course it's not all right. Now tell me what happened."

I ran her through our discovery of the body. She kept returning to the moments when Jason and I had been separated—him at the rear of the building, me inside Reign.

Finally, exasperated, I said, "You can't think I killed her while Jason was outside?"

"I think you've made a real problem for him," she snapped. "As usual."

"What does that mean?"

Her jaw clenched. "You shouldn't have gone inside that damn shop alone. What the hell is wrong with you?"

"The door was open," I said weakly.

"Did you even think about what this might mean for his career?"

"His career?" I asked.

She rolled her eyes. "Question answered. Now get out

of here before I decide to arrest you."

"But—"

"Get!"

I scuttled down the sidewalk. Had I caused problems for Jason? It had seemed simpler to go through inside and let him in at the rear. Or was that just a neat excuse? Had my urge to snoop gotten Jason into trouble?

I paused outside an Irish pub and called him.

It went to voicemail, and my midsection tightened.

Guilt-stricken, I left a message for him to call and hurried to the alley behind the museum, where my pickup waited.

Light streamed from the windows above Mason's motorcycle shop. I was swamped by an urge to run up those concrete steps, knock on his apartment door.

I didn't want to be alone.

Ridiculous. I was a grown woman and a paranormal museum owner, not some damsel in distress.

I climbed into my pickup and drove home.

In my driveway, I sat for a moment in the cab and listened to the ticking of the metal cooling. The bare branches of a nearby oak rubbed against each other, clicking like bones.

I drew deeper into the seat, zipping my hoodie to the top. My aunt's house was dark, her driveway empty. Dark fields stretched around me, and I realized how isolated I was in my little garage apartment.

The gibbous moon vanished behind a cloud, plunging the scene into blackness.

Swallowing, I stepped from my pickup and shut the door.

Two slim shadows detached themselves from my front porch.

My fist clenched on my keys. Had Laurel changed her

mind? Was I going to be arrested? Did the killer have an accomplice?

"Maddie?" Harper called.

Smiling with relief, I trotted up the stairs. "What are you two doing here?"

"Harper told me what happened." Adele unbuttoned her long coat, exposing an ice-blue dress dotted with white flowers. "We thought you might need some support." With one hand, she brandished a wine bottle from her parent's vineyard. The other held a brown-paper gift bag.

"I know I wasn't supposed to tell anyone." Harper combed her fingers through her dark hair. "But it's Adele. And ... wine!"

I let them inside my apartment and flipped on the lights. While they shed their coats and uncorked the bottle in my kitchen, I conducted a quick, secretive search, pulling open the closets, checking beneath my queen-sized bed. No one hid beneath it.

Self-conscious, I smoothed my T-shirt and returned to my small, nautical-themed living area.

Harper and Adele lounged on the gray-blue couch, glasses of red wine in their hands. Someone (I guessed Adele) had shoved aside a stack of paranormal-themed magazines and set out a cheese platter.

I dropped into the matching lounge chair. "Who brought the gorgonzola?" I felt the urge to say *something*, to fill the room with noise and humanity. I wasn't hungry but leaned forward and snagged a crumbly green-veined wedge.

"I did," Adele said. "I thought it would make a nice break from wine and chocolate pairings."

"I always get a little tired of chocolate this time of year," Harper agreed, one leg tucked beneath her jeans.

A crumb of cheese garnished the chest of her coffee-colored turtleneck sweater. She grinned. "But I get over it fast."

"What happened?" Adele adjusted her dress around her legs.

I drew a shuddering breath. "I got a call from Tilde to meet her at Reign," I said. "It sounded weird, so I called Jason. He met me there, but there was a *Closed* sign in the window, and no one answered our knocks. So he went around the back. It turned out, the front door was unlocked, so I went inside and let him in through the back door. Then we found her. It was just like Atticus."

"She was covered in chocolate?" Harper asked.

"No." I rubbed my hands on my jeans. "No, she was stabbed." *Pinned like a butterfly*. The cheese turned to lead in my stomach.

"You mean, it was like Atticus because you found the body in the same chocolate shop?" Adele asked. "Of course it reminded you of his murder."

"No," I said slowly. "It was more than that."

"More than what?" Harper asked.

Unseeing, I moved my arm, imitating the position of Tilde's, sprawled on the floor.

"Is that sign language for give me a drink?" Adele asked. "Is a wine glass supposed to magically appear in your hand? Because I put your glass on the table right next to you."

"No, it's just ... Her arm." I straightened, eyes widening. "It was her arm. We assumed Atticus had knocked over the chocolate when he fell. But there wasn't any chocolate on his arm nearest the melanger. If he'd grabbed the vat and tipped it over, there would have been chocolate on his hand or arm, wouldn't there?"

Adele wrinkled her forehead. "I guess."

"Think about it," I said. "The melangers tip forward so workers can pour out the chocolate. If Atticus had grabbed one and fallen beneath it, there would have been chocolate on his sleeve."

"So you think someone put Atticus there and tipped the chocolate on top of him?" Adele shuddered. "That's sick."

"Or someone was trying to send a message about the victim." Harper sipped her wine.

"But don't you see?" I asked. "It means it's all connected. Everything. The murders. The firecrackers at the vigil. The bomb threat at my museum."

"I don't get it." Adele set her wine glass on the coffee table and propped her elbows on her knees.

"It's the same mind," I said, leaning forward in my chair. "They're all dark pranks. Maybe Atticus fell near the melangers, maybe he was dragged there. I don't know. But someone dumped that chocolate on him *after* he was dead or unconscious. And using a receipt holder to stab their accountant—"

Harper choked on her wine. "A receipt holder? One of those metal pointy ones?"

"Yeah," I said. "And it was …"

"Awful." Adele paled.

"Wrong." Harper shook her head, her glossy black hair cascading around her shoulders.

"Both," I said. "I mean, sure, Atticus makes chocolate, so maybe it pointed to chocolate making being the reason behind his murder. But why would a murderer leave hints about the motive?"

"Because he's crazy?" Adele asked.

"Obviously, the killer's disturbed," I said. "But I think it's more than that."

"If the killer wasn't leaving a message, then why dump

the chocolate?" Harper asked. "And why the other pranks?"

I sank back in the soft chair. "I don't know." I plucked a glass of wine from the nearby end table and sipped absently. "I should have figured it out sooner. But Jason banished me to the sidewalk—"

"What?" Adele asked, outraged.

"And then Laurel interviewed me—"

"Laurel?" Adele asked. "Not Jason?"

"Laurel." An uncomfortable flush of heat rolled through me. "I guess it would have been weird for him to interview me, since we're dating." I bit my lower lip. *Had* my actions gotten him into trouble? I'd been so set on helping him find the killer, I hadn't thought through the ramifications for Jason.

"But why did Tilde call you to Reign?" Adele asked. "Not to find her body."

"She said something about an invoice, but I'm not sure I believe her."

"She must have known something about Atticus's murder," Adele said. "Why else would someone kill her? But if she saw or knew who killed Atticus, why not tell the police?"

"Could she have been blackmailing someone?" Harper asked.

"Or maybe she was unsure of what she'd seen," Adele said.

"Maybe someone overheard her call you and decided she knew too much?" Harper asked.

My stomach turned, the wine souring in my mouth. If Harper was right, that would make me partly responsible for her death.

"Okay," Adele said, "let's assume you're correct and the bomb threat is connected to the murders. Why target you and your museum?"

"I don't know," I said. "Except I found Atticus, and I thought I heard something when I was alone with him."

"Heard something?" Harper cocked her head. "You mean, you might not have been alone? The killer could have still been there?"

"Maybe," I said. "But at this point, they must know I'm no threat."

"Unless the killer thinks you know something that you haven't told the police," Harper said.

My mouth went dry.

A bomb threat.

A near hit-and-run.

They were right. I'd become a target.

seventeen

There are people who visit the Paranormal Museum for a laugh, or because they're stuck drying out between wine tastings. But a surprising number are genuinely interested in the strange and supernatural. Maybe something happened to them they can't quite explain. Maybe they grew up on a diet of Tolkien or Harry Potter and have loved the mystical ever since. More rarely, the visitors are true believers in the supernatural. But most have a story to tell. I love hearing those stories.

Usually.

"I don't believe in ghosts," the middle-aged blonde assured me. She twisted the bangles on her wrist. "But I just can't explain what happened in that apartment." She shuddered. "The weird shadows. That creepy hand ..."

"Uh huh," I said. The line at the counter was six deep. Something crashed from the Fortune Telling Room, and I winced.

Leo, in a Paranormal Museum tee and torn jeans, handed out tickets and brochures, bagged tarot cards and chocolate.

I worked the register, and I was wearing the exact same tee. Maybe it *was* time for a fashion upgrade.

"Trust me." I keyed in the blonde's chocolate bars. "I get it. It's hard to trust your senses. And it's smart to ask if there are alternate explanations for the phenomena. Not every bump in the night is a ghost."

"I know. But what do you believe?" she asked. "I mean, is the museum really haunted?"

"Not the museum itself," I hedged. This was always a tricky question. I wasn't sure what I believed, but I couldn't exactly advertise my agnosticism. "The way these things work, it's the objects inside that are haunted. My experts say ghosts or psychic energy attach to items that have meaning for the prior owner. Like the molinillo." I nodded to the Gallery.

I handed her the change and Leo passed her bag across the counter. "Have a great rest of your day." I beamed.

The blonde winked. "The wineries are next on our list. How could the day be bad?" She swaggered outside with her boyfriend.

The bell above the door jingled in her wake.

Jason caught the open door with one hand and walked inside. My favorite detective took in the crowds. "Bad timing?"

"Uh ..." I rang up a T-shirt.

"I got a hot lead on the molinillo," he said. "I'll come back later." He ducked out the door.

"Wait. What—?"

The door jangled shut.

What lead? With the sleeve of my hoodie, I wiped a handprint off the glass counter. I was more interested in leads on the murders than on the molinillo. But violent crime was his business, the molinillo mine.

"Do you know anything about, um, shadows?" a gangly twenty-something at the counter asked.

"What kind of shadows?" Leo asked briskly, wrapping a T-shirt.

"I've been seeing shadows moving up and down my apartment stairs." He scratched his narrow chin. "And there's no reason for them. I've checked everything. Reflections, window angles ... But they're just ... there."

"Shadow people," Leo said. "No one knows what they are, but most think they're not ghosts."

"Are they dangerous?" he asked.

Leo reached beneath the counter for a dented metal recipe box and pulled out a business card. "Do a search for shadow people on the Internet. If you think you need to do something about them, you might want to call this woman." He handed the customer the card and bagged the T-shirt.

"Thanks." The young man pocketed the card and left, bag in hand.

"We should talk about shadow people on our podcast," Leo said to me.

"Maybe," I said, sweating, and handed a woman a box of chocolate Tarot cards.

We worked through the line. Finally, around lunchtime, the crowd eased, in quest of food more substantial than chocolate.

I slipped into the Fortune Telling Room to check for damage.

A clear glass bottle lay shattered on the floor.

Cursing beneath my breath, I retrieved the whisk broom from a low cabinet and swept up the pieces. I plucked its placard from the shelf:

Mrs. Antoinette Matteson was born Antoinette Wealthy in 1847. This Buffalo, New Jersey, spiritualist and psychic healer, or "clairvoyant doctress," grew into her mediumistic powers after the death of her husband, when she became the sole support for her family.

This bottle once contained one of her custom herbal remedies, compounded from recipes Antoinette discovered during trance states. In her book, The Occult

Family Physician, *she wrote: "During the twenty years of my mediumistic experience, many hundreds, in fact I may say thousands, of remarkable cures have been made through the aid of my spirit guides." She died in 1913.*

I grimaced. I'd liked that bottle, a relic of America's spiritualist movement, and from a time when women had to get creative if they wanted a career. Options for women working outside the home during the nineteenth century had been limited. In a way, I was following in Antoinette's footsteps with the museum.

Returning to the main room, I dumped the shards in the waste bin. I sagged against the glass counter, my elbow nudging GD's tip jar. "Wow."

"Wine and Chocolate Friday," Leo agreed. "Lunch?"

"It's your turn to make the run. What are you thinking?"

He scrunched up his forehead. "Burrito?"

"Fine by me." The day Mexican food gave me heartburn was the day I was packing it all in. I handed him cash.

He pulled on his motorcycle jacket and sauntered out the door.

I grabbed my cell phone from beneath the counter and called Jason.

"Maddie?" His deep-timbered voice rumbled through me. "How are you doing? I'm sorry I didn't get a chance to talk to you after …"

"Tilde," I said heavily.

"I'm sorry you had to see that."

"Me too. And I'm sorry … Did I make things worse for you?"

"No," he said, his voice firm.

"Jason, Laurel suggested—"

"I know what she suggested," he said in a neutral

voice. "Laurel is protective of her partner, just like I'm protective of her."

But had Laurel been wrong? I had a sick feeling she hadn't.

"You can't plan for finding a body," he said. "Well, you can plan for it," he corrected, "but things happen. You stayed calm and you gave a clear statement. You did good."

I wasn't convinced, but I let it drop. "So, what do you mean you have a lead on the molinillo?"

He chuckled. "I thought that would get your attention. My friend in Oaxaca said he'd look at the files. I'm supposed to call him today."

"Oh," I said, weirdly disappointed. I was glad Jason was taking an interest, but I'd hoped to talk to the Mexican detective myself.

"What if I come to the museum and we call him together?"

I brightened. "I'd love that!"

"When's a good time?"

"Any time this afternoon should work."

"How about now?" He strolled into the museum.

Grinning, I leaned across the counter and kissed him. His cheek was rough against mine, and I had to restrain myself from throwing my arms around him. We weren't alone, and I'm not a big PDA fan.

GD sneered, whiskers twitching, from his perch on the haunted rocking chair.

"Do you think your friend in Oaxaca learned anything?" I asked.

Jason pulled his phone from the pocket of his navy suit jacket. "Let's find out."

The bookcase swiveled open and Adele stalked into the museum on skin-toned sling-backs. She wore a matching pencil skirt and white blouse beneath her Fox and Fennel apron. Strands of inky hair escaped her chignon. She moaned, "This is a disaster."

"What's wrong?" I smothered my frustration. I loved Adele, but Oaxaca! Detective! Molinillo!

"The wedding cake. My second, third, and fourth choices don't have enough time to make it now."

Jason frowned. "The wedding's not until June. What's the problem?"

She braced her elbows on the counter, her head in her hands. "You explain."

"Wedding cakes need to be booked four to six months in advance," I said. "We're just past the window."

"It's only a cake," Jason said. "How tough can it be?"

Adele raised her head and glared. "Only a cake?! The cake is the focus of the entire wedding!"

"I thought the happy couple was." His mouth quirked.

"You don't understand," she said. "What am I going to do?"

"There must be a solution," I said. "Maybe we could simplify. Maybe there's an amazing cake decorator at Ladies Aid—"

She made a squeak of horror.

"Take it from someone who knows," Jason said. "The wedding is the least important part of the marriage. And it doesn't predict future success."

"I know you're right." Adele gripped the hair close to her scalp. "But there's knowing, and there's *knowing*. No matter how logical I try to be about it, it's my wedding!"

"We'll figure something out," I said, soothing. "I'll call my mother. She's been to tons of weddings. Maybe she'll have an idea."

"Fine. Call her." Shoulders slumped, Adele trooped through the open bookcase into her tearoom. It snicked shut behind her.

Jason smiled grimly. "Want to call your mom?"

"No! I want to call your buddy in Oaxaca." I also really liked saying *Oaxaca*. I wanted to visit the place because of the name alone.

Jason's smile broadened. "Then let's do it." He made the call and put the phone on speaker.

"*Bueno?*" a man's voice floated, tinny and broken, from the phone.

"Alejandro, it's Jason."

"Jason! I have what you were looking for."

"I've put you on speaker," Jason said. "My friend Maddie is with me."

Friend? I made a face at him. "Hi, Alejandro," I said.

"Ah, the lady with the haunted museum. *Encantada.*"

"What did you find?" Jason asked.

"The Miss Ocasio case is officially a suicide."

"Officially?" Jason's face tightened.

The man laughed shortly. "*Officially.* I spoke with the lead detective, however, and unofficially, he liked her *bastardo* boyfriend for her death."

"Why?" Jason asked.

"The boyfriend dealt in narcotics. And people had a habit of disappearing around him."

"What was his motive for killing Felicitas?" I asked.

"She was pregnant."

"Oh," I said softly. How awful. "How exactly did she—?"

The man swore. "*Lo siento.* I must go. An emergency. Call me later." He hung up.

Jason pocketed the phone. "It's stories like that that made me leave the big city."

"You're not getting much of a break from murder and mayhem in San Benedetto."

"At least the public doesn't see me as the enemy. What did you think of Alejandro's story?"

"I wonder if there's more to it, since we got cut off. Do you think Felicitas knew her boyfriend was dealing drugs?"

"Why wouldn't she? They were together. She'd have to know."

I shot him a look. Yeah, in a perfect world, there'd be no secrets. I squirmed, thinking of my own recent investigations I'd been keeping secret from my mother. "If the molinillo legend is rooted in fact, and rattles when lies are told, that would imply her boyfriend was keeping things secret."

"Lying to her about his drug dealing?"

The front door jingled and swung open.

"At least we don't have any dark secrets from each other." Jason smiled, wry.

Mason walked inside, stopped short. A flush of red swept from the collar of his black T-shirt to the roots of his hair. "Dark secrets?"

I straightened off the counter. "The case of the haunted molinillo."

"Are you sure about that?" The muscles beneath Mason's motorcycle tee tensed.

Confused, I shifted my weight. "Well, yeah, I'm ..." I trailed off, realizing that Mason thought we were talking about his situation—the son he hadn't known about. But that wasn't his fault. Belle had given birth to their son while he was overseas in the military, and she hadn't told him until recently. And he and Belle had never married.

"Why would she lie?" Jason asked, his arms loose at his sides. "It's a haunted molinillo."

Mason turned to me and his hands unclenched. "You don't have to protect me, Maddie. I get it. The situation with Belle wasn't kind to you."

"It's fine." My cheeks warmed. "It was no one's fault." Well, maybe Belle's, but ... whatever.

"You wanted something?" Jason asked him.

He hesitated. "Someone's been using my dumpster. I thought it might be Dieter. I'd ask him myself, but I haven't seen him since the vigil, and he doesn't answer his phone."

"He screens his calls," I said. It was super irritating. "But I don't know why he'd use your dumpster. He hasn't been doing any construction work here—not that it would be an excuse if he had," I added quickly. I hoped we weren't in for another bout of dumpster wars. It was amazing how touchy people could get over dumpster use and positioning. Though I'd thought Mason and I were past that.

"Have you seen anyone else around?" Mason asked.

"No," I said, "and Adele certainly wouldn't abuse your dumpster. I know I haven't." Heh heh. Dumpster abuse. Maybe San Benedetto needed a dumpster protective services division.

Mason glanced at Jason.

The detective raised his hands, palms out. "Hey, I'm not getting involved."

Mason grunted, turned on his bootheel, and strode out.

"That went well," I muttered. When I'd first met Mason, he'd been on a tear about dumpster issues as well. Was our relationship regressing?

I glanced at Jason, who was watching the slowly closing door. The two men had completely different temperaments. As fun and exciting as Mason was, I preferred Jason's easygoing demeanor. And it was time I told him my theory about the murders. I drew a breath.

"Has he been coming around much?" Jason asked.

My head jerked back. "Who? Mason? No more than usual."

"What's usual?"

"We're neighbors. Jason, have you noticed—"

"—that Mason came here to tell you something, and he backed off when he saw me here? Yeah, I noticed."

"What?" I adjusted the hem of my T-shirt. "No. He left because he was embarrassed. He thought 'dark secrets' meant his situation with Belle."

Jason eyed me skeptically. "Yeah, but he came here for a reason. He's been hanging around your museum a lot lately. Is everything okay between him and Belle?"

Heat, made of mingled embarrassment and annoyance, flushed my face. "I don't know. Why would I? Mason and I are over."

"I know that." Jason's eyes darkened with annoyance. "But I'm not sure he does."

"What's that supposed to mean?" I asked sharply. Mason and I had broken up. He was with someone else. And I wasn't a cheater.

"I mean—"

The door opened and Leo clomped in. "Hi, Jason. Here's your burrito, Mad. Grilled veggies with refried beans and hot salsa." He set a small paper bag on the counter.

"Thanks," I said. "Jason, about—"

He leaned across the counter and kissed me lightly. "I know. You haven't done anything wrong, and I'm not jealous. But for his sake, you need to shut this down."

Shut it down? I hadn't started anything! "But—"

"You know I'm right."

"Right about what?" Leo asked.

"Nothing," I muttered, looking away.

Jason slid a tattered business card across the counter. "Here's Alejandro's number. Feel free to call him again."

"Thanks. I will." I watched him leave.

"Who's Alejandro?" Leo asked.

"A detective in Oaxaca," I said. "He may have more information on the molinillo."

Leo grinned. "Cool."

I flopped against the counter. I hadn't had a chance to tell Jason my theory—or profile—on the killer. It was a day of bad timing.

"What's wrong?" Leo asked.

"Nothing. Something I forgot. It's not important." But I felt a chasm of things unsaid growing between myself and Jason. And I wasn't sure how to fix it.

eighteen

"A fake cake?" Adele paced in front of my counter. "What does that even mean?"

My gaze darted to the computer screen. "Um, are you sure that's what my mom said?" It was the end of that long day, and I'd settled in to do online research on Atticus and Orson. I'd just found a magazine profile about the two when Adele walked into the museum.

"A fake cake and then a sheet cake to serve the guests," Adele said. "She said it would save the baker time."

I set down my pen, resigned to doing no research until Adele got the cake business off her chest. "Why didn't any of the bakers suggest that?"

"Maybe because they knew I'd say no? I can't have a fake cake! It's bad karma. What does that say about the marriage? That it's a fake too?"

"Why would it say anything about your marriage?" I asked, trying for a reasonable tone.

She shooed GD off the haunted rocking chair and dropped onto the seat. "I don't know."

"And when did you care about karma? Isn't that more Harper's bag?"

"I've always cared about karma. I just didn't call it that."

GD leapt into Adele's lap and coiled into a silky black ball.

Distractedly, she stroked his fur. "Maybe I'll see that

fortune-teller of yours tomorrow for advice."

Now I knew something was seriously wrong. Adele thought anything to do with the paranormal was a waste of time. "Adele, this seems like it's about more than a cake. What's really bothering you?"

She stared at the ceiling. "Do you have any idea how many people have told me recently that opposites attract?"

"No-o."

"They keep reminding me how different Dieter and I are. When we're together ... we always seem like a good thing. He's so relaxed, and I'm ..."

"Not."

"Right." She leaned forward. "But we agree on the most important things, like family and money and morals. I didn't think these personality issues would bother me. But ... this wedding! It feels like everything's on my shoulders. I wish he'd get more involved. Dieter doesn't even seem to care!"

"I'm sure that's not true. Have you talked to him about it?"

"Of course I have. And he's offered to do more work, but ..."

"But what?"

She winced. "I'm not sure I trust him with the job."

"Adele ..."

"I know!" Her fists clenched in GD's fur. "But a wedding is so important, and he's just so casual about everything. All he wants is to get married. He doesn't care how."

"And that's a bad thing?"

"It is when you're trying to please two extended families full of demanding people."

"Maybe Dieter has the right idea. If you can't please

everybody, why try?"

She glared at me. "Honestly, Maddie, you're as bad as Dieter. And you're in customer service!"

"Huh?"

Adele set GD on the linoleum floor and stalked to the bookcase. "I'll figure this out somehow." She slipped into the tearoom and shut the bookcase behind her.

I half rose from my seat to go after her, but I sat back down. This was something Adele and Dieter needed to work out on their own. Besides, murder research was calling.

I read the profile.

"There's something highly suspicious about someone who doesn't like chocolate." Atticus Reine, in his San Benedetto chocolate factory/store, grins beneath his impressive beard.

Five years ago, Atticus and his best friend, Orson Malke, began experimenting with chocolate in their San Francisco apartment. They crushed cocoa beans to make their chocolate from scratch and added nothing but pure cane sugar. Their simple brown wrappers stood out in a sea of chic graphics. But it's the chocolate—the alchemy of heat, cocoa beans, and sugar—that has taken the chocolate world by storm.

"I won't say that we make the best chocolate in the world," Orson says. "But if we don't, then who does?"

Orson's wife, Lola, insists on a tasting in their updated Victorian home. We sit in their elegant dining area, the French windows open to their organic garden. The tasting is complemented with local cheeses and central California wines. Lola talks about the chocolate as if it were a fine wine, complete with forward flavors, complexity, and balance.

Many purists prefer their plain chocolate bars, which

are identified by country. But I confess I'm partial to the bars enhanced with local ingredients. Sea salt from the Pacific. Lavender. Dried, locally grown citrus and nuts.

"We keep it simple," Orson says. "The ingredients should enhance the experience of the chocolate, rather than be the experience. Because in the end, it's all about the chocolate."

But evaluating chocolate—like wine—is subjective. Expert Donald Warner insists Reign chocolate is prized more for its clever marketing than the quality of the chocolate itself. "Not a single bar is perfect," Warner complains. "There are always defects."

"The bars are made by hand," Orson insists. "And the imperfections are part of their beauty, and, frankly, of the organic process. What's important is taste, and Reign chocolate is among the top in the world."

I drummed my fingers on the glass counter. Orson was right. People expected glossy perfection when they bought things. We were used to standardized items made in factories. But that wasn't reality in the world of handmade products.

GD leapt onto the counter, his tail lashing the screen.

Annoyed, I brushed it aside. Returning to the search page, I clicked on the next article, this one a profile of Lola and Orson and Reign:

While others sampled wine in quaint farmhouses, I sat with chocolate maker Orson Malke and his wife, molecular biologist Lola Emerson. We tasted chocolate ...

I frowned. Atticus had barely been mentioned in the articles I'd turned up. There should have been a *bit* more about Atticus, shouldn't there? Had Atticus been that modest? Or had he kept a low profile for a different reason?

I needed to learn more about him, and the Internet wasn't cutting it. On impulse, I called the chocolate shop.

"Hello, this is Reign," Lola said.

"Oh, hi," I said, surprised to hear her answer the phone. "This is Maddie from the Paranormal Museum."

"Hello, Maddie. What can I help you with?"

"You're working at Reign now?"

She laughed shortly. "God, no. But whenever a phone rings, I can't stop myself from answering. If you want to speak to Orson, I'm afraid he's busy training the new assistant."

"Oh. It's about my chocolate display here at the museum. I wanted to put something up about Atticus, to honor him." I winced. It was a lie, but honoring him wasn't a bad idea. I should have thought of it sooner.

Something rattled in the Gallery. Brow furrowed, I leaned across the counter. That wasn't ... the molinillo? Or could someone be in there? Hairs rose on my arms. I'd thought all my guests had left.

"You mean like a eulogy?" Lola asked.

I rose and walked around the counter for a better view of the Gallery. "Something like that, but I didn't want to bother India. I was thinking a small placard, with something about his life and work with Reign. I've been searching online, but most of the articles are about you and Orson." I edged to the open doorway and peered around the corner into the Gallery.

No one was there.

The molinillo sat at an innocent angle in its tall ceramic bowl.

"That was all Atticus's idea. He thought the chocolate maker made for a more compelling story than the marketer."

Then how did Lola end up in so many of the press

pieces? "That makes sense," I said. "I wish I could have talked to him about his marketing strategies, and how he put you and Orson front and center."

"I wouldn't say front and center, but you've seen our home … You know, I was just leaving for the day. Why don't you stop by my place? I'm sure we have something at the house you can use."

"At your house? Not the chocolate shop?"

"The office was the domain of Atticus and Tilde." Lola paused. "Orson does most of his paperwork from home. He won't be coming home until late tonight, so I'd love it if you could join me. As much as I enjoy our place, it can get lonely at night."

My lips pursed. "May I bring a friend?" Because I was definitely not going to meet a murder suspect alone.

"The more the merrier," Lola said. "Can you meet me there in an hour?"

"Sure. Thanks."

We hung up.

I glanced at the bookcase that led to the tearoom. Adele could use a break. But I had a feeling she'd view an impromptu invitation to Lola's as an annoyance.

I called Harper, and she agreed to meet me at the Malkes' home.

When I arrived, Harper's BMW was parked in the long gravel driveway. Light glowed from the two-story Victorian, transforming it into a fairytale confection. Behind its floor-to-ceiling windows, Harper and Lola gestured animatedly inside the home's extension.

Parking behind the BMW, I stepped from my pickup. Rows of barren grapevines cast long, twisted shadows in the front yard. They shifted in the moonlight, stretching their long fingers toward me.

I pulled my hooded jacket tighter. The night had

grown cold, the stars above dimmed by the lights from nearby Sacramento.

Something rustled in the nearby hydrangeas.

I stilled. If Lola and Harper were in the house, then who—?

A striped gray-and-black tail whisked across the drive. My muscles relaxed. A raccoon.

Annoyed by my jumpiness, I crunched loudly down the driveway and up the steps to the peak-roofed extension. I noticed an old-fashioned bell pull beside the French doors and reached to tug the rope.

Lola met my gaze through the glass and moved toward me. My hand dropped to my side.

She opened one of the French doors. A gust of wind billowed her long blond hair, tangling strands across her cable-knit sweater. Her jeans were narrow, tapering into suede knee-high boots, and once again, I felt underdressed in my schlumpy paranormal museum tee.

"Maddie! Thanks for coming," she said. "And thanks for inviting Harper."

Harper raised a glass of red wine in my direction. Its rich color almost exactly matched her turtleneck. "Maddie's thoughtful that way." She winked. Harper knew exactly why I'd invited her.

A cheese platter sat on the rustic wooden table alongside a bottle of zinfandel and a bouquet of white flowers. A folded sheet of paper lay beside the sky-blue vase. Benches ran along the long sides of the table. On one wall stood a tall, white glassed-in sideboard. Magazines lay artfully scattered atop it, open to pages with photos of Lola and Orson and their home. Opposite, hung a framed, over-sized magazine cover featuring the Victorian.

"Would you like a glass of wine?" Lola asked.

"Thanks," I said.

She poured from a bottle of a local zinfandel and handed the goblet to me. "To Atticus."

"And to Tilde." An ache speared the back of my throat. If I hadn't stopped to call Jason, or if we'd figured out that the door was open sooner, would she still be alive?

Lola blinked. "Of course. And to Tilde." She took a sip. "I still can't believe what happened."

"What did happen?" Harper asked.

"I'm not sure," Lola said. "I only know what I read in the papers." She shivered. "I'm not sure I want to know more. How are things at that museum of yours, Maddie? I heard someone called in a bomb threat."

"Ah. That." I turned the wine goblet in my hands. So far the bomb threat hadn't affected foot traffic in the museum. "I think something like a paranormal museum tends to attract pranksters." I really hoped that was all it had been. But the timing was too coincidental, and a prickle of fear raced up my spine.

"That's the problem with boring, small-town life," Harper said. "The kids need to get creative to have fun."

Lola smiled. "And we can't have that."

"In spite of our small-town atmosphere, I never had the chance to get to know Atticus," I said. "What was he like?"

Lola sobered, staring into her wine goblet. "He was funny. Charming. Clever."

"Honest," Harper said.

Lola looked up from her wine.

"I knew him and India," Harper explained.

Lola nodded. "My husband likes to think it was their chocolate that put Reign on the map. But Atticus was as important to the company's success as Orson. Maybe more so. I don't know what we'll do without his marketing skills. I've been trying to fill in, as you know, but I'm an amateur."

"Why is the company called *Reign?*" I asked.

"It was named after Atticus," she explained. "Well, not *after* him, but the idea came from his last name, and then the crown imprint on the wrappers from that."

"And the plain brown wrappers?" Harper asked.

"Atticus felt the contrast of something simple and the crown had an impact," she said. "He was a genius."

"How is India holding up?" Harper plucked a piece of cheese from the white ceramic tray on the wooden table.

"As well as can be expected, after losing her husband and then her cousin in such an awful way," Lola said. "Maybe I should have invited her tonight, to get her mind off this double tragedy." She rubbed the rim of the wine glass against her bottom lip. "It's hard to know what to do when someone is grieving."

"Were she and Tilde close?" I asked.

"Close enough for Tilde to follow her to California, I guess," Lola said. "I assumed ..." She adjusted the cheese platter on the table. "I guess I assumed a lot of things," she said in a subdued voice.

"Do the police have any idea why someone would have killed both her and Atticus?" I asked.

Lola rubbed her arms, rumpling the sleeves of her thick sweater. "It must be some sort of grudge against Reign, don't you think? I've asked Orson to come away with me, take a vacation. But he won't. And now he's insisting that he can do Tilde's job and manage the accounts too. He's going to give himself a heart attack."

"Who might have a grudge against Reign?" I asked.

"Sam Reynolds." Lola's delicate face pinched. "I've

noticed he hasn't returned with his picket lately. He was harassing us all and our customers. I heard he bothered you one day," she said to me.

I nodded. "He let me know he was upset with Reign's management."

Lola's mouth compressed. "Tilde told me he was lurking at the back door when she left one night and followed her all the way to her car, cursing and making threats."

"Why was he fired?" I asked, curious if the story would change.

"He ..." Lola blew out her breath. "It just wasn't a good fit. Atticus should have fired him long ago, for all our sakes, Sam's included. Retail isn't easy, and the work's not for everyone."

"Is Sam from around here?" I asked, dissatisfied.

"He's a local," Lola said.

That would make it easier for me—er, the police—to track him down. I cleared my throat. "Atticus's death has affected so many people." I hesitated. "There seemed to be some tension between you and Tilde at the chocolate shop."

Harper shot me a warning look.

Lola flushed, her words coming more rapidly. "She thought because she was India's cousin she could slack off. But Tilde was making mistakes. Or at least, that's what Orson told me. Of course, it's horrible that she's dead. But that doesn't negate her poor performance."

"No," I said. "I guess not."

"But you said you wanted to talk about Atticus." Lola's gaze narrowed. "Not our accountant."

"You're right," I said. "I suppose in my mind, the two will always be linked now that they're both dead."

The three of us stood silently for a long moment.

Outside, a wind chime tinkled, faint and musical.

Harper shook herself. "I love what you've done with your home. This extension really updates this old Victorian."

"Thanks," Lola said. "We worked hard on it, and we used reclaimed materials wherever we could."

Seemingly mollified, Lola regaled us with tales of the remodel and restoration—the horrors of outdated plumbing, wonky electrical wires, and tiny rooms.

I tried to look interested, nodding and mm-hmming at appropriate moments.

After we'd discussed Harper's business, the weather, and my museum's next exhibit, arty photographs of ghosts, I finally got to the supposed reason for my visit. "About that tribute to Atticus—"

"I found the eulogy that Orson's been working on." Lola lifted a folded sheet of paper off the table and handed it to me. "Maybe you can develop something for your museum from that."

I folded the page into quarters and slid it into the back pocket of my faded jeans. "Thanks." We hashed over the weather some more, and then Harper and I said our goodbyes and escaped.

My friend and I walked down the curved driveway, the gravel rattling beneath our shoes.

"Did you get what you wanted?" Harper asked.

"I'm not sure. I feel like ..."

"Like what?"

"Like everyone's lying or keeping things back." And Lola had said something that had left my nerves jangling.

Now all I needed to do was figure out what.

nineteen

Outside the museum, iron streetlamps flickered on in the Sunday night gloom. Inside the museum, GD slept, his head and paws dangling off the edge of the haunted rocking chair.

I handed a bag of chocolate-covered almonds across the counter. "Have a good night," I said to my final customer.

She clasped the bag to her ample chest. "Thanks!"

Relieved, I followed her to the door and flipped the sign to *Closed*. Tonight was officially the end of Wine and Chocolate Days. I rubbed my aching neck. As much as I'd enjoyed the chocolate inspiration, I'd already moved on to thinking about what came next. An exhibit of faerie art. Experimenting with a paranormal museum podcast. Solving a murder.

Ursula, the buckles on her scarlet corset clinking, peeked from the Gallery. Wisps of brown hair escaped from beneath her steampunk hat. "Is it over?" she squeaked.

"Yep, we're closed," I said. "Rough crowd?"

She smiled. "Not at all. I made six hundred dollars today, and that's after what I owe you. If you ever want to do this again, let me know."

"There's always the Wine and Chocolate Days next spring." I would need to figure out a new twist for my chocolate exhibit. But I had twelve months to figure it out.

She pressed her hands into the small of her back and stretched. "I've got one packet of chocolate left. How would you like a reading?"

I *definitely* wanted a reading, but she had to be exhausted. "Are you sure you're up for it?"

"Come into my parlor," she intoned.

I followed her into the Gallery. The black shelves were denuded, great gaps where tarot cards and chocolate bars used to stand. Wine and Chocolate Days might be over, but my *Magic of Chocolate* exhibit would run through the end of the month. I needed to restock.

She motioned to the canopied table. "You know the drill. You'll have to make your own drink."

I made myself a cup of cocoa and stirred, while Ursula wrote a receipt and counted the museum's share of her take.

"Where's Leo today?" she asked.

I smothered a yawn. "He had a big exam to study for, so I gave him the afternoon off." I sipped my drink, warmth cascading through my veins, and leaned back in the chair. "Ah. I needed this." The chocolate didn't make my stomach lurch, so at least I was getting over my cocoa trauma.

"I could see how busy you were, but don't tell me about your day. It might taint the reading."

"How does this work?" I asked and took another gulp.

She raised a wide, empty cup. "Chocolate dregs left along the rim refer to something immediate. The middle of the cup represents the near future, and the bottom is the key to your situation. I look for symbols within the dregs and use my intuition to interpret them." She peered into my cup. "Leave a teensy bit of liquid, maybe a tablespoon, in the bottom."

I finished the hot chocolate and hoped she'd tell me something good. Not that I believed in fortune-telling, but I didn't exactly disbelieve either. Not after all the odd things I'd seen in the museum.

"Swirl your cup three times in a clockwise motion," she said.

I swirled and handed her the white cup.

She clapped a saucer on top and flipped the cup over. "I need to drain the liquid, and that creates the pattern." Careful not to spill, Ursula removed the cup, turning it right-side up and setting the saucer on the table.

She studied the dregs. "There's conflict swirling about you now. You'll have a difficult time seeing your way through, but you'll get there, so persevere. And ..." Her face scrunched.

A shiver of apprehension rippled through me, and I leaned closer. "And what?"

"See this stain here, shaped like a knife?"

"Yes," I said. Once she'd pointed it out, the chocolate shape *did* look like a dagger, complete with blood dripping from the blade. An image of Tilde flashed into my head and I shuddered.

"Usually, that means danger. Real and immediate." She shivered. "Sorry, I don't usually have such dark readings."

I frowned. I'd gotten feedback from all her customers, and none had left frightened or disturbed. They'd all been delighted with their readings.

Her face cleared. "Of course. It's the museum, all these objects that you're connected to, the photos of murders and haunted things. Are you researching anything in the museum now?"

"Yes," I said, embarrassingly relieved. "As a matter of fact I am."

"That's likely what this is about then." She tilted the cup and studied the dregs. "The object you're researching is connected to someone who died violently, correct?"

"It looks that way, but I'm not sure. My research isn't finished."

She nodded. "There was violence in that death. Trust the chocolate. And it looks like murder. And here ..." She pointed to a splotch of chocolate shaped like a dog. "This means the support of friends. A friend of yours will need your help in the near future, within the next four weeks, I think. It will be a big ask, but you'll both feel good about it in the end."

Adele. It didn't take a Nostradamus to predict more wedding insanity in my future.

"You're in a relationship now," she said, "but it's complicated. Both parties have shields up because of other attachments from the past."

"*Both* parties?" What was Jason shielding?

And hold on. Did *I* have shields up? What if I hadn't completely gotten past my breakup with Mason? Maybe Jason was right, and I needed to cut things off more cleanly. After all, why *was* Mason hanging around the museum so much?

"Remember," the fortune-teller said, "honesty really is the best policy ... And this closed book." She pointed to a smudge of chocolate. "There are still mysteries to be revealed." She angled the cup. "Strange," she muttered. "There's a key at the bottom."

I rubbed the back of my neck. "What does that mean?"

"Mmm? Oh. The bottom of the cup is where I find the key to unlocking the story. It's the element or personality trait that will help you to move forward, or figure things out, or be successful. And I see a key at the bottom of your cup."

"I don't understand."

"A key symbolizes a secret that will unlock the mystery, so basically it's saying the key is the key. Sorry. Whatever the secret is, it's still hidden." She sighed. "This was my worst reading of the day."

I straightened, alarmed. "What?"

She reached across the table and touched the back of my hand. "I didn't mean the worst fortune, just my worst telling. I guess I'm more tired than I thought."

"No, no. I enjoyed the reading. And I'd love to have you back for future events." But anxiety jittered my insides. I didn't believe in fortune-telling. Or at least I didn't *believe* believe. So why was I getting so worked up?

"I read wine dregs too."

I laughed. "I'm keeping your number on speed dial."

She paid me the museum's cut and I helped her pack her things into cardboard boxes. After seeing her to the door, I locked it behind her.

A hidden mystery was the key. Well, there was *one* mystery I might be able to unlock. I found the phone number for the detective in Oaxaca and called.

"Bueno?" he asked.

"Hi, Alejandro? This is Maddie Kosloski from California."

"Oh, hello, Miss Maddie. How are you this evening?" Something clattered in the background.

"Fine. Is this a good time to continue our conversation   about Felicitas Ocasio's death?"

He sighed. "Why not?"

"You said officially her death had been ruled a suicide.

But your friend suspected Felicitas's boyfriend might have had something to do with it." There was a loud noise on his end, like a truck rumbling past, and I raised my voice. "How exactly did she die?"

"What?"

I repeated myself.

"Drug overdose," he shouted. "Everyone said she was not a user, that she'd never taken drugs before, and my friend believed it. Felicitas was a good woman, a good Catholic, and suicide is a mortal sin. She worked hard, took care of her parents, was top of her class. More importantly, she only had one needle mark, the one that took her life. Perhaps it was her first time and she made a mistake. But there were bruises on her neck, as if someone had held her down."

One of the fluorescent lamps flickered above me, and I glanced up. Photos of convicted murderers stared down at me from the museum walls. "And your friend thought someone had injected her against her will?"

A horn blared in the background.

"What?" he shouted.

"As if someone had injected her against her will?"

"Yes, yes." He erupted in a stream of Spanish. I picked out a curse.

I swallowed, sickened. "Then why was it ruled a suicide?" I asked over the street noise.

"What?"

"Why a suicide?"

"Because the bruises were inconclusive," Alejandro said. "And witnesses said she had been distraught the day before her death. Her family did everything they could to get the finding changed to murder, but ..." I could almost hear the shrug over the phone. "Politics."

"But it sounded like there was clear evidence of foul

play. How could politics—"

"You have politics in America too, I think," he said shortly.

"Yes, of course," I said. I would like to think it didn't influence criminal investigations here, but that was naive. Still, it was strange politics that would cover up a drug murder. "Maybe she was distraught because she learned her boyfriend dealt in drugs?"

"Her relatives said he told her he worked as a driver for a cocoa company. It turned out he was delivering a different kind of coca."

"You mean, cocaine? Was that what killed her?"

"Yes. Injecting is a much more dangerous method of using the drug, but it causes the most intense effects, so fools take the risk. Now you see why it was easy to call her overdose an accident."

I gnawed my bottom lip. This was getting worse by the second, but I couldn't stop. "What happened to the boyfriend?"

"He disappeared after her death."

That sounded suspicious.

GD hopped onto the counter and brushed against the tip jar.

"We found his body a week later," the detective continued. "He'd been beaten to death, we guessed by one of his colleagues. He was in trouble, and he knew it and ran."

"Do you know how long he'd been dead before his body was found?"

A long pause. "I thought you wanted to know about Felicitas."

I hesitated. Had I imagined the edge to his voice? "I do, but if her boyfriend was the killer, that's part of the story. Isn't it?"

"Is it?" He coughed.

I waited, hoping I hadn't offended Jason's friend.

"He was dead roughly a week," he finally said.

So, the boyfriend had died not long after Felicitas. "I see. Thank you for telling me about the murders."

"I hope it is helpful." He cursed in Spanish. "I must go. Good luck with your museum." He disconnected.

Feeling drained, I sat back in my chair. What a brutal story, ugly and cruel. Poor Felicitas.

I looked toward the Gallery, and the molinillo in its ceramic bowl. Felicitas probably hadn't known the truth about her boyfriend's drug dealing until it was too late. Was that the key to the molinillo's mysterious rattling—a lie that had killed Felictas? Or perhaps the lie was that her boyfriend had ever loved her?

I massaged the heel of my palm against my chest. I'd write out the story for the molinillo display, but I'd leave Felicitas's name out. She'd been betrayed in the worst way, and she deserved privacy.

Heavyhearted, I called Jason.

"Maddie," he said, his voice warm. "Is everything okay?"

I laughed shortly. "I hope I don't only call when I've got a problem."

"Of course not. It's just ..." He cleared his throat. "I don't like the way we left things the other day."

"Me neither." I leaned one hip against the glass counter. "You're right. Mason has been hanging around the museum more than usual. I thought he was trying to get back to being friends, and it was awkward, so I avoided asking him what was going on. But I will, next time I see him. And if it isn't clear to everyone already, Mason and I are over. For good."

"I know. I trust you. One of the things I love about

you is your honesty. Though you tend to bend things a bit when it comes to murder investigations."

There was that L-word again. And I wasn't sure if I was ready for it. "That's not fair. Whenever I learn something, I tell you right away."

"I know, I know. I just wish you wouldn't *accidentally* come across so much relevant information. But people are more willing to gossip to civilians than cops. And you seem to have a knack for ... whatever it is you do."

Lightly, I bit my bottom lip. "So, are we good?"

His voice lowered to a rumble. "We're good."

Relief slumped my shoulders, because I didn't want to fight, and I didn't want to give up what I was doing either. I coughed. "I've been thinking about the murders—"

"Maddie ..." he began, in a voice reinforced with rebar.

"You've probably already considered this," I said quickly, "but hear me out. Don't both these murders seem like they were done by the same sort of ... *mind* as the bomb threat at the museum and the firecrackers at the vigil?"

A cautious pause. Then, "Go on."

"Stabbing an accountant with her own receipt holder. Death by chocolate for a chocolate maker—"

"He was bludgeoned," Jason said. "The chocolate didn't kill him."

"Even so, dumping chocolate on him after he'd fallen—"

"You think someone dumped it on him because his sleeve was chocolate-free?"

I deflated. "Um. Yeah. Am I wrong?"

"No. I'd come to the same conclusion."

GD meowed. Tail high, he brushed against my arm.

Okay, maybe my detecting brain wasn't exactly unique. "Right, but doesn't it seem almost childish, as childish as—"

"A bomb threat and firecrackers. I agree."

"You do?" So, he *had* thought of the connection. I didn't know whether to feel disappointed I wasn't dazzling him with my brilliance or relieved my idea wasn't crazy.

"Here's the thing. When we catch the killer, the defense will have a field day if the lead detective had a relationship with a material witness."

My heart sank. "Material ... Are you saying I'm a material witness?"

"You discovered the body," Jason said. "You were with me when the second body was discovered. And if the bomb threat is connected to the murders, you took the call. You're the only person who can testify to what you heard."

"Oh." My throat tightened. Where was all this going? "Have I made things harder for you? I haven't wrecked the case or anything, have—?"

"No," he said. "You haven't done anything wrong. But from now on, if you get any brainstorms, talk to Detective Hammer."

"To Laurel?" Was he nuts? She *hated* me. She'd never listen to anything I had to say. My stomach spun. "Are you saying they pulled you off the case?"

"I've never been on it. Not since you discovered Atticus's body."

"But I thought—Why didn't you tell me?"

Silence.

"What?" I asked. And I swear I could *hear* the look Jason was giving me over the phone, which, yes, I know is technically impossible.

"Are you actually complaining that I don't keep you in the loop about police investigations?"

"Ah …" Yeah. That probably wasn't realistic.

"I didn't think so. Don't sound so glum. Me being yanked is just bad luck. You were the first on the scene at a murder. And it didn't help that you were covered in chocolate."

"From the CPR!"

"Don't worry. We have a tape of the 911 call. We know what happened."

"The police don't really think I'm a suspect, do they?"

"Why would you be a suspect?"

"No reason," I said quickly. "I just wish you hadn't brought up my murdery chocolate coating."

"Mmm," he said in a velvet-edged voice. "That has possibilities."

We weren't talking murder anymore, and my pulse sped.

"Damn, I have to go," he said. "Sorry, I'll call you later."

"You'd better." Because I was starting to get over my chocolate phobia.

twenty

A gray wall of fog pressed against the Gallery's windows Tuesday morning. I stooped to refill GD's food and water bowls. Licking his chops, the cat nudged me aside and got busy crunching kibble.

I rolled up the sleeves of my fitted blouse—white with tiny blue flowers that matched the color of my jeans. "You're welcome." *Cats.*

In the Gallery, I surveyed its black shelves. They were delightfully empty. I made notes on my inventory list, then retrieved boxes of chocolate and tarot cards from Adele's storeroom.

GD came to supervise as I constructed pyramids of chocolate bars. He leapt to the top of my alchemy display and wound sinuously between fake cocoa pods and grinding stones.

I adjusted a stack of chocolate-themed oracle decks. Wine and Chocolate Days had been a good promotion. I needed to thank Penny at the Visitors Bureau for organizing the event.

Penny, who knew all the wine-related business gossip. Penny, who I suspected had been holding back when she'd taken me to Lola's tea. Penny, who like me was obsessed with her work and would no doubt be locked away inside the Wine and Visitors Bureau, which, like my museum, was closed today.

Oh yes, a thank you call was definitely in order.

Purring with satisfaction, I ruffled GD's fur.

The cat hissed with surprise.

"See ya!" Grabbing my blue faux-leather jacket off its peg, I sauntered out the front door. I had to jump to sidestep Mason on the brick sidewalk.

"Oh, hey." He stuffed his fingers into the front pockets of his worn black jeans. "Going somewhere?"

"To …" *Shut it down.* If only I knew how, or even what I was shutting down. "Uh huh."

"How's the haunted milano you've been promoting?"

"The molinillo?" I asked, surprised. "Good. I mean, it's an inanimate object, so it doesn't have an emotional state, but I think I have most of its story." With both Felicitas and her boyfriend dead, it was unlikely I'd learn more. But that was life. Not every mystery was completely resolved. Sometimes you had to rely on guesswork and intuition.

He crossed his bulging arms over his chest. "What's the story?"

"It looks like Felicitas—the woman who owned the molinillo—was murdered, likely by her boyfriend."

"So why does it rattle when someone lies?"

I was starting to hate this story. "Because her boyfriend lied to her. He kept it secret that he was a drug dealer. But the real betrayal was that he lied about loving her. You don't murder someone you love because they get pregnant." I shivered in the fog. Poor Felicitas. I couldn't even imagine the pain she must have felt. Her lover's hands around her throat, the breathless agony …

Okay, maybe I could imagine it a little *too* well. "If only he'd just let her go."

Mason smiled faintly. "Like you let me go."

"That wasn't the same," I said, feeling myself color. "I—" I'd had real feelings for Mason. But had I been in love? Letting him go hadn't been easy, but maybe it should have been harder. "Anyway," I said, brusque, "honesty is better than the death-by-a-thousand-cuts of little relationship dishonesties." Or in Felicitas's case, it was better than actual death.

His gaze shifted to the brick sidewalk. "Right. Hey, there's something—"

The door to the motorcycle shop opened and Belle leaned out, her hair swinging past her shoulder. "Mason, a customer has a question I can't answer."

He nodded to her. "Right. I'll be right there." He turned to me, a question in his eyes.

"Mason ..." *Get it over with. Ask him what's going on.*

He glanced over his shoulder toward the motorcycle shop. "Yeah?"

I chickened out. "I've got to go. Good luck with the customer." I hurried to my pickup and drove off.

At the Wine and Visitors Bureau, I walked through the twisting fog to the brick building's side door. I tested the latch. The metal door creaked open, a melancholy whine that raised the hair on my arms.

"Hasn't anybody in this town heard of oil?" I muttered.

I leaned inside the long hallway. Cardboard wine boxes sat stacked along its walls. "Penny? It's Maddie." My voice echoed off the tile floor.

I walked inside. "Hello?"

Above me, a fluorescent lamp flickered and pinged. Penny's office was at the far end of the hall, which was lined with closed doors.

"Penny?" I called more softly.

I crept down the hallway. Penny's office door stood open. Inside—a desk overflowing with papers. Stacks of boxes. A purple cardigan slung over the back of her rolling chair.

But no Penny.

Maybe she was in the restroom.

I edged from the office and toward the opening to the tasting area. My thigh struck a box, rattling the bottles inside. I cursed, rubbing the muscle, and limped forward.

The overhead light flickered, and I glanced up.

Motion blurred at the edge of my vision. A woman shrieked.

I gasped and stumbled backward, shielding my face. "No!" When I didn't get clobbered, I peeked through my fingers.

Penny lowered a near-black wine bottle and clutched one hand to her heaving chest. "I thought you were a burglar!"

I straightened out of my crouch. "I called out. Didn't you hear me?"

"I was in the ladies' room." She placed the bottle on a nearby box. "What are you doing here?"

"Looking for you." I eyed her. Penny's long-sleeved black tee read: *Wine Rack*. The sentiment seemed racy for grandmotherly Penny. But she took her duties at the Wine and Visitors Bureau seriously.

"Did you need something?" she asked.

"Sort of. I felt like there was something you wanted to tell me last week about Reign, but that you were being polite."

"Ah." She tugged down the front of her tee. "Come into my office."

I followed her inside.

She shifted a stack of manila folders off a chair, then settled herself behind the desk. Primly, she folded her hands. "What did you want to know?"

"What didn't you want to tell me at Lola's?"

"I probably told you too much," she fretted. "I never should have been talked into joining that wine tasting beforehand, but they were old college friends of mine. It seemed wrong to refuse. I always gab too much after a glass or three."

"Would you like one now?" I half-joked. Maybe it would unstick her tongue.

She stared over her cat-eye glasses. "No, young lady, I would not."

"Look, if you don't want to tell me, then tell the police. Two people are dead, and someone phoned a bomb threat in to my museum."

"You think the bomb threat is connected to the murders?"

"I'm not certain, but ... yes, I do."

She frowned. "But you're an associate member of the Wine and Visitors Bureau!"

"Ye-es."

"That's outrageous! An attack on one member is an attack on all. We're like NATO."

Whoa. Maybe Penny took her duties a little *too* seriously. I hoped I hadn't unknowingly signed on to any containment pacts. "So, will you help me?"

She leaned back in her chair. It creaked beneath her bulk. "I wish I could."

Oh, come on. "Penny, please. NATO!"

"It's not that I don't want to. I just don't think I'll be much help. I told you about the late payments from Reign to that farmer?"

"Yes."

"Well, as you know, I've been working with the wineries to help them organize the wine and chocolate tastings."

I nodded, encouraging.

"And since Reign is such a big name, getting their shop on board seemed like a huge coup. I mean, they've been in national newspapers and magazines."

"Sure." I nodded encouragingly.

"But Orson could be difficult to work with."

"Orson?" I asked. "Not Atticus? I thought he'd be the liaison with the Visitors Bureau."

"Atticus was our point man, and he was a dream, but he wasn't always available. They're still a small shop, you know."

So small they were artisanal. "And Orson?"

"I suppose he was so busy with the chocolate-making, having to deal with the sales side was frustrating."

"Hmm." Disappointed, I studied my tennis shoes. She was right. This didn't exactly illuminate the crimes.

"And then there was that argument."

My spine snapped into alignment. That sounded more promising. "What argument?"

"I stopped by Reign one morning. It was early. They'd just opened for the day, and they weren't expecting me. But I needed their approval on some flyers."

"Yes?" I asked, bracing my forearms on the knees of my jeans.

"I mean, I couldn't print it without approval. What if something was wrong? We couldn't afford to reprint. Do you have any idea how much color printing costs?"

"Roughly a dollar a page." I'd become a fixture at the local copy shop with my flyers promoting Gallery exhibits.

"Exactly! It's crazy! But I can't use our printer." She motioned toward a corner of the office and a printer buried beneath a Vesuvius of paper. "The colors always get strange."

I crossed one leg over the other and jiggled my foot. "Penny, what was the argument about?"

"Orson and Atticus were shouting. Atticus said something about being compromised. And then they noticed I was there and clammed up. Orson told me some of the cocoa beans had been ruined—that's what had been compromised. Apparently, cocoa beans are even more expensive than color printing."

"You're sure it was Atticus who said they were compromised?"

"I might be getting older, but I can still tell who's who." She glared over her glasses.

"I just meant ..." I sucked in my cheeks. "It seems a little strange Atticus was complaining about cocoa prices and bad beans. He was marketing, not chocolate-making."

"They were business partners. A financial loss would affect them both." Penny twisted in her chair and plucked the purple cardigan from its back.

"Hmm ..." It was my go-to noise of dissatisfaction. Something wasn't right.

"I attended one of their chocolate-tasting workshops." She shrugged into her cardigan. "Honestly, I couldn't tell the difference between one bar and another. I thought I had a good palate—I used to be a sommelier, you know."

"I didn't know that," I said, impressed. Becoming a sommelier wasn't easy.

"But my favorite chocolate is still See's."

It was mine too, and we paused, silent, lost in misty recollections of those white chocolate boxes.

"Butter creams." I sighed.

"Summer berries."

"Cranberry truffles."

"And wine," we said in unison, and laughed.

"I don't suppose that gives you any better idea of who killed Atticus and that poor woman," she said.

"Not really. Have you told the police about any of this?"

"Do you think I should? The argument I heard seemed so minor. Maybe you could tell that boyfriend of yours. If he thinks it's important, he can call me."

"Actually, Detective Hammer is in charge of the case."

"Oh." A look of consternation crossed Penny's broad face. "Maybe I'll call the police hotline then."

"Call the police about what?" my mother asked from behind me.

I started guiltily in my chair.

In the doorway, my mother gazed down with a forbidding expression. She folded her arms over her pale blue wool coat.

"Something odd I overheard at the chocolate shop," Penny said. "Maddie was giving me some advice."

My mother's brows pinched. "Was she now?"

I shrank in my seat. *Eeek!*

"Because I was under the distinct impression," my mother continued, "that she had promised to stay out of the Reign murders."

"Had I?" I squeaked.

"You had."

My chin dipped to my chest. "I don't actually remember that," I mumbled.

"I do. Quite clearly."

Penny cleared her throat. "Well. What brings you to the Wine and Visitors Bureau, Fran?"

"Ladies Aid."

"Ah, yes," Penny said. "The charity event." The two

began rattling off statistics on ticket sales and table costs.

I lifted myself from my chair and attempted to make like a ninja and slink past unnoticed. But that was impossible in a room this small, especially with my mother blocking the door.

"Just one moment, Madelyn." She raised her index finger. "Are you free for lunch today?"

"Um—"

"Good."

I waited awkwardly beside a tottering pile of boxes. Honestly, I was an adult. It's not like I needed my mother's permission to talk to Penny about the murders.

Finally she and Penny wrapped up their conversation, and I followed my mother into the mist-shrouded parking lot.

She stopped beside her Lincoln SUV. "I hope you know why I asked you to lunch."

To yell at me some more? "I have no idea."

Her brows lowered. "Madelyn, we need to talk."

twenty-one

Lunch with my mother. Normally, I enjoyed spending time with her. All the other Kosloskis were off doing exciting things in amazing places, and now that I'd given up the wild international life (*ha*), I figured the remainders had to stick together.

But lunch today was frosty. I sat at the table in the breakfast nook in her kitchen, poking my chicken Caesar salad with a fork.

Outside the paned windows, the front yard was gray, a low mist dampening the hood of her new SUV. Her old Lincoln had been blown up last December. That had sort of been my fault, so in fairness, she had reason to be annoyed.

I cleared my throat. "Have you heard from Shane yet?" I could usually distract my mother with gossip about one of my siblings.

"You're changing the subject," she said.

Usually distract. Not always. "Well ..." At a loss, I turned the fork between my fingers. "I guess I am. Mom, I don't understand what's going on here. You practically dragged me into two murder investigations last year. You said I was good at it."

"You are. You're good at everything you do. Well, nearly everything. Those piano lessons were a disaster."

"I never wanted to take—" I clamped my jaw shut. *Never mind.* "So, what's different now?"

"What's different is, last year I saw someone aim a

compound bow at you. You were shot!"

"Only grazed."

"*And* we were both nearly blown up. Just because you have a talent for something doesn't mean you have to do it." Her shoulders hunched. "No, it isn't that. I was arrogant. This town ..." She motioned toward the SUV. "I thought nothing really bad could happen to us here. But that was ridiculous. Places change, and so do people. I thought I was in control of things." She laughed hollowly. "What a rude awakening last winter was."

I swallowed, my throat dry. My normally unstoppable mother had hit a wall. "But you were right about getting involved then. Things worked out."

"Shane's being transferred to Afghanistan."

Stunned, I flopped back in my chair. "What?" Our embassy there was still a frequent target of attacks. Shane might be annoyingly perfect, but he was my brother, and my stomach burned with worry.

"As you can imagine, there aren't many volunteers to go to that embassy. Your brother said he doesn't have a choice in the matter, and ..." Her voice hitched. "He wants to go."

"I'm sure he'll be safe," I lied. "They have lots of protection at the embassy, plus Marine guards." *Afghanistan. Good God.* It had been a year since I'd last seen my brother.

I stared out the window at the oak by my mother's SUV. Mist twined in its bare limbs. As kids, we would gather mistletoe from that oak, build precarious tree houses in its branches. My throat thickened.

"I'm *not* sure about his safety." She knit her fingers together on the table. "But we all must do our duty. You, however, have no duty to insert yourself into these murders. In fact, as a good citizen, you should let the police do their jobs."

I could have argued it was my duty to make sure the police had all the facts. But that seemed churlish. My mother couldn't make sure Shane was safe, so she was going to make sure I was. Dammit.

"I don't want to have to worry about you both," she continued.

"Mom, I'm not going to do anything crazy," I hedged. What would I do if she demanded I promise to drop things?

She rose and took our plates to the sink. "No, I suppose you won't. You've always been more risk-averse than Shane and Melanie."

My mouth flattened. More risk-averse? I owned my own business, a paranormal museum. That was risky! But I wasn't going to argue.

Silent, I cleared the table and washed the dishes in the kitchen sink. Fortunately, my mother didn't press her point. I helped her clean the kitchen, and we talked about next month's ghost photography exhibit.

I grabbed my jacket. "Well, thanks."

"Wait. Take this."

She forced a frozen chicken Alfredo casserole on me, and I escaped with it to my waiting pickup. My mom hadn't made me promise to stay out of the murder investigation, and that was good. I didn't want to worry her, and I sensed I was getting close to the answer. I couldn't give up now.

Drawing a deep, guilty breath, I glanced at the foil-wrapped baking dish on the seat beside me. My mother knew I didn't like chicken Alfredo. What was I going to do with this huge casserole?

Give it to someone who could use it.

Someone like … India.

I called Adele's father.

"Maddie? What's going on?" he asked.

"I have a casserole for India. Is she working today?" I glanced at the dashboard clock. It was just past one o'clock. The wineries would be getting busy.

"No, she's at home as far as I know."

"Great, thanks. If she's not, I'll leave the casserole on her porch," I said. "Can you give me her address?"

"Sure. Let me dig it out." After a minute, he rattled off her address and phone number, and I scribbled it into my notepad.

"Thanks. Er, how's the wedding planning going?"

He chuckled. "Fantastic, since I've been banned from helping."

"I hear you," I said, wistful. I was glad to be assisting Adele with her big day. But there was an awful lot to do. "I'll talk to you later."

We rang off, and I drove slowly down the fog-bound roads. Wraiths of twisted grapevines stood like sentinels along the roadside.

Would my brother be in danger? You didn't hear much about Afghanistan in the news anymore, but we still had troops there. I wasn't sure if no news was good news, or if we'd just grown indifferent, uninterested. My stomach twisted. I wasn't indifferent any longer.

India lived in a sprawling ranch house in a neighborhood tucked between vineyards.

I parked on the sidewalk beside her emerald lawn. The circular driveway was empty, which didn't bode well for finding her at home. But I walked up the concrete drive, past a barren dogwood tree and to the front door. A wreath of dried grapevines knotted with twinkle lights encircled the brass knocker.

Casserole balanced on one hip, I rang the bell. Its

solemn tone echoed through the house.

I waited a few minutes. Finally, I dug into my purse and retrieved a pen and notepad. Setting the casserole on the low bench beside the door, I scribbled a note and tucked it beneath the baking dish.

I waited another minute or two, then slowly walked down the drive. A gust of damp wind tossed my hair, and something banged behind me.

My neck tensed. I looked over my shoulder.

A tall redwood gate at the side of the house drifted open, banged shut.

My mouth pursed.

It would only be neighborly if I made sure the gate was shut fast. What if India kept a dog in the back yard? It might escape, run into the street, and get hit by a car.

Deliberately, I walked to the tall gate. It creaked open, horror-movie-inviting. A narrow concrete path threaded between the house and a high wooden fence. A dust-covered barbecue leaned against the stucco wall.

"India?" I called.

My heartbeat sped. Paranoia had become an old friend, but I'd stumbled across two too many dead bodies recently. What I felt now wasn't paranoia. It was rational fear. I *really* didn't want to find a third corpse.

"Hello?" I whispered and crept down the path. The hem of my jeans brushed the yellow mustard flowers growing between the concrete and the fence.

I rounded the corner of the house. Neatly swept wooden deck. Wood-beam awning. Elegant outdoor chairs. Beside the kidney-shaped pool, near the diving board, was a single large cardboard box. The grounds seemed recently landscaped, with a low-water selection of lavender bushes and not a leaf out of place.

But the cardboard box was a sour note in the

immaculate yard, and I walked toward the pool. *Affaire* was printed on the side of the box.

There was a soft noise behind me. I started to turn.

Something struck the center of my back, knocking the wind from my lungs. I pitched forward, arms windmilling helplessly, and plunged into the pool.

The water was cold as knives. I came up sputtering, eyes blurred and stinging with mascara.

A strong hand grabbed the top of my head and forced me beneath the surface.

I clawed at the sides of the pool. My fingers scraped cold concrete. My legs kicked, useless.

My hands scraped across the rim of the pool. Heart exploding in my chest, I grasped at it, straining to pull myself up. But I didn't move, didn't break the surface. I hadn't taken a breath when I'd gone in and didn't know how long I could last without air. *Breathe. I had to breathe.*

Stars sparked in front of my eyes. *If not up, then down?* I pushed away from the side of the pool.

But whoever held me had a firm grasp of my hair. A chill wracked my body.

I flailed beneath the water.

My lungs burned, the demand for air unbearable, overwhelming. This couldn't be happening. Shane was going to Afghanistan, and I was going to die in a California swimming pool. And it hurt, hurt, hurt, an agony of cold and fire in my chest. Black flames flickered at the edge of my sight.

I gasped, sucking in water. Then I really knew agony. My lungs seemed to tear, slashed by rough blades. Distantly, I felt my limbs writhing. My vision telescoped.

My final thought was that my mother was going to be furious.

Then the darkness closed in, complete.

twenty-two

I awoke in water, my arms pinned to my sides. I jerked away, coughing, lungs aching, and vomited water into the pool.

India let go like I was radioactive, and she floundered backward in the water, splashing. "It's okay. You're all right."

I found my feet and stood, hip deep in the pool. Coughing, I scraped my wet hair from my face. "What the hell?"

She raised her hands in a warding gesture. Her green and blue yoga outfit was soaked to the collar, her ponytail plastered to her neck. Water beaded her delicate face. "I found you in the pool. What were you doing in my pool?"

Shivering, I sloshed toward the pool steps. My legs collapsed after the first one, and I crawled up the remainder and onto the wooden deck.

"What were you doing in my pool?" India repeated more sharply.

I rolled off the deck onto the pavement and sat, staring at the gray sky. Someone had tried to kill me. I shuddered. They'd come too close to succeeding.

India trudged out of the pool and stood over me, dripping. "You haven't answered my question. What are you doing here?"

I coughed. "The gate was open. You weren't

answering your door. I thought …" My lungs ached, and I rubbed my chest.

"What did you think?"

Cold seeped from the concrete into my bones, and a deeper chill settled into my heart. Someone had tried to kill me.

Violently. Hands-on.

I began to shake, my trembling having nothing to do with the cold air on my wet clothes. I rolled onto my side and sat up. "I guess I thought you might be dead."

Her legs folded beneath her and she sat hard on a deck chair. She clasped her arms. "Oh."

My teeth chattered. "With everything that's been happening—"

"I get it."

We said nothing for a long time.

"How did you get in my pool?"

"I was looking at the box. Over there." I pointed, hand wavering, to the diving board. The box had vanished.

"What box?" she asked.

"There was a cardboard box," I rasped, my throat raw. "It seemed out of place. The rest of your yard is so neat."

"Thanks," she said dully.

So where was the box now? "Someone pushed me into the pool and held me under."

She quirked a skeptical brow. "So, you trespassed in my back yard, examined a box which isn't there, and then someone tried to drown you?"

A bout of coughing wracked me and I pressed my hands to the cold cement, bracing myself. When I looked up, her expression hadn't changed.

"Someone killed your cousin and husband." I sucked

in a deep breath, working to calm myself, and started hacking up a lung instead. "I'm not lying. Something's going on," I said more quietly, "and it's connected to your family."

She rose. "Come inside. I'll get you a towel."

Thoughts jumbling, I trailed after her. My feet squelched in their sneakers. At least she trusted me enough to let me into her house.

The interior was a disappointment of unmatched furniture and movie posters. I'd thought India would have more flare, like Lola, but maybe I was holding her to unfair standards.

She opened a closet door and tossed me a beige towel. "I'm not sure if I should call the police."

"Neither am I." I peeled off my sodden jacket and grimaced. Faux-leather probably liked water about as much as real leather. I rubbed my arms with the rough towel. India hadn't trusted my story. But I was in her house, so she hadn't completely disbelieved me either. "How did you find me?" I asked.

"I came home and saw the gate was open. I thought I heard a noise, so I called out and walked into the back yard. You were face-down in the pool." A quick gust of air escaped her, half laugh, half sob. "You weren't faking being nearly drowned."

"Do you have any idea who's behind this, India?"

"No." Turning away, she grabbed another towel from the closet and wrapped it around herself like a cloak. "I don't know."

"Someone was here, at your house—"

"The only person who I know for sure was here is you."

"Then who took the box?" I asked.

"What box?!"

"The box that ... ." Hell. What was the point? "I left a casserole on your doorstep," I finished weakly.

She walked to the front door, opened it, stooped. She returned inside with the foil-wrapped casserole. "Thanks."

"It's chicken alfredo. Let it defrost, then reheat for thirty minutes at 350. Now, putting aside how weird it looked that I was floating in your pool, why would someone be lurking in your back yard?"

"Aside from you?"

I repressed a scowl, icy fear replaced by hot, welcome anger, though not toward her. Someone had tried to snuff me out of existence, as if I didn't matter. It was insulting. "Aside from me."

She pulled her hair free from her hairband and rubbed her head with the towel, obscuring her face. "Sam's been here." Even muffled by the towel, I could hear the strain in her voice.

"Sam?" I asked. "You mean the guy Atticus fired?"

"Orson fired him, not Atticus."

"Then what did he want?"

She emerged from beneath the towel and clutched it to her chest. Her slim shoulders hunched. "Justification," she whispered. "His job back. I'm not sure. He was ..." She swallowed. "He was angry. Unbalanced."

"Unbalanced?" I squeaked. Was he unbalanced enough to push someone into a pool and hold them under? But if so, what did he have against me?

India smiled, wry. "Let's just say I didn't let *him* inside the house."

I guessed she didn't think I was crazy. "Did you tell the police?"

"It didn't seem worth it." She shook her head.

Droplets from her hair struck the closed closet door. "Should we call 911?"

"That's for emergencies. This one is kind of over. But you should call them about Sam." I looked around. "My purse."

"Is at the bottom of the pool."

I groaned. *Dammit.* I doubted my phone had survived underwater. And I really didn't want to go for another swim. In all the excitement, I *might* have peed in the pool.

"We can fish it out with the net," she said. "Come on."

Towel draped around my shoulders, I followed her outside. My purse lay at the bottom of the deep end. Beside it on the pale blue pool floor was my phone. A pen and candy wrapper floated on the water's surface. My face heated. How long had *that* been in my purse?

India was adept with the pool net, and after a few attempts she retrieved all my things, including the wrapper. I stuffed it into my ruined purse.

"Let it dry out before you turn it on," India advised, nodding to the phone.

"I will." How long would that take? "Do you know where I can find Sam?"

"I'm not sure finding him is such a good idea."

I was too angry to care. "I need to know if he was here earlier."

"You should call the police about today."

My heart sank. Laurel wouldn't believe me. In her mind, any disaster was always my fault. But I couldn't *not* report the attack. "I'll call Detective Hammer when I get home. But do you know where Sam might be?"

She angled her head and sighed. "Atticus has his address in his office files. Wait here." She went back through the sliding glass door into the house.

So, she trusted me in the house, but not in her husband's office. I could hardly blame her under the circumstances. Rubbing my chest, I studied the pool. I couldn't have been unconscious in the water long, or I wouldn't have ...

... survived.

I'd been lucky. My limbs trembled, and I slowed my breathing. I was alive. Now wasn't the time for the hysterics I sensed shrieking at the edge of my awareness.

I scanned the yard. Where had my attacker gone?

India must have gotten to me fast. She said she'd come through the same open gate I had, but she hadn't seen the person who'd been holding me under.

The yard was surrounded by a six-foot redwood fence—not impossible to get over, but not easy either. I walked around the other corner of the house to a side yard with a decrepit swing set and tetherball pole. At its end stood another gate. My would-be killer could have heard India coming down the walk and escaped that way.

Five minutes later, she emerged with a slip of paper in hand. "Here." She held it out to me.

Composed, or at least pretending to be, I took the paper.

She didn't loosen her grip.

"You *are* calling the police, aren't you?" she asked.

"Of course. You should too. About Sam, I mean."

"About Sam." She nodded, her brandy-colored eyes serious, and she released the slip of paper.

"In case you forget, the directions for heating the casserole are on the note I left."

"Right. Let me know if you find anything, will you?"

"Sure. Thank you for saving my life."

"You're welcome." Her face crumpled. "I only wish

you could have …" She pressed a hand to her mouth and fled into the house.

I looked down at the concrete, stained with pool water dripping from my jeans.

I wished I'd been able to save Atticus too.

Feeling sick, I got into my pickup, tossed my ruined jacket on the passenger seat, and turned on the heater. My clothes stuck to my flesh. Inside my sneakers, my feet would soon start to itch. I should go home and change, but I couldn't, not yet. There was something I needed to find out first.

I drove to the address India had given me—a bungalow on the wrong side of the tracks. The yard was knee-high with weeds. A Honda faded to a sullen pink squatted in the driveway.

I squelched to the Honda and laid my palm on its hood. The metal was cold. If Sam had been at India's drowning me, he hadn't taken this car.

I peered through its window. Wrappers from Reign, crumpled fast food cups and boxes, and flyers protesting the chocolate shop lay scattered on the passenger seat and floor. Yup. This was Sam's car. So he probably hadn't tried to drown me, and since I was here …

I walked to the house and pressed the cracked plastic doorbell. It buzzed, setting my teeth on edge. I studied the paint peeling off the front door.

A curtain flicked sideways.

Sam opened the door. He was barefoot and bare-chested, a paunch riding over the hips of his faded jeans. His gaze traveled from my toes to the top of my head. "What happened to you?"

"Uh." I looked down at myself. My blouse had gone sheer, my blue bra visible beneath it. I crossed my arms over my chest. "I fell into a pool."

"Fell?" He sagged against the door frame.

Maybe honesty was the best policy. "Someone pushed me in and tried to drown me. At India Reine's house."

He quirked a brow. "India pushed you in?"

"I don't think so. She was the one who pulled me out." She'd saved my life. Had I even said thank you? I couldn't remember.

"So, she's a hero." He sneered and crossed his arms, mirroring me. "What do you want?"

"Where have you been for the last hour?"

"Here." His soft jaw jutted forward. "Why? Do you think I pushed you in?"

That tracked with the cold car, but I took an involuntary step backward. "Atticus and Tilde are dead. Someone called in a bomb threat at my museum and then tried to drown me."

"And India didn't notice someone trying to drown you in her own pool?" His eyes rolled.

"She wasn't—it's a long story. But something's going on with that chocolate shop, and you're the only one who might be impartial enough to tell me what." Because sometimes flattery is the best policy.

He straightened. "Damn right I'm impartial."

I waited. "So?"

"So, what?"

A new ache spread up my neck and behind my eyeballs. "You said your firing was unfair. Why don't we start with that? What happened, exactly?"

He shrugged. "Beats me. All I was trying to do was learn the roaster. I was in the storage room, grabbing a few beans from one of the plastic bins. Orson walked in and pitched a fit."

"Why?"

"Probably because the beans looked moldy. I figure he panicked—those beans are expensive—and took it out on me."

Moldy? Were they the ruined cocoa beans Penny had mentioned? "Did he know you were practicing with the roaster?"

Sam licked his lips. "No one else was using it. You'd think he'd be happy I was trying to work things out, become a better employee. But he was totally possessive of the whole chocolate-making process. I'd signed a nondisclosure agreement. It's not like I was trying to steal any chocolate-making secrets."

In other words, Orson didn't know Sam had been playing around with his equipment.

"I figured he'd cool off by the next day," Sam continued. "But when I got to work, he handed me my paycheck and told me to get out. Just like that. I told you it wasn't fair."

"That does seem a little extreme," I admitted and rubbed my jaw. "Did anything else happen?"

He stiffened. "You think I'm lying?"

"No." My mouth went dry. "I'm only trying to understand what happened."

"I *told* you what happened."

"What about Tilde, the accountant?"

Sam slouched against the door frame and his stomach bulged forward, his spine folding. "What about her?"

"Did she have any enemies? Were there any conflicts?"

He snorted. "Orson didn't like her. I heard him tell Atticus she was nosing around where she didn't belong."

"Nosing around where?"

"How should I know? You think Orson was ever in the mood for my questions? Besides, that accountant was a blackmailing snake."

"Blackmail?" I asked, startled. This was the first I'd heard of that.

A dog barked from a nearby yard.

"Tilde caught me coming in late once. It was only a few minutes, so of course I wrote on my timesheet that I came in on time. I mean, I'd practically forgotten about the whole thing by the time it came to submit timesheets. She threatened to tell Orson I was cheating unless I gassed up her car."

"Did you?"

"I wanted to keep my job, didn't I? I put three hours of pay into her gas tank." He spat a curse.

"And Lola?"

"The rich wife? I only saw her in the chocolate shop when she was swanning around getting her picture taken."

"I mean, did she ever have any problems with Tilde?"

"Not that I heard."

"Did you see India around the shop much?"

His expression turned wistful. "India would come by to bring Atticus lunch. Always had a smile for everyone. I'm sorry for her. She didn't deserve to lose her husband that way, even if he was a jerk."

"She didn't only lose her husband. Tilde, the accountant, was her cousin."

Sam's expression smoothed. "Was she?"

He'd known. Why was he lying about something so trivial? "Were you at the vigil for Atticus?"

He snorted. "Why would I be? I like India, but that only goes so far."

Now I *knew* Sam was lying. I'd seen him at the vigil. What else was he lying about? "Tilde said you followed her to her car one night when she left work and threatened her."

"*Tilde* said? Tilde's dead. Doesn't much matter what she said." He stepped backwards into the squat house and slammed the door.

twenty-three

I stared at the computer in the museum's dim light. Friday evening stragglers drifted through the main room. Clutching chocolate bars, they muttered over the creepy dolls, examined the placards beneath the exhibits.

I was so in trouble.

The week had passed, blessedly uneventful. No one was murdered. My *Magic of Chocolate* exhibit had gotten a mention in a Sacramento paper, and the museum had been packed all week. I felt kind of guilty about not telling Jason of my near-drowning. But he'd made it clear that this sort of info was for the officer in charge, Laurel Hammer.

Unfortunately, I hadn't talked to Laurel either. Or at least not directly.

When I'd returned, soaking wet and with a drowned cell phone, to my garage apartment three days earlier, I'd discovered that my wall phone was out of order. So I went next door to my aunt's. She admitted she'd disconnected the phone since I never used it. Then my aunt drafted me into cleaning out her garage. When she'd finally lent me her cell phone, she watched me dial, and I ended up leaving Laurel a vague message. My aunt would have told my mom about my near-death experience in a New York minute.

The next day, from the museum I'd left another, more detailed message for the detective about my near-drowning. Then I went to buy a new cell phone, which ended up being on a new system to save money. Museum ownership had turned me into a penny pincher.

Thursday, when Laurel didn't call, I phoned the desk sergeant from my new cell phone. He told me she was off work that day.

I braced my head on my fist and scanned the Affaire website for the fifth time. The box with that name on it had to be important somehow, or the person who'd tried to drown me in India's pool wouldn't have removed it. Affaire was a chocolate-making company in the San Francisco Bay Area. It sold wholesale blocks of chocolate to bakeries. Had Atticus been researching the competition? But Reine was artisanal – they wouldn't be competing with wholesalers. And could I believe that India hadn't know anything about the box? The weather hadn't been great that week, so it was possible she hadn't been in her back yard. But it seemed weird.

"Hi, can I buy this?" a woman asked.

My head jerked up from my phone, where I'd been programming my mother's number. A sale! "Sure!" I sold her the tarot deck and shuffled the last happy customers out the door.

The bookcase swung open. Adele leaned against the door frame. "You need a break. Instead of the microbrewery, why don't we go to the wine pickup party at Plot 42?"

I flipped the sign in the window to *Closed* and eyed her. Wisps of jet hair had come free of her chignon, and her face looked worn. "Rough day?"

"Oh, you know. Friday."

"Friday," I agreed. Though unlike most people I had to look way ahead, to Monday and Tuesday, for my time to run errands and relax.

Dammit. And I needed to call Laurel again.

"So?" Adele asked. "Will you come?"

"Are you kidding?" I dropped a pen on the counter. I couldn't wait to thrash over what I'd learned about Reign with my friends. "I've got so much to tell you."

"Great! You can bring Jason."

I eyed her. "Bring Jason to girls' night?"

She blushed. "Dieter's coming."

I'd suspected girls' night might not survive Adele's wedding. But all good things must come to an end. "All right. I will."

She straightened off the door frame and her shoulders relaxed. "Perfect. Harper will meet us there."

Promising myself I'd clean the museum in the morning, I refilled GD's food and water bowls, double-checked the locks, and called Laurel. At this point I had her number memorized. It was only one digit off from Jason's. Maybe the police had a special deal for partners.

"This is Detective Hammer. Leave a message. If this is an emergency, call 911."

"Um, hi. This is Maddie. Listen, I've left a few messages. I guess I'll just tell you again in case you didn't get them ... Someone pushed me into India Reine's pool and tried to drown me on Tuesday. I didn't see who—"

Beep!

I pressed the phone to my forehead and breathed deeply. Okay. Forget Laurel. She *must* have gotten at least one of my messages by now. I debated programming her number into my new phone – at least that way I could screen her calls. Instead, I called Jason.

"Maddie," his voice purred. "I was just thinking of you."

My insides warmed. "Good things, I hope?"

"The best. What's going on?"

"I'm headed to Plot 42. Their wine club pickup party

is today. Do you want to come?"

"I've got to finish a report, but I'll meet you there."

I grinned. "Great. See you then."

We hung up, and I strolled through the shared hallway to the alley and my pickup.

Two shadows moved behind the blinds in Mason's upstairs apartment. Annoyed with myself, I looked away. Would there ever be a day I didn't glance up when I left my museum?

Adele emerged from the building. She rattled the heavy metal door behind her, making sure it was locked, then stepped inside her Mercedes.

We caravanned down fog-bound streets, beneath the San Benedetto arch and out into farm country.

Tires crunching, I trailed Adele's taillights down the gravel drive to Plot 42. Light gleamed from the converted barn. Cars packed the lot, but I followed the Mercedes into the private family lot behind the barn.

I hopped from my pickup and stretched, inhaling the scent of damp earth.

Adele joined me and stretched too. "I'm glad we can just relax here."

Raucous music flowed from the barn.

I pointed to her chest. "You might want to take that off."

Adele looked down at her Fox and Fennel apron and her cheeks darkened. "You should have told me earlier." She whipped the apron over her head and tossed it on the seat of the Mercedes.

"I've learned some interesting things about Reign," I said.

"Oh?"

We strolled into the barn, and I flinched at the blaring music. At the far end, a local cover band played

"Rhiannon." Twinkle lights swagged the rafters. People jammed shoulder-to-shoulder at the tasting bar. Clusters of tall chairs surrounded wine-barrel tables.

Adele scanned the crowd for Dieter.

Harper waved, alone at one of the small tables, and we joined her.

"I wasn't sure I'd be able to hold your chairs," she shouted over the music, and I promptly claimed one.

"This place is a madhouse," she finished.

"I'll get the wine." Adele disappeared into the crowd.

Harper pointed at her full wine glass, beside a bowl of chocolate. "I've already got …" She sagged in the chair. "Never mind. Long day?"

"The museum was pretty busy."

"I remember when you complained about just the opposite when your museum was floundering." She smiled.

I raised my hands. "Hey, I'm not complaining. I'm just ready for a break."

On the low makeshift stage, the musicians paused between songs and conferred.

Lola and India strolled past. India offered a tray of chocolates to passersby and looked miserable. Lola walked arm-in-arm with San Benedetto's mayor and with Mike, our intrepid local reporter.

"Try that dark chocolate from Tanzania with the cab," Lola was saying, pointing to India's tray. "Notice how it brings out the fruit flavor in the chocolate? It's eighty percent."

The mayor nodded enthusiastically.

I braced my elbow on the table and shielded my face. "Tell me when Mike's out of sight," I muttered.

"The reporter?" Harper's gaze tracked Lola and the mayor's progress. "I thought no publicity was bad publicity."

"He keeps asking me about the bomb threat. That's not the sort of publicity I want."

"Uh huh," she said doubtfully.

Lola released the mayor's arm to snap a photo of him, glass raised to his lips.

Mike scribbled in a leather-bound notebook. "Eighty percent … ?"

"Cocoa," Lola said.

India shifted her weight and glanced toward a table surrounded by middle-aged couples.

The mayor leaned close and muttered something in Lola's ear.

"Don't worry." Lola laughed. "If you don't take a picture, it didn't happen."

"Not exactly in mourning, is she?" Harper asked.

"It wasn't Lola's husband or cousin who died," I said.

Frowning, Adele materialized at our table cradling three wine goblets filled with ruby liquid. "The estate cabernet." She frowned at Harper's glass. "Why didn't you tell me you already had a glass? Oh well, someone will drink it."

"Dieter can have it," I said.

"He's more of a beer person," Adele replied.

"Dieter?" Harper raised her brows. "I thought this was girls' night."

"Oh, you know," Adele said vaguely, watching the open barn door.

"Whatever." Harper leaned left, watching Lola and the mayor vanish into the throng.

"I thought Wine and Chocolate Days were over," I said. "I know I'm keeping my exhibit up all month, but what's with these chocolate tastings?" I nodded toward India.

"We had some Reign chocolate left over," Adele said, "and Lola offered to play chocolate sommelier."

"What did you decide about the wedding cake?" I asked her.

Adele's face crumpled. "Sheet cake and a fake tiered cake. I had no choice. I just hope some kid doesn't decide to try to eat the fake one. He'll end up with a mouthful of Styrofoam."

"I thought the reception was adults-only?" Harper asked.

"It was," she said, "until Dieter told me about all the kids on his side of the family. We'll hire some nannies and set up a separate play area for the children on the other side of the house."

"I've been thinking about these murders," I said. "Sam said Tilde was into petty blackmail. I wonder if she was killed because she knew too much? But if so, what did she know? Did she witness Atticus's murder, or did she somehow suspect who was behind it?"

"What's the mayor doing talking to Lola?" Harper's brow wrinkled.

"Who cares?" Adele replied. "I've got bigger fish to fry. Do you know any good babysitters?"

"No," I said, impatient. "Now about the murders—"

"I thought you'd decided to drop that business," Adele said.

This is what came from not telling them about my near drowning. But the only way to make sure it didn't get back to my mother, was to keep it to myself, India, and Laurel—if I ever managed to track down the detective.

I squirmed on my chair. "Not *drop*, not entirely. But I heard there was some conflict between Orson and Tilde. Orson told Atticus she was snooping. And if he told Atticus, he may have told others, like the killer." Assuming Orson himself wasn't the killer. I hadn't forgotten the insurance policy that resulted in him benefitting from Atticus's death.

"What are they telling that reporter?" Harper toyed with her wine glass.

I frowned. What was wrong with Harper? I understood Adele's obsession with her wedding, but Atticus had been one of Harper's clients. I thought she would've cared more about his murder.

"Lola's a publicity hound," Adele said. "Of course she's talking to a reporter. She doesn't have Atticus around anymore to manage her promotions."

"It sounds like you know Lola better than I do," I said.

"You can't avoid knowing Lola." Adele sipped her cabernet. "She's made sure of it by inserting herself into every single article connected to Reign. *And* everything else to do with this town."

"Is she a wine club member?" I asked.

"Yep," Adele said, white lines appearing at the corners of her lips. "And look how she's taken over the party. India works for my father, not for Lola."

"I'll be right back." Harper rose and plunged into the crowd.

"What is *with* her?" Adele asked. "You'd think she didn't care about my wedding."

"Well, we do talk about it an awful lot."

The band segued to David Bowie.

Adele glared. "Of course we do. How do you think you plan a wedding? You manage events at the museum. You know what sort of planning is required."

"Yes, but—"

"And those events are nothing compared to a

wedding. It's only the most important day of my life."
She gulped her wine.

I winced. "I know, I know. Sorry."

Adele set down the glass and hung her head. "No, I'm
sorry. I shouldn't have blown up at you like that. This
wedding is making me lose my mind."

"Your wedding's going to be fabulous. I mean—a
vineyard! It will be gorgeous! And in the end, all anyone
cares about is you and Dieter."

"And the cake." She moaned.

"Ply everyone with enough wine and they'll forget the
cake."

"I don't want a bunch of slobbering drunks at my
wedding. What will the children think?"

There *was* that. Thoughtful, I snagged a piece of
chocolate from the bowl on the table and popped it into
my mouth. It stuck in my throat and I washed it down
with wine. Maybe I hadn't completely gotten over my
recent aversion to chocolate.

"I could organize a petting zoo," Adele mused.

"Sure. Kids love petting zoos." There had to be a way
to get her to stop obsessing over the wedding and start
obsessing over my murders. Okay, that might have been
a *tad* selfish.

I cleared my throat. "I'm sorry, I keep thinking about
the murders. You're my best friend. I should be giving
your wedding more attention, but I haven't been able to
get these deaths out of my head."

Adele laid a hand on mine. "Of course you can't. You
found the bodies! And all I can think about is myself.
Enough. How can I help?"

"Is there anything else you know about Lola that you
haven't told me?"

"For starters, I don't know why Harper has become

so obsessed with Lola and the mayor tonight. It's like my wedding isn't even happening."

Agh! Enough with the wedding. "Someone tried to drown me in India's pool on Tuesday," I blurted. It was the only thing I could think of to get her attention. And if I couldn't trust Adele and Harper to keep their mouths shut, who could I trust?

She blinked. "What?"

"What?" Jason asked from behind me.

I winced. Turned. "Oh … hey, you made it."

In his blue suit and tie, Jason glowered. "What's this about someone trying to drown you at India's?"

"Why didn't you tell me?" Adele asked.

"I wasn't hurt," I said weakly. "I was waiting to tell Laurel."

"You mean you haven't told her either?" Jason's nostrils flared. "Unbelievable. You didn't think to report an attempted murder at the home of a material witness?"

"I tried!"

He scowled. "Not hard enough. We could have gotten the alibis of everyone involved. Now days have gone by."

I'd left four messages for Laurel! How could he think I'd blow something like this off? "I already checked," I ground out. "India could have pushed me in, but she's also the one who pulled me out. Sam doesn't seem likely—his car engine was cold when I drove to his house right after the incident. And Orson and Lola were at the chocolate shop." I'd gone there after drying off Tuesday afternoon, and Lola had told me they'd both been there all day.

"You checked? I could have you arrested for interfering in an investigation," Jason fumed.

"But—"

"You withheld evidence. When Laurel finds out, she'd be within her rights to arrest you."

"But I left her messages!"

"Messages." Adele angled her head. "I'll bet they were vague, or she would have gotten back to you. Honestly, Maddie. What were you thinking?"

"I was detailed!" This was so unfair. Maybe I *could* have asked Jason to pass the message on to Laurel. But I hadn't, because it seemed like tattling on Laurel, plus ... I hadn't wanted him to tell me to stay out of the murders. Annoyance and reason warred inside me. "Fine," I finally said. "I'll call her again tonight."

"Now would be good," Jason said.

I slid from my chair. "I'll go outside to do it." *And leave another message, no doubt.*

"I'll come with you," he said grimly.

He didn't trust me to follow through? *Ouch.* Just for that, I wouldn't program his number into my new phone either.

Harper appeared at my elbow. "So much for girls' night. No offense, Jason."

"None taken," he said.

"What did I miss?" she asked.

"Maddie's about to be arrested for withholding evidence," Adele said tartly.

"Huh?"

"Long story." I trudged from the noisy barn.

Jason followed.

"I did leave messages, you know, and I *did* say someone tried to drown me in India's pool."

He didn't respond.

I dialed. "You know, the reason I have her number memorized is because I've called it so often. Also, it's only one digit off from yours, which I only realized after—"

"This is Detective Hammer."

Laurel didn't sound happy to hear from me. But ordering me to the station seemed to lift her spirits.

I pocketed the phone. "I'm going to the station."

"I heard," he said.

"I'm sorry," I said stiffly. "I should have told you right away." Jason seemed to have a hard time believing Laurel had ignored my messages.

"Why didn't you?"

"You told me to tell Laurel this stuff first, but she never got back to me."

He just looked at me.

"I left her four messages."

"She should have called you back for something like this."

"Well, she didn't. Jason, Laurel really—" *Hates me.* I exhaled slowly. He and Laurel were partners, and if I complained about how she'd messed with me again, I'd look like I was the one with the problem. But he was a cop. Shouldn't he be able to tell who was being honest?

He shook his head. "Is that all that's going on?"

I screwed up my face. "My mom would flip out if she heard about the attack. Especially if it made the papers."

"You're a grown woman, and you're still afraid of your mother?"

"My brother's being sent to Afghanistan," I snapped. "She's worried. And yes, I know that's no excuse. But I left—"

"Messages," Jason said, stone-faced. "Got it. You said India saved you. What happened, exactly?"

Did he get it? I had my doubts, but I explained about the casserole, the open gate, the pool.

"Why didn't India call the police?" he asked.

"I don't know." And I *had* sort of been trespassing in her yard. But if India had tried to kill me, why then had she revived me? Had she had second thoughts? No, it *couldn't* have been India.

"Well." I scuffed the gravel drive with my toe. "I should probably go to the station."

"I'll follow you in my car."

My heart bottomed. He didn't trust me to do that either. Swallowing the angry lump in my throat, I nodded.

Jason walked me to my pickup and watched while I slithered inside and locked the doors. His sedan followed me all the way to the squat brick police station.

I met him on the front steps. Silently, he perp-walked me inside the sickly green reception area.

Laurel stood beside the reception window chatting with a beefy uniformed policeman. A shark-like smile spread across her face. "Well, well, well. Kosloski. Let's have a chat about withholding evidence in a police investigation."

twenty-four

Adele winced and rotated the white teacup between her hands. "Laurel kept you overnight?" Her hair was done up in a prim chignon, and she wore an ice-blue silk blouse beneath her Fox and Fennel apron.

Slouched across from her in the booth at the tearoom, I nodded and examined the white teeth marks GD had left in my palm that morning. "No, only for a few hours. And she didn't charge me with interfering with a police investigation." Like me, Laurel seemed to believe the attempted murder-by-drowning was connected to the Reign murders.

I'd clung to that bright spot all weekend. Jason and I still hadn't spoken, and my mouth twisted. I wasn't sure if I should apologize or break up with him for not believing me. My ego told me to break up. But the thought squeezed my neck and chest, brought despairing tears to my eyes. I looked past the gauzy curtains to the sidewalk outside and blinked away the heat. Jason was usually so … sensible. I wanted to give him a chance to make things right. "I can't believe Jason didn't believe me." My grip tightened on my cup.

"I'm sorry I didn't, but I was …" Adele briefly closed her eyes. "As self-obsessed as Lola. Jason will come around. Everyone knows Laurel is totally irrational when it comes to you and GD. I wouldn't be surprised if she deleted your messages."

"Thank you!"

"Give Jason a chance. It's got to be complicated for him. She's his partner, and if she did ignore your report of a crime – that's serious."

"Yeah," I said heavily. I'd wasted so much time agonizing about whether we were in love or not. Perversely, now I was certain I did love the man. And just as certain if he didn't trust me, I had to end it.

"But why didn't you just tell Harper and me about the attack at India's?" Adele asked.

Swallowing, I fiddled with the cuff of my olive blouse. "I wanted to tell Laurel first. But first she was off work, and then she didn't answer, and then one thing led to another …"

"Why didn't India call the police?" Adele folded her arms.

"I'm sure Laurel will ask her that." I checked my watch. "What time did you say our appointment with the caterer was?" I'd officially rededicated myself to Adele's wedding. Detecting was only getting me into trouble, and since it was finally my day off, I had the time.

"In fifteen minutes, and don't change the subject."

I scooted from the booth, my jeans squeaking on the faux-leather. "Then we should get moving. Do you want me to drive?"

Adele shuddered. "In that old jalopy? No thanks. We can take my Mercedes."

"My truck's not old," I said loftily. "It's vintage." But my shoulders relaxed, relieved the subject had been changed. I gulped the last of my mint tea and followed my friend's clicking heels to her Mercedes. In the foggy alley, I did *not* glance up at Mason's windows. At least that was progress.

The caterer's business was located in an industrial park on the outskirts of San Benedetto. Thick mist hugged the low, corrugated metal building sandwiched between a wine tasting room and a sign shop.

"Don't say it." Adele eyed the door beside the retractable garage door and smoothing her tulip skirt. "This caterer really is the best in fifty miles."

"I believe you." Adele was choosy when it came to pretty much everything. It was one of the reasons she was so successful.

She walked inside without knocking, and I followed her into a small room. Oversized framed photographs of successful catering events lined the rear wall. Good smells—bacon and cheese and something sweet— floated from a back room. A small round table covered in an elegant white cloth sat in one corner. High-backed wooden chairs with inviting cushions surrounded the table. On its top stood a cut-crystal vase filled with multicolored ranunculus flowers.

A door behind the counter opened and a plump, middle-aged woman in a black apron hurried from the back room. "Ms. Nakamoto?" She smiled.

Adele stuck her hand across the counter. "That's me. This is my friend Maddie Kosloski. She's helping me plan the wedding."

"Moral support is important," the woman said, grinning, "but we'll try to keep things painless." She grasped my hand. "Nice to meet you. I'm Margaret."

"Hi, Margaret," I said, smothering a wince. Margaret had a grip.

From beneath the counter she pulled a slim binder, its spine labeled *Nakamoto-Finkielkraut.* "Are you ready to finalize the menu?" She motioned us to the table.

The three of us sat, and I eased back against the cushions.

Adele and the caterer finalized the menu and the head count, occasionally looking to me for confirmation. This part of the job was easy—I agreed with everything Adele wanted.

"What about wedding favors?" the caterer asked. "Have you decided if you'd like us to provide them?"

Adele glanced at me, and I nodded. We'd already hashed this out and agreed to let someone else do the work. "Yes," she said. "But we want to keep the costs low. What do you recommend?"

"Candied almonds are traditional for many weddings," Margaret said. "The bittersweet taste represents life. The sweet coating is a wish for the newlyweds to experience more sweet than bitter. Our almonds are organic and locally sourced. But we're doing a new twist—coating almonds in Reign chocolate." She winked. "You may not know this, but chocolate is considered an aphrodisiac."

Oh, I knew. I canted my head. "Reign is providing you with bulk chocolate?" I asked, intrigued. "I thought they only sold retail." If they were going into the wholesale business, maybe Affaire was a competitor after all.

Adele shot me a warning look.

I shrugged. I wasn't investigating, just curious. "Since one of the owners is, um, gone," I said to Adele, "we want to make sure they'll be able to fulfill their future orders. Who knows what'll happen to Reign by the time your wedding rolls around?"

"Mr. Malke has assured me Reign won't experience any disruptions," Margaret said. "After all, it's Orson

Malke who makes the chocolate. Poor Mr. Reine was responsible for the marketing."

"How long has Reign been supplying you with bulk chocolate?" I asked.

Adele cleared her throat.

"Only two months," the caterer said. "We've never had a problem with the orders, and I don't expect any in the future."

"I'm sure it will be fine," Adele said, "but—"

"Is Reign selling their chocolate in bulk to anyone else?" I asked.

Margaret's face pinked. "No. We're exclusive. So exclusive that …
Well …" She leaned forward, her gaze darting toward the industrial door. "We got lucky. Orson made the deal with us, and we didn't think anything of it."

I nodded, encouraging.

"Apparently," the caterer continued, "Atticus didn't know about it until after it was done. He wasn't happy about the arrangement. He thought Reign should stay purely retail to maintain the brand. But we'd already signed a contract. So we're the first caterer to use their chocolate." Her brow creased. "Of course, now that Orson is on his own, he may decide to sell to other restaurants or bakeries."

Reign was a small operation. Wholesaling chocolate seemed like a big shift. No wonder Atticus had been upset that the decision had been made without him. Did the shop even have the facilities to produce the quantities needed for wholesaling?

"The chocolate coating would go well with the wine we'll be serving," Adele said. "But June gets awfully hot. Although the reception won't be until evening, when it's cooler, you'll be setting up the tables earlier. Won't the chocolates melt?"

"We can put the favors out last, and usually we pack them in Reign's boxes—"

"Reign has boxes sized for wedding favors?" I asked. They must have been serious about wholesaling.

Adele kicked me beneath the table and I sucked in a gasp of pain.

"Oh, yes," Margaret said blithely, "Orson was quite proud of those boxes. We have to pay for them, of course."

"Of course." I rubbed my shin and silently cursed Adele's penchant for pointy-toed shoes.

"What sort of cost are we talking about?" Adele asked.

The two talked price points, and Adele shook her head. "I know Reign chocolate is popular, but this is a little outside our budget."

"We could drop the price by putting them in net bags," Margaret suggested.

"And making them more susceptible to melting in someone's pocket," Adele said. "What about the more traditional candied almonds?"

"We can, of course, do that too," Margaret said smoothly. She flipped a page in the binder to a photo of candied almonds in net bags and named a price.

Adele's smile faltered. "I'll need to discuss this with Dieter. Can I call you in a few days with a decision on the favors?"

"Of course! I'll be right back with a final menu printout for you to sign." Margaret escaped into the back room.

"Are you seriously interrogating my caterer?" Adele hissed at me.

"I'm sure it all has nothing to do with the murders," I said quickly. But why had Orson been making deals behind Atticus's back? "I didn't know Reign was selling wholesale. Did you?"

"That's not the point. You promised your mother you wouldn't investigate."

"I doubt the caterer is involved in the murders." And I hadn't promised. Not exactly.

"Of course she isn't!"

I grimaced. "So, there's no harm. This is only background information. Like researching the history of my haunted molinillo." Why couldn't I seem to stop myself from turning things into an investigation? This was Adele's time, not mine.

Margaret returned with the menu, and Adele signed it. Then Adele and I drove to town in silence and she dropped me at my closed museum.

GD lifted his head from his spot on the rocking chair. He gave me a hard stare, then tucked his head beneath a paw and resumed snoozing.

"Nice to see you too." I dug out my water stained notepad, pulled out my new cell phone, and called India.

"Hello?" she asked, caution dampening her voice.

"Hi, India, this is Maddie."

"Oh," she said. "I just got back from the police station."

Uh oh.

"The detective wanted to know why I didn't report your near-drowning," she said.

I covered my face with one hand. "What did you tell her?"

"That I didn't witness what happened, and you said you'd call the cops. Why didn't you?"

"I did, but … it's a long story. I'm sorry if I caused you problems." I wasn't actually sorry, but I didn't think telling her that would get me what I wanted to know.

India blew out a shaky breath. "My husband was murdered. And then my cousin. There's nothing anyone can do to make things worse."

"I'm sorry," I said quietly, and this time I was sincere. Outside the museum's window, cars drifted past in the mist. "Is there anything I can do *for* you?"

"If I could think of something, I'd ask. Why did you call?"

"Does Reign have any other production facilities beside the one in their San Benedetto shop?"

"No. That's the whole point of artisan chocolate. Reign is small, and everything's made by Orson. Why?"

"I was just curious. Thanks." I paused. "How are things going?"

Her laugh was mirthless. "They released my husband's body."

"Oh. I'm serious about that offer of help. Just let me know what you need."

"The mortuary's taking care of nearly everything."

"That's good." I remembered my father's funeral. There had been so many decisions to make, and though none of them had been earth-shattering, they'd seemed that way through my haze of grief. A remembered ache pinched my heart. "Let me know if—"

"Sure." India hung up.

Thoughtful, I pocketed the phone. Reign wholesaling. Did it mean anything?

My pulse quickened.

I thought it might.

twenty-five

The microbrewery was quiet Monday night. A few older couples staked out booths, their conversations echoing softly off the dark tile floors, the pressed-tin ceiling, the giant copper vats.

I slid into the red booth beside Harper. Her dark hair cascaded over the shoulders of her coffee-colored turtleneck.

Adele's heels clicked across the tile floor. "As much as I love girl time, I hope this is important, Maddie. I've still got tons of wedding planning to do." She neatly swiveled into the booth, her pale blue tulip skirt flaring around her knees.

"How did it go at the caterers?" Harper asked.

Adele slewed her gaze in my direction. *"Someone* turned it into an interrogation."

Harper's full lips quivered. "Did she?"

"The caterer is buying chocolate wholesale from Reign," I said. "I was surprised, that's all. I thought Reign only sold retail."

They stared at me.

"Okay, yes, I may be obsessing," I admitted. But the wholesaling *meant* something. I needed to talk to Orson. Or Jason. My heart pinched. But there was always Laurel. I really didn't want to talk to Laurel, but for the first time, the prospect was more appealing than facing Jason.

Harper sighed. "Denial ain't just a river in Egypt,

Maddie."

"What's that supposed to mean?" I asked, indignant. I'd already admitted I was obsessing.

"It means—"

A waiter materialized at Harper's elbow. "Hi, I'm Paul. Can I get you started with drinks?"

"The Hefeweizen," Harper said.

"The IPA," Adele said.

"Hefeweizen," I said.

"And beer-battered artichokes," Harper added.

Impatient, I shifted in the booth. I wasn't in denial.

"Anything else?" the waiter asked.

"What are your specials today?" Adele asked.

He checked his notepad and rattled off the list.

"We'll need a few minutes, I think," Adele said. "Thanks."

The waiter strode away.

"What do you mean, denial?" I asked.

Adele pressed her index finger onto the wooden table. "You're turning into your mother."

"My—what?" I sucked in a breath. *No. No way.* "That's a bridge too far."

"Is it?" Adele asked.

"Explain," I said, crossing my arms.

My friends shared a look.

"Oh, come on," Harper said. "You must have noticed."

"Noticed what?" I asked.

Another long look.

Harper turned to me. "Your mother has her finger in every pie in San Benedetto. And you manage to get yourself involved in every murder, which puts you in the intriguing position of knowing everything that's going on."

"I found two bodies!"

The waiter returned with the beers and deep-fried artichokes. "Are you ready to order?"

"I think so," Adele said.

I sat, heels bouncing, while the others ordered.

"Blue-cheese burger and garlic fries," I rapped out when the waiter got to me. "Medium rare." I was so not my mother. I jammed an artichoke into the ceramic bowl filled with ranch dressing and popped it in my mouth. The damn thing was scalding and I gulped my beer, feeling blisters rise on the roof of my mouth.

"Careful," the waiter said. "They're hot."

"Mmph!" No kidding.

He ambled toward the kitchen.

I brandished an artichoke heart. "And I'm not my mother." That was just crazy.

"Your mother is San Benedetto's unofficial queen bee," Harper said. "No offense. I like your mother. She gets things done. In fact, when I run for town council, I'm going to ask for her support. But let's face it, she's involved in San Benedetto business in a way that just isn't normal."

I stared, thunderstruck. "You're running for town council?"

"That's amazing!" Adele shrieked. "You're going to be perfect for the job! Who's in charge of your campaign? Can I be in charge of your campaign?"

Harper's cheeks turned dusky rose. "Yeah, I'm running. I've been thinking about it for a while now."

"But why didn't you tell us?" Adele asked.

She lifted her shoulders, dropped them. "You've been busy with the wedding. Maddie's been busy dealing with dead bodies. The time never seemed right. But something's changed in San Benedetto, don't you feel it?"

"Change is inevitable," Adele said.

"No," Harper said, "it's more than that. Our crime rate has gone up. People are on edge. We need to find the money to hire more police, put up more streetlamps."

"We're going to get you elected," Adele said. "It's about time there was new blood on the town council."

"I'll help too," I said. "You're going to be great. You know the town. You understand what it's like for small business owners. And you're smart and organized and honest."

Harper turned her beer mug on the table. "Thanks. But I'm not on the council yet."

"You will be," Adele said confidently. "First though, we need to get my wedding out of the way and deal with Maddie's little problem."

I scowled. "I don't have a little problem."

"It's bigger than you think," Adele said.

"Fine," I grumped. "Tell me what my problem is."

"You *want* to investigate these murders," she said. "You want it so badly that you're sneaking behind the backs of the people who care about you the most."

I slumped. Maybe they weren't crazy. I had been making a lot of friends and family mad lately. "All right. I get the point. Laurel's in charge, and I'm no Nancy Drew." But that didn't let Jason off the hook for not believing me about those phone messages, and misery tore at my heart.

They glanced at each other.

Harper's brow furrowed. "That isn't what we're saying at all."

"You need to figure out a way to be true to yourself," Adele said. "You *are* like your mother in a way. Both of you are good at helping people solve problems. Sure, you're great at the museum. I'm almost not embarrassed anymore about having my tearoom next door to it. But if you can't figure out a way to get involved in the things you care about *and* be honest with the people around you, you're never going to be happy."

They were right. I'd been dancing around my mother like a nervous colt. And the fact Jason had taken Laurel's side over mine really hurt me. The beer glass burred, and I swiped at my eyes with the back of my hand. If he didn't believe me, we didn't have a relationship to lose. I needed to face him.

The waiter stopped beside us, a tray on his shoulder. He whisked our plates onto the table. "Can I get you anything else?" The tray dropped to his side. "More beer?"

"No thanks," I said, lifting my half-full mug.

"Not right now," Harper said.

"Okay. Enjoy." He bustled away.

"I need to talk to Jason," I said slowly. "And to my mother."

"Not if you're eating those garlic fries," Adele said, pointing at my plate.

Right. I needed to lose a few pounds anyway. Appetite gone, I shoved the basket away and sipped my beer. "Any suggestions?" I asked.

"Blunt honesty," Harper said.

Adele nodded. "If Jason doesn't believe you, he isn't right for you."

I stared at my hands, wrapped around the cool mug. "I don't get it," I said. "I left four messages for Laurel, and she ignored them. And I'm frankly … pissed off that he's taking her side." Sure, they were partners, but I was his girlfriend.

Adele's brows drew together. "Are you sure she ignored them? I mean, I believe you left the messages. I just wonder if there could have been some mistake. Laurel's never liked you, but I always thought she was a good cop."

"I even left a message with the desk sergeant!"

"But that's ..." Harper's face creased with worry. "I know you and Laurel have issues, but that's dereliction of duty. If she ignored your messages about a crime, this whole town has a problem."

And Jason had a partner he couldn't rely on. My throat tightened and I suddenly found it hard to swallow. I was going to lay it on the line with him about my relationship with Laurel and why she'd ignored my messages. And if he didn't want to hear it, I needed to know that now.

Our conversation shifted to lighter things: Adele's wedding, Harper's plot to rule San Benedetto, the museum's upcoming ghost photos exhibit. Finally, crumbs scattered across the table, we paid the bill and emerged on the dark sidewalk. The fog had lifted, stars faint above the glow of the iron lampposts, the low buildings.

We lingered on the brick walk in front of the Bell and Brew, and I leaned one hip on the wrought-iron fence that marked off the restaurant's outdoor tables. I wasn't looking forward to my conversation with Jason. But now that I'd decided to have it, a weight seemed to have lifted from my shoulders.

Tackling my mother wouldn't be easy either, but—

"Maddie?" Penny waddled up to our group.

I straightened off the fence and smiled at the older woman, her thick parka buttoned to her chin. "Hi, Penny. Where are you headed?"

Expression strained, she canted her head toward the microbrewery. "It's good to see a friendly face. I'm picking up takeout for myself and a friend."

"A friendly face? Is something wrong?" I glanced down the darkened street.

Her gaze followed mine. "These murders have made me paranoid." She laughed uneasily. "For a moment I thought I was being followed. I almost got back in my car and drove home, but it was just Mr. Sanderson with his beagle."

"The murders have unnerved everyone," Adele said. "It's no fun thinking a killer is out there, someone we might even know."

"That's an understatement," Penny said. "This afternoon I got it into my head that someone had snuck into the Wine and Visitors Bureau after it closed, and I was there alone." She looked over her cat-eye glasses at me. "I've taken to locking the side door."

I laughed. "Noted." No more sneaking into the Center and giving Penny a potential heart attack.

A Mazda drifted down the road toward us.

Penny's grip tightened on her oversized purse. "Have you learned anything—"

A bang. A flash on the opposite side of the street.

Penny and Adele shrieked. Harper leapt backward, stumbling against the low iron fence.

The Mazda swerved toward us, brakes squealing. The car screeched to a halt six inches from the sidewalk. Behind the wheel, the elderly driver's eyes bulged.

Two dark figures ran down the street.

"Call the police!" Unthinking, I raced across the road after them.

Adele shouted something. But all I could make out were the pounding of my feet on the pavement, the gust of my breath, the roar of blood in my ears.

The figures turned a corner.

I lengthened my strides, my anger giving way to anxiety. But I kept on anyway, rounding the building.

A teenager, hands on his knees, leaned against the wall of the bank. A second laughed and punched his friend on the shoulder.

"What did you two do?" I snarled.

They straightened, whirling.

I knew these two, and I got mad all over again. They were regulars in the museum—Gary Matthews and Walter Wiggins.

"A firecracker. You two idiots set off a firecracker," I said, realization dawning.

Gary paled, his freckles going gray in the amber light. "It was only a joke."

My teeth ground together. "You nearly caused a car accident. What if someone got hurt? It wouldn't have been so funny then."

Walter's narrow shoulders curled inward. "A car accident?"

"Mr. Thorenson was driving down the road when your firecracker went off. He nearly plowed into us on the sidewalk."

"We didn't mean for anyone to get hurt," Gary said. "It was only a firecracker. He wasn't hurt, was he?"

"No," I admitted, my fury fading. "He looked okay. Did you set off that firecracker at the vigil in the park a few weeks ago?"

"What?" Walter looked at his friend. "You mean, at the vigil?"

I nodded.

"I wasn't anywhere near the vigil," Walter said. "I wanted to go, but my dad made me stay home and do homework. He even helped me with history."

"Gary?"

"It wasn't me," Gary said. "I was grounded for cow tipping."

"Cow tipping?" Kids still did that? "Look, I know it can get a little boring out here, but think, will you?"

"Are you going to tell our moms?" Walter asked.

I was tempted. But as pranks went, theirs hadn't been that awful. I was angry mostly because it had scared *me*. "I'll try to keep your names out of it. But if I catch you or hear about you doing anything else, all bets are off."

"Thanks." They raced down the street and vanished around a corner.

Frowning, I trudged back to Main Street. Mr. Thorenson's Mazda was parked at an angle on the road, its headlights illuminating the sidewalk. People had spilled from the brewery and stood in a grim circle.

I ran toward the crowd, my view blocked by the heavily clothed backs. I tapped our waiter on the shoulder. "What's going on?"

He looked over his shoulder. "Looks like a heart attack. I called 911."

"A heart ..." Suddenly, I found it hard to breathe. Not Mr. Thorenson. He'd looked fine! I pushed past the waiter.

Penny sat slumped against the wrought-iron fence. She clutched her chest. Her face was gray, her breathing shallow, her eyes closed.

Adele crouched beside her. She looked up at me. "An ambulance is on the way."

"Not Penny," I whispered. Was fear about to claim another victim?

twenty-six

Gray dawn light filtered through the hospital windows. Yawning, I stretched in the waiting room's thin-cushioned chair and tried to work the kink out of my neck.

My mother strode through the sliding glass doors. "How is she?"

Even at five a.m., my mom's jeans were perfectly pressed, the razor-sharp collar of her blouse positioned with millimeter precision over the lapels of her corduroy jacket. But the fragile skin beneath her eyes was the color of a bruise.

Relieved, I stood. I hadn't known whom to contact on Penny's behalf besides my mother, so I'd left a message last night. For once I was glad my mom was an early riser. "The doctors said she had an anxiety attack but they're keeping her for observation," I explained. "They're moving her from Emergency into a room. I'm just waiting to check in on her once she's moved."

My mother's shoulders slumped. "What a relief. What happened?"

I explained. "Penny told me she was anxious about the murders," I finished. "On the way to the microbrewery, she even thought someone was following her."

"Someone's imagination running away with them?" my mother asked dryly and folded her arms. "Hard to believe."

My cheeks warmed. My mom knew me too well. I had a tendency to imagine the worst too. "She must have thought the firecracker was a gunshot or bomb and panicked." The scene had been awful, Penny gasping for breath, her face purpling. It was hard to believe fear could cause that much pain.

My mom shook her head, her squash-blossom earrings swinging. "Penny's not the only one who's tense. You should hear the talk at Ladies Aid. All of San Benedetto is jumpy. This murderer needs to be caught." Her mouth pinched. "But that doesn't mean you have to do it."

"Mom, I'm sorry I've worried you. But if I have a chance to learn something, I'm going to."

"Madelyn—"

"It's important. People tell me things they wouldn't tell the police. All I'll do is pass it on to Jason. Or Laurel."

She raised a skeptical brow. "You're actually going to help Laurel?"

"Of course, because …" Because if Jason thought I was a liar, we were breaking up. "I have to. And I like investigating. The fact is, as much as I love the museum—and I do love it—there's more to life than work."

"Have you thought of joining a gym?"

"I swear I haven't gained any weight—"

"Your weight is fine. I meant there are other productive hobbies you could enjoy aside from sticking your nose into murder investigations. You could join Ladies Aid."

I shuddered. *No, no, a thousand times no.* "But sticking my nose into murder investigations is what I *do.*"

She stared at me, then pressed her hand to her mouth. Her shoulders quaked. "Oh, Madelyn, you really are your father's daughter," she gasped, laughing. Then she straightened. "All right. I didn't tell your brother not to go to Afghanistan. I don't suppose it's fair of me to tell you to stop ... whatever it is you're doing. But that doesn't mean I have to like it."

I hugged her. "I know, Mom. Thanks."

"Now go home," she said gently. "You're exhausted. I'll stay and see if there's anything Penny needs."

I yawned again, my eyes gritty from lack of sleep. "Thanks. Tell her I'm thinking of her."

I left the hospital, stopping at the museum to check on GD's food and water. Startled by my early morning appearance, he scowled from his perch on the haunted rocking chair. Then the ebony cat tucked his paw beneath his head and resumed napping.

I drove home, kibble duty done. Stumbling upstairs to my apartment, I kicked off my tennis shoes, tugged off my clothes, and tumbled into bed.

I startled awake, blinking, confused.

My front door thundered beneath someone's fist.

Outside my bedroom window, sun and blue sky had broken through the morning's gloom. Puffy cartoon clouds floated above my aunt's house.

I staggered from bed and tugged on a cotton robe. "Keep your pants on!" Annoyed, I jerked my belt tight and scraped a hand through my hair. I stormed into my nautical-themed living room, smothered a yawn, and yanked open the door.

Jason stood on the steps in faded blue slacks and a white shirt open at the collar. "Thank God."

"What's wrong? Has something happened?" I

stepped aside and he strode past me.

"I heard you were at the scene last night. And then you   weren't answering your phone this morning. I thought—" He pulled   me into a hug.

"I might have done something crazy?" My words were muffled against his muscular chest. Pulling away, I dropped onto the soft, blue-gray couch. "And what do you mean, 'at the scene'? I told the officers it was just some kids with a firecracker. I saw them running away. I told them it was Gary Matthews and Walter Wiggins. And they told me they had alibis for the vigil, by the way. Gary was doing homework with his dad and Walter was grounded for cow tipping. Or maybe Gary was grounded. I can't remember."

Jason lifted a single brow. "So that's really all that happened?"

"Of course. I wouldn't lie about it."

Jason dropped onto the couch beside me. "I know. I talked to the desk sergeant. He told me you left a message for Laurel last week about the attack at the pool."

"Oh."

"I don't know what happened. He left the message on her desk."

"I left other messages too," I said pointedly. "On her voicemail."

"She told me she's been having problems with her phone."

Sure she was. I lowered my head. Jason would never believe she'd ignored those messages intentionally. "I don't trust Laurel."

"I know," he said. "But she's a good cop. I believe her." He flushed. "I checked her phone records, okay?

And if you tell her that ... don't tell her that. The point is, I'm sorry. I shouldn't have jumped on you."

"You didn't believe me."

"That's not true. I did believe you left the messages."

I opened my mouth to argue.

"Detailed messages," he amended. "But I can't ... not believe Laurel without evidence. We're partners. That means something."

"I thought we meant something too," I said quietly.

"We do. Which is why I took time to sort this out before reacting."

Before reacting? He'd— I thought back to that evening at *Plot 42.* Jason had been upset I'd been interrogating potential murderers. He'd been annoyed I hadn't told him about the near drowning, and ... He'd never accused me of lying. He'd been pissed, but he'd been thoughtful too, trying to sort things out, waiting to gather evidence before reacting.

Like a good cop.

I *liked* that he was a good cop.

"So why did you follow me outside that night, like you didn't trust I'd call Laurel, or find my way to the police station on my own?"

"You told me someone tried to kill you. I wasn't going to leave you alone."

Well, that was just ... reasonable, dammit. "But you were definitely avoiding me afterward."

"Can you blame me? I could see you were furious. I thought we both needed some time to calm down. And I needed to figure out what was going on with Laurel."

"Well," I replied, grudging, "Laurel and I aren't exactly besties, and I assumed the worst about her motives. I could have asked you to deliver the message when it was obvious mine weren't getting through."

"Maybe. But I get why you didn't. And I shouldn't have gone into cop mode that night at the winery. You're my girlfriend, not my suspect." His brows furrowed. "Sometimes it's hard to turn it off. But you've never lied to me. I do trust you."

So, he wasn't perfect. Jason hadn't reacted exactly the way I would have liked that night. But I wasn't flawless either. I just needed to make sure we could both live with each other's imperfections. I rose and walked around the coffee table. "There's something else. I know you're not happy about me collecting town gossip and talking to murder suspects either."

"True."

I paused beside his chair. "But …" I drew a breath. "San Benedetto is my home, and people tell me things, and I'm not going to pretend I'm not interested if I can help."

"So you're not backing off," he said flatly and stood.

"No." I grimaced.

"Okay."

I blinked. "What?"

One corner of his mouth quirked upward. "I said, okay. We're not going to change each other, Maddie. Well, I like to think you bring out the best in me, but it's still me. And I wouldn't want to change you. I love your curiosity and stubbornness and inventiveness, even if it does make me crazy sometimes. And as long as you don't cross the line into interfering with an investigation or withholding evidence, we're good."

"Oh." I rubbed my jaw. Stale makeup sloughed off beneath my palm. I thought I'd brushed after last night's blue-cheese burger, but my teeth felt furry. What did I smell like? "Well, good. I wouldn't want to change you either."

Jason's strong arm encircled my waist and he pulled me closer. "Good? Is that all you have to say?"

I clapped a hand over my mouth. "I need to brush my teeth."

It turned out Jason didn't care about my dental hygiene. The heady sensation of his mouth, hard against mine, sent shivers of desire racing through my body. Blood coursed through my veins like a river in the spring.

After we broke apart, panting, but he didn't release his grip around my waist. He cleared his throat. "Are we still going slow?"

"I think it's best," I said weakly. "Obviously, we're still figuring some things out in our relationship."

"Right," he said. His forehead crinkled with concern. "I heard you were at the hospital most of the night. How's Penny?"

"I think she'll be okay," I said. "But if you knew I was at the hospital, why were you so panicked this morning?"

"Morning? It's two o'clock. Usually you're at the museum by now checking inventory or investigating a haunting." Humor glinted in his tawny eyes.

My stomach rumbled. "It's two already? That explains why I'm so hungry."

He grinned. "I'm off duty. Want to grab lunch?"

"Yes." I wriggled from his grasp and escaped into the bathroom. Ugh, my mascara was smeared beneath my eyes. It must be love since Jason hadn't burst into laughter when he'd walked through my door. I stilled. *Love.* I did love Jason. But I'd recently been thinking of ending things, so clearly, my feelings weren't to be trusted. I scrubbed violently at the dark makeup. I'd table the love issue for later.

At record speed, I cleaned myself up and changed into a pair of khaki slacks and a white blouse.

He drove me to my favorite taqueria, because good boyfriends know where you like to get your Mexican food. We sat outside, enjoying the unseasonably warm weather.

I took a careful bite of my veggie burrito, and for once, beans didn't cascade down the front of my blouse. "Will Laurel follow up with the boys from last night?"

Tiny black birds, eager for crumbs, hopped beside our red plastic table.

"She'll have to, if she's going to keep up with my high standards." Jason grinned.

"Tell me you two aren't competing."

"We're not, because I'm clearly the better cop."

I choked down a laugh, and I think, a bean. "Don't make me do something I'll regret."

"Like what?"

"Like defend Laurel."

"A sure sign of the coming zombie apocalypse. Seriously, though, Laurel's good." He aimed a nacho at me. "You can trust her."

"Then she's going to check the boys' alibis for the night of the vigil?"

"Of course."

Rats. "Their parents are going to kill them."

"Maybe that's not such a bad thing."

I peeled back a strip of foil and dunked one corner of my burrito into a plastic cup of green sauce. "Did you know that Reign Chocolate is wholesaling to Adele's caterer?"

"Who is Adele's caterer?"

I gave him Margaret's name.

Jason shook his head. "I hadn't heard about it. But I'm surprised an operation that size—one that makes everything by hand—has the bandwidth to wholesale."

A warming glow flowed through me. It felt good to talk this over with him. I should have pushed the issue sooner. "It surprised me too. And I was thinking of that box I saw in India's yard, the one that disappeared after the pool incident."

"Incident?" He grimaced. "Is that what we're calling it now?"

"That's what I'm calling it. The box was from a chocolate company in the Bay Area called Affaire."

Jason frowned. "Was Atticus checking out the competition?"

"I don't know. Affaire is strictly a wholesaler, selling to restaurants and bakeries and other candy companies. If Reign's getting into the wholesaling business, maybe that's all it was. But that wouldn't explain why whoever pushed me into the pool took the box."

"No," he said. "It wouldn't."

"Personally, I never thought Reign's chocolate tasted that spectacular, but I'm not a chocolate connoisseur." I shifted my basket of tortilla chips and leaned closer. "But there's another reason that box might have been there, and why someone might have wanted to cover it up."

"Oh?"

"Do you think they could have been cheating? Passing off Affaire chocolate as their own instead of making it themselves from the bean? That would explain how such a small shop could have jumped into wholesaling to a caterer like Margaret."

"That's a leap. Reign may have another production center."

"They don't," I said. "I asked India. And remember the table in the storage room, where they sort the cocoa beans by hand?"

"Yes," he said cautiously. He reached across the table

and wiped the corner of my mouth with his thumb.

"Whoops." Because sour cream dribbling down my chin was always a good date look, I flushed and grabbed a napkin. "Moving on—"

"Do we have to? Because you've got another little bit there …" He leaned closer. Slowly he brushed his thumb across my upper lip.

I scrubbed at my mouth and glanced at the napkin. It was pristine white. "There was nothing on my—" I sputtered. "You're a laugh riot."

"Made you look."

"Moving *on*," I said more loudly. "The plastic that lined the garbage bin at the end of the table was dusty, like it had been there a while. But there were no bad cocoa beans or bits of leaves or rocks inside the bin— which is what they were sorting for, remember? There was only a paper cup from a fast food restaurant."

Jason nodded. "As if they weren't sorting cocoa beans at all. Orson is the chocolate-maker. If Atticus had found out—"

"It might have been a motive for murder. Orson would want to stop Atticus from blowing the whistle. It might also explain why Sam was fired after he tried to figure out how to roast beans on his own. He told me the beans in the temperature-controlled room looked moldy. What if they were moldy because they'd been lying around for a while? What if those sacks of cocoa beans are just for show?"

"It's possible," Jason said, noncommittal.

Possible?! My theory was solid. "Tilde, the accountant, would have known whether payments were going to Affaire or to buy cocoa beans from overseas."

Jason raised a single dark brow. "And you think Orson killed her because of it?"

"He seems the obvious candidate. But wait, there's more."

"A set of Ginsu steak knives?"

"Ha ha. I overheard Orson and India talking about an affair. I assumed they were talking about an *actual* affair. India and Orson admitted she and Orson used to be together and suggested that was the affair they'd been talking about. But what if Orson and India were arguing about Affaire chocolate? Maybe Atticus brought the box back to his house for some reason—maybe he needed it to move some junk—and then he became suspicious, or realized what it meant?"

Jason popped a nacho into his mouth. "But if India knew about the chocolate scam—let's assume Atticus told her what he'd learned—why wouldn't she have come forward?"

I gnawed the inside of my cheek. Good question. If India knew the truth, she was in danger.

Unless she was in on the con.

Unless *she'd* been the one who held me under in the pool. Then when I'd lost consciousness, she'd somehow ditched the box – maybe threw it over the neighbor's fence. And then she'd decided a corpse floating in her pool would be too difficult to explain away and revived me. Uneasy, I shifted on the scarlet fiberglass bench.

"It's speculation," Jason said. "We examined Reign's books and didn't find anything unusual."

"But were you looking for regular payments to an outside chocolate company?"

"Our forensic accountant looked at the accounts, and she looked again after Tilde's murder. Trust me, she would have found something like this."

"Oh," I said, disappointed. Of course the police would have looked into it. A dollop of beans and rice dropped onto the side of my palm. I wiped it off with a napkin.

"But there could be a second set of account books." Jason pulled out his phone. "I'll call Laurel."

I smiled, relieved. Maybe my theory wasn't crazy after all.

twenty-seven

Jason had been right about my work schedule. I normally did put in an hour or two at the museum on Tuesdays. So after my very late lunch, I zipped over.

I filled GD's bowls. The cat sniffed my ankles, considered his line of attack, and then seemed to decide against it. He sneezed and hopped onto the glass counter.

Feeling reckless, I ruffled his fur. There might be less than two weeks left on my *Magic of Chocolate* exhibit, but I could still update the information on the molinillo. I booted up my computer.

While the computer whirred and pinged, I straightened a pyramid of chocolate bars on the counter. Did I really want to write out Felicitas's story? It seemed too tragic, too recent, too real.

I shook myself. Truth was a good thing, even if it was sometimes painful. "It isn't right for her death to be written off as a suicide or an accidental overdose," I told GD.

The cat's tail twitched. He stared at an empty spot three feet to the left of the counter.

A wave of cold air flowed through the museum, and goose bumps stippled my arms. I glanced out the window. The sun was still shining. I fiddled with the heater dial on the wall above the register.

With a shiver only partly due to the cold, I reached for a museum hoodie on the shelf behind me.

The cat howled.

"I just fed you. What more do you want?"

GD batted my hand with his paw.

"Whatever." I typed up a new placard for the molinillo—the suspected murder of Felicitas, her boyfriend's lies, and his murder after her death. If I was an eye-for-an-eye type of person, I'd say justice had been done. But something didn't feel right.

Fingers stiff with cold, I printed out the new sign and laid it on the counter to check for typos. "What do you think?" I rubbed my hands together and blew into them.

GD sat on the paper and sneezed.

"Thanks," I said dryly and shooed him off the page.

I laminated the sign and brought it into the Gallery, GD trailing behind me. My breath misted the air. What was going on with the heater today?

The heater rattled and GD started, his green eyes widening.

I hooked the sign onto the hanger pin on the side of the pedestal. Cocking my head, I listened for … I didn't know what I was listening for. They say ghosts suck the warmth out of rooms, but my museum was in an old building, and there probably wasn't any such thing as ghosts.

Cold fingers crawled up my spine. Uneasy, I slipped my hands into the pockets of my hoodie. "I don't care if a ghost *has* dropped by for a chat," I told GD. "I'm working."

Someone banged on the front door and I jumped, missing the cat's tail by a millimeter. GD yowled and streaked into the main room.

The new molinillo sign popped off its hook and slipped to the checkerboard floor. I scooped it up and hurried to the front door.

Orson Malke peered through the glass.

I hesitated, then unlocked the door and peered out, my foot wedged against it in case Orson tried anything funny. No, I wasn't paranoid. Not at all. "Hi, Orson. I'm sorry, but the museum's closed today."

The chocolate-maker colored and rubbed his neat beard. "That's not actually ... I wanted to see you, not the museum. Though I hear it's a great museum," he added quickly. "Can I come in?"

Could the man at the top of my murder suspect list join me inside a lonely museum?

Um. No.

"Things are kind of a mess in here," I said. "Why don't we go to the Fox and Fennel?" Where a horde of tea-sipping little old ladies were ready to deliver a beatdown with their handbags if he tried anything.

He wavered, then nodded. "Sure."

Grabbing my purse from the counter, I walked outside and locked the door behind me. I followed him into the tearoom.

The Fox and Fennel was packed. Women braced their elbows on crisp white tablecloths and lounged on soft ivory couches. Customers lined up beside the tiled mint-green counter and waited patiently to pay for a brushed-nickel tea tin from the wooden shelves.

A harried-looking Adele hurried up to us. "I hope you're not here to eat. I don't have a single table free."

"That's okay," I said slowly. "Orson and I can talk in the museum." I still didn't like the idea, but I didn't think Orson was crazy enough to try anything now that Adele was a witness to him being with me.

"I'll send your order over." She gave me a significant look—*message received*—and handed us paper menus.

We ordered tea. I pressed the spine on the bookcase,

and Orson's eyes widened when it swung outward. "No way. You've got a secret passage? Cool!"

"It was Adele's idea. But yeah, it is cool."

He followed me into the museum.

I arranged Leo's tall chair in front of the counter and sat in my own chair on the opposite side. "So, how can I help you?"

Orson frowned. "I heard you had an accident at India's house."

I hung my purse on the back of my chair. "I wouldn't call it an accident. Someone pushed me into the pool and held me under until I passed out."

GD hopped onto the counter.

Orson stroked the cat and didn't meet my gaze. "What were you doing at India's?"

Now that was an interesting reaction—no curiosity about the attempted murder, just my trespassing.

"Looking for India," I said.

"In her back yard?"

"The gate was open. With everything that's been going on ..." I shrugged. "I guess I was paranoid." Though clearly I hadn't been paranoid enough.

He shifted on his chair. "Did you ... see anything?"

I raised a brow. "See anything?"

"Was anyone else there?"

"No."

His expression relaxed.

"All I saw was a box from Affaire Chocolate."

He blanched.

I plunged in, heart pounding. "Given the size of the box, the fact that you're wholesaling to caterers in spite of your small facility, and the argument I overheard between you and India about an 'affair,' I'm guessing you and Atticus were using Affaire chocolate and pawning it off as Reign's original chocolate."

GD purred. His tail lashed the tip jar.

Orson shook his head. "No. You have no proof."

The lament of someone who really *was* guilty. "Not yet," I said in a steady voice. "But the deception would explain Tilde's death. As the accountant, she would know where the money was going."

His shoulders collapsed. "Using Affaire chocolate was only temporary. But I didn't kill Atticus. Or Tilde."

"So you were passing off Affaire chocolate as your own?"

"You don't understand," he said miserably.

"Fraud?" I asked, darting a glance at the closed bookcase. "I think I can understand that. You killed Atticus and Tilde. Now that India knows, do you plan to kill her too?"

Orson's eyes widened. "What? No! I would never hurt India!"

"Because she was in on it with you?"

"Because I'm not a killer. And ... I love her." He crumpled on his chair. "That argument you heard—it wasn't about the chocolate."

Whoa. What? "You mean—"

The bookcase creaked open. A waiter shuffled inside carrying a tray with two small pots of tea. He set it on the counter between us. "Will there be anything else?"

"No thanks," I said.

The waiter departed, leaving the bookcase ajar.

I leaned across the glass counter and dropped my voice. "Do you mean you two were having an actual affair?" I'd been right the first time? How often did *that* happen?

He nodded.

Well, damn. "That doesn't really help your case. An

affair with Atticus's wife is an even stronger motive for murder."

"No, you don't understand. I was with India when Atticus was killed."

I arched a brow. "The woman you were having an affair with is your alibi?" That just meant they could have done it together, or India was covering for him. On the other hand, he could be covering for India.

Orson groaned. "I know how it sounds. And it's only a matter of time before the police find out."

Sooner than he thought. I'd have to tell Laurel.

"Call India. Call her now," he urged. "Ask her about the alibi."

Twisting on my seat, I excavated my phone from my purse. "Are you sure about this?"

"I'm sure. Call her."

"Sorry, what's her number?"

He told me, and I made the call.

"Hello?"

"Hi, India. It's Maddie."

"Yes?"

"I'm in the museum with Orson." I coughed lightly. Asking Orson about the Affaire chocolate was awkward enough. Asking the two of them about a real affair was a whole other level of uncomfortable. "He asked me to call you. He said the two of you were together at the time of your husband's death."

A long silence. "He did?"

"Is it true?" I asked.

"He asked you to call me? Why?" a faintly hysterical note tinged India's voice.

"I think he wants you to confirm his alibi. And yours."

Over the phone, her breath came soft and quick.

I waited. When she didn't respond, I continued, "He said you two were romantically involved."

"No," she said wildly. "No! It isn't true! I loved Atticus. Why is he doing this to me?" she sobbed.

"India—Orson needs an alibi."

"No, he doesn't. Orson didn't do anything. It was Sam, don't you see? Losing his job the way he did sent him over the edge. He keeps coming around the house harassing me, and Lola, and he bothered Tilde too. Why do you think my gate was open that day? Sam must have opened it. He must have been inside. He's after us all."

I straightened in my chair. I'd nearly forgotten about Sam. "Have you told the police Sam's been bothering you, like I suggested?"

"Of course I told them. Do you know how easy it is to get a restraining order?" She gulped. "Not at all. You offered to help me. Can you help me with that?"

I didn't miss the sarcasm. But maybe I could help. "I could talk to—"

She hung up.

Or not. I set the phone on the counter.

"Well?" Orson asked.

"She said you weren't having an affair."

"She's lying!"

GD's head swiveled toward him. The cat growled, a menacing sound that raised the hair on my arms.

Slowly, Orson exhaled and set down his cup. "She's lying." His tone was low, urgent. "She feels guilty now that Atticus is dead, don't you see?"

I saw that *someone* was lying.

Somebody pounded on the front door, and I jumped in my seat. GD flowed like quicksilver off the counter.

Detective Laurel Hammer and two uniformed officers glared through the window. "Open up," Laurel shouted.

"Um," I said, "I'd better." I rounded the counter and unlocked the door.

The cops marched inside.

"Orson Malke?" Laurel asked. "You need to come to the station with us."

Above his beard, his face turned the color of cement. "What? Why?"

"We've got more questions."

"Am I under arrest?"

Laurel flashed a counterfeit smile. "Not yet. But if you don't cooperate, you will be."

He rose, his limbs shaking. "All right. All right. It's fine. I'll come."

Laurel stared down at me. "Well?"

"Uh," I said, "do you want me to come to the station too?" *Say no. Say no!*

"Don't you want to know how we found him here?" she asked.

Did I? "Okay, how did you find us?"

"I asked at the chocolate shop," the detective said. "The assistant said Mr. Malke had gone to see you at the museum."

Which meant he hadn't come to kill me. Murderers generally prefer not to advertise.

Her eyes narrowed. "Now why would Orson want to talk to you so badly that he'd leave his work in the middle of the day?"

"We were just …" I floundered.

"Interfering with an investigation?" she asked.

Had I been? But this wasn't fair! Orson had come to me. "I wasn't interfering," I said.

Her lip curled. "We'll see."

"Wow," a man said behind us. "This cat is really

friendly."

The color drained from Laurel's face. "The cat …"

We turned.

GD sat perched on one of the uniformed officer's shoulders. The cat's green eyes gleamed, malicious. He hunched, his shoulder muscles flexing, his paws kneading the cop's shirt.

"GD, no!" I shouted.

The black cat launched himself at Laurel.

She shrieked, ducked, and covered.

I lurched sideways, trying to catch GD mid-air. The cat passed harmlessly through my outstretched fingers. I overbalanced and tripped over Laurel.

The detective and I collapsed in a tangle of arms and legs and slammed against the counter.

Chocolate bars cascaded from above. They pelted us, sprawled on the checkerboard floor.

"Got him," Orson said.

Laurel and I glared up at GD, smirking in Orson's arms.

The cat purred.

A muscle pulsed in Laurel's jaw. "That. *Cat.*" She said the word like a curse.

I scrambled to my feet and slipped on a chocolate bar. I grabbed the antique cash register for balance, then snatched GD from Orson. "Bad cat!" Did he really hate Laurel, or was he just trying to get me in trouble? Or was it a sort of two-for-one deal?

"He's possessed," Laurel rasped, struggling to her feet. "A menace!"

"He's only a cat," I squeaked.

GD squirmed, and I clutched him tighter.

Orson cleared his throat. "So. Police station?"

I shot him a grateful look. Murder suspect or not, he'd

stopped GD from assaulting a police officer. If the cat had succeeded, I was sure Laurel could have found a crime to charge me with if she'd tried hard enough.

Laurel's nostrils flared. "Stop gawking," she said to the cops. "Let's move!"

With the uniformed officers flanking Orson, they marched him out the door.

The bookcase creaked open and Adele peeked inside. "Are you all right? What happened?" She sidled into the museum.

"GD tried to kill Laurel again, and I think Orson's about to be arrested." One-handed, I gathered the chocolate bars off the floor.

"Oh, GD." She took him from me and the cat snuggled against her Fox and Fennel apron. Twin lines appeared between her brows. "I hope the police have got it right. I really thought India had done it."

"Atticus's wife?" I asked, surprised.

"The spouse is usually the killer. Isn't that what they always say? It's got to be someone close to the victims. I've got two cousins I wouldn't mind murdering right now. One is demanding a gluten-free menu at my wedding. Another wants to bring guests I don't even know. And I just got half a dozen RSVPs from distant relatives even though they knew darn good and well the deadline was three weeks ago! It's almost as if they think because we're family, they can act like divas. Now I have to go back to the caterer and change the headcount."

"Ouch." Absently, I poured tea into my cup and stirred, my spoon clanking on the side. "I'm sorry people are being such pains."

"I should be used to it by now," she said. "So, what did Orson want? Or did you call that little meeting?"

"He did. India said the ex-employee, Sam, was

harassing her and Lola," I said, evasive. I wasn't sure if Orson's story of an affair was real, and even though I knew Adele wouldn't blab, I wasn't comfortable sharing it. "Sam was also bothering Tilde."

"Hmm. I thought you decided Sam couldn't have pushed you into India's swimming pool because his car engine was cold."

"Well, I did." But I still didn't like what I was hearing about the man. Could I have been wrong?

I straightened my blouse, which had gotten twisted in the scrimmage. India had said this time that she'd reported Sam to the police. The investigation was Jason and Laurel's job. I would tell Laurel what Orson and India had each told me. I'd done my part.

For now.

twenty-eight

In the Fortune Telling Room, GD and I eyed the round table loaded with electronic equipment. The table wasn't quite an antique, built in the groovy sixties with a circular Ouija board painted on the wood. But it was vintage, and I didn't want it scratched.

"Maybe I should get a tablecloth," I said, anxious.

Beside the spirit cabinet, GD lashed his tail and growled. The cabinet's tall doors stood slightly ajar. I edged them open, making sure Herb wasn't inside.

GD sneezed, derisive.

"And I do *not* want to hear your opinion," I told him.

"Uh." Leo looked up from fiddling with the computer and eyed me askance. "Are you talking to me or the cat?"

"GD."

"Okay. Then everything's set up for the podcast."

The bell over the front door jangled, and I frowned. I thought I'd locked it after Leo arrived.

"Maddie?" Mason called out.

I hurried into the main room. "Hi. Is something wrong?"

My neighbor jammed his fingers in the front pockets of his jeans. "No. Why would anything be wrong?"

"Because …" I glanced at the open entry to the Fortune Telling Room. "Let's go outside."

Mason followed me onto the sidewalk. The moon was

full, the light from the streetlamps reflecting like mini-moons in the shop windows. I rubbed my arms in the evening chill.

"What's up?" he asked.

"I could ask you the same thing. You keep coming around and acting weird. What *is* it?"

He opened his mouth to speak and I raised my hand, palm out, to stop him.

"No," I said. "On second thought, I don't need to know."

"But I'm—"

"You're a good guy, Mason. But whatever's going on is none of my business. And you need to stop coming around and giving me the skunk eye."

He blinked. "The what?"

"You know what I'm talking about. I mean, you're not a skunk, but … I'm with Jason, and I'm happy with him." My heart warmed. And Jason was happy with me, even if I still thought his partner was a jerkface. So I wasn't going to overanalyze what we had. For now.

"I can't get drawn into whatever's going on between you and Belle," I continued. "You and I need to spend less time together, even if I do like and respect you. So, unless you've got information about the murders—"

My cell phone rang, and I dug it from my pocket, recognized a familiar number. *Jason.*

"If you know something about the murders," I said, "tell Detective Laurel Hammer. Sorry, but I need to take this." I turned away from him and put the phone to my ear. "Hi, Jason. What's going on?"

A sixties-era van drifted past.

"Orson Malke's been released."

"Really?"

"Lack of evidence."

"You mean you didn't find a second set of books?" I asked, dismayed.

"Lack of evidence," he repeated evenly. "We did put a tail on him, but he's slipped it."

"What?" Slipped it? But that made him look totally guilty! Was he?

"Look, I can't get over there right now, but I've got a bad feeling. Are you alone?"

I glanced at Mason. "No."

"Good. Try to keep it that way. Are you still at the museum?"

"Yes. Leo and I are doing our test podcast tonight."

"All right. Call me when you leave."

"Why?" I asked. "If they released Orson, it must mean there was good reason. Is something else going on?"

"India Reine has disappeared too."

"What do you mean, disappeared?" I yelped.

"Just what I said. Look, I can't talk about this right now. Just stay with Leo, okay?"

"I will." We said our goodbyes, and I hung up.

"Problem?" Mason asked.

"Um, no." Mason might be ex-military and twice Leo's size, but I couldn't ask him to stay, not after what I'd just told him.

"Belle and I aren't having problems," he said.

"Oh." Self-conscious, I shuffled my feet on the cold sidewalk. "That's good." Then why had he kept coming around looking like a lost puppy?

"We're getting married."

"Oh!" Oh wow. Married? That was quick. No, it wasn't. They had a history, a son. And I was happy for them. "Congratulations!"

"I wanted to tell you how grateful I am to you for

ending things between us the way you did and letting Belle and I rebuild our relationship." He scratched his temple. "But I guess I felt kind of guilty. I mean, what kind of guy has a kid and doesn't know about him? And I realize finding out the way you did hurt you."

My face heated. "It was fine," I said. "It all worked out. For everyone."

"I know. But it might not have if you hadn't cut me loose. Anyway, Belle's been itching for me to tell you we're engaged, but it never seemed like the right time. That's why I was giving you the, uh, skunk eye. And that business about the dumpster ... It didn't happen. Sorry, but it just felt like the wrong time to tell you and I couldn't think of what else to say."

I laughed. "Since I didn't follow up with Dieter, you're forgiven. But I am happy for you both. This is wonderful news."

He backed down the sidewalk. "Well. Thanks. I'll be seeing you. But not too often."

"Right!"

He turned and strode down the street.

Married! There must be something in the air. First Adele and Dieter, and now Mason and his girlfriend.

Feeling lighter, I returned inside the museum and locked the door carefully behind me.

GD sat waiting at the counter. He slipped to the checkerboard floor and followed me into the Fortune Telling Room.

I rubbed my hands together. "So?"

Leo checked his phone. "Right on time. You ready?"

"Wait. We're going to start *now*?"

"I posted on social media that we'd be starting at seven. It's six fifty-eight."

"You posted on social media?" I bleated. "I thought

this was only a test run!"

"It is, so we can test the caller system. Don't worry, I doubt we'll get many callers on our test night."

Great. I pulled out the folding chair and sat down, checked my podcasting notes, zipped up my hoodie. It was even colder inside the museum than outside.

"Don't look so worried," Leo said, dropping onto the metal chair beside me. "It's only a beta test. It's not supposed to be perfect."

"Right." A beta test. How bad could it be?

Maddie: Welcome to—Is this on?

Leo: It's on.

Maddie: Welcome to our beta test of the Paranormal Museum Podcast, live from the San Benedetto Paranormal Museum. I'm your curator, Maddie Kosloski.

Leo: And I'm Leo.

Maddie: Aren't you going to use your last name?

Leo: Then people would know who I am.

[PAUSE]

Maddie: [Clears throat] Right. Well, San Benedetto's Wine and Chocolate Days are over, but our Magic of Chocolate Exhibit will continue through the end of the month. So be sure to stop on by. We're giving away a free tarot card to each guest.

Leo: And we've got a caller.

Maddie: What do you mean, we've—

Leo: Hi, you're live on the Paranormal Museum Podcast.

Male Caller: I'm calling about the cursed molinillo.

Maddie: [Laughs uneasily] Cursed? It's not cursed. It's only haunted. For people who aren't familiar with the term, a molinillo is a kitchen instrument used to whisk

Mexican hot chocolate. The molinillo in our exhibit was once owned by a woman in Oaxaca who died tragically. It's haunted.

Male Caller: Then why have there been two chocolate-related deaths since you've put it on display?

Maddie: Wait a minute, is this Herb?

Herb: No names! The cops may be listening.

Maddie: Herb, as you *well* know, the molinillo rattles when someone nearby tells a significant lie. That's not a curse, that's a haunting. The prior owner was murdered by her boyfriend after she learned he was dealing drugs and he learned she was pregnant with his child. He was killed not long after … [PAUSE]

Leo: Is something wrong?

Maddie: I think … my story might be. Her boyfriend was killed almost immediately after she was. What if her boyfriend didn't kill her? What if she threatened to expose his secret, that he was dealing drugs, and in turn expose his fellow criminals? What if his partners killed them both?

Herb: Does it make a difference? The molinillo's still cursed.

Maddie: It's haunted, not cursed! Her death was ruled a suicide in spite of the evidence that she'd been murdered. I was told that was a political decision, but I think it was really a coverup. She didn't commit suicide. Maybe that's what the molinillo was trying to tell us. Maybe that's why it rattles when a lie is told. The public story about her death is a lie.

Herb: But it *could* be cursed.

Maddie: *Goodbye* Herb. [Whispered] Leo, end the call.

Leo: Thanks, Herb, for calling in.

Maddie: Is he off the line?'

Leo: Yes, when the red light goes off, it means he's off the line.

Maddie: If he starts another curse scare—

Leo: We're still live.

Maddie: [Hurriedly] Okay, so let's talk chocolate. *Cocoa* means, "food of the gods."

Leo: We have another caller.

Maddie: What? I thought you said hardly any—

Leo: Hello, you're on the Paranormal Museum Podcast.

Female Caller: I want to talk about lies.

Maddie: Um, this is the Paranormal Museum Podcast. Tonight, we're talking about the magic of chocolate.

Female Caller: [Laughs] There's no magic to murder.

Maddie: No, I suppose there's nothing magical about what happened to the molinillo owner. I'm sorry, I shouldn't—

Female Caller: I'm not talking about that. [STATIC] I'm talking about Atticus and Tilde.

Maddie: Who is this?

Female Caller: I saved your life. Don't you recognize me? [STATIC]

Maddie: India?

India: They say if you save someone's life, you're responsible for them forever.

Maddie: India, are you all right? You sound, um, distraught.

Leo: She sounds drunk.

Maddie: Shhh! India, where are you?

India: The two people I loved best died because of a lie. Maybe that molinillo of yours really is cursed, because history is repeating itself.

Maddie: India, why don't you call me on my cell phone? We can talk privately.

India: You ... know. You saw.

Maddie: I know what? India, call my cell.

India: You know it all. I told you. [BREAKING GLASS]

Maddie: India? Are you okay? Look, I'll call—

[LOUD ELECTRONIC NOISE]

Maddie: GD! Get off the keyboard!

Leo: We lost the connection. Sorry.

Maddie: Okay, I think we're going to have to cut this podcast short.

Leo: We've got a caller. Hi, you're on the Paranormal Museum Podcast.

Maddie: India?

Detective Laurel Hammer: Kosloski!

Maddie: Cut the podcast. Cut the podcast!

"What have I told you about interfering with an investigation?" Laurel's voice crackled over Leo's computer.

I leaned toward the microphone. "It's not my fault India called. At least you know she's still alive." I frowned. "Why were you listening to my podcast?"

"Why do you think? Whatever you do, mayhem follows. India Reine said you knew everything. What do you know?"

"Nothing! I don't know what she was talking about."

"What did she mean about history repeating itself?"

Sweating, I unzipped my hoodie. "I'm not sure. She was saying something about a lie? We know Orson was lying about the chocolate."

"Tell her we can give her the audio file," Leo whispered.

"We can give you the audio file," I said.

"Email it." She hung up.

Leo and I stared at each other.

GD meowed.

"At least we know your social media promotion worked," I said weakly.

"I'm not so sure," he said. "Herb is basically stalking the museum. Hammer's probably got our phones tapped—she really hates you. And India … Okay, I don't know why she was listening."

I stilled. Was India tracking me too? "She sounded off, didn't she?" I asked, worried. I also didn't like the way that call had ended. "Like she'd been drinking."

"Or on drugs."

My scalp prickled. That was how Felicitas had died. History couldn't be repeating itself, could it? And the molinillo … Was Herb right? Was it really cursed? I shrugged out of my hoodie. *No such thing as curses. No such thing as curses!* "Has it gotten hot in here?"

"Yeah," Leo said. "It happened during the podcast. I guess the heater finally started working."

"It's always been working," I said grumpily.

On the spirit table, Leo's cell phone rang. He answered. "Yeah? Where … yeah … I'll be right there." He hung up. "Sorry, I gotta go."

"Is something wrong?"

"A friend of mine's car broke down. She's stuck on the side of the road."

"She?" In spite of my anxiety, my ears pricked. Leo had never mentioned a girlfriend.

He blushed. "I can't leave her there."

So, she *was* a love interest! "No, of course not. Go." *And then bring her to the museum so I can interrogate her.*

"I'll come in early tomorrow to put this stuff away." He motioned to the equipment on the table.

"I'll put it away. Don't worry about it."

"Thanks." Leo ducked his head and hurried from the Fortune Telling Room.

I shut down the computer and unplugged the cables. Careful not to damage the vintage table, I removed the equipment and hid it under the counter in the main room.

Beneath GD's critical gaze, I fanned out the tarot deck atop the painted spirit table and returned the crystal ball to its place.

Houdini seemed to wink at me from his vintage poster. The room seemed brighter, somehow, almost as if a spell had been broken ...

I chuckled softly. *Broken spells? No way.* I was starting to buy my own ghost stories. If Felicitas Ocasio was at peace, it wasn't because I'd publicized the truth of her murder. I wasn't even sure I had the truth.

Returning to my own computer, I rewrote the molinillo sign with a new story—that both Felicitas and her boyfriend had been killed by drug dealers and the story swept under the carpet due to local "politics." It was just guesswork, but it felt right.

I laminated the paper, punched a hole in the top, and strolled into the Gallery. The molinillo sign I'd put up that afternoon had fallen again to the checkerboard floor. Brow pinching, I whisked it up and hooked the new sign onto the pedestal.

I stared hard at the hook in the pedestal. How had the old sign fallen off? There were no tears or breaks in the laminated sign. It *could* have been knocked off by a passerby, but the museum had been closed today. Only Leo and I had been inside the Gallery.

Unless Felicitas hadn't liked my first version of her story, and had ...

Hair prickled my scalp.

Nah.

I thunked my palm on my forehead. Jason had asked me to stick with Leo tonight, and in the excitement of getting raked over the coals by Laurel, I'd forgotten.

Digging in my purse, I found my phone and called Jason.

"This is Detective Slate. Leave a message at the tone. If this is an emergency, call 911." *Beep.*

That was a new greeting. Jason and Laurel now even had matching messages. "Hi, Jason, it's Maddie. Look, something came up, and Leo had to go. I'm leaving the museum now and headed home. Call me when you can."

GD howled.

"All right, all right." I refreshed the cat's food and water, double-checked the locks on the front door, and exited through the bookcase.

The hallway I shared with the tearoom was pitch black. I felt my way to the heavy metal door and shoved it open.

The dim silhouettes of garbage bins and my pickup faded into the gloom. I glanced up at Mason's windows. They were dark, and I smiled. He was probably at Belle's, telling her he'd finally broken the news about their wedding.

The metal door clanged shut behind me. "Gagh!" My shoulders twitched. *Calm down, Maddie.*

In the alley, something metallic rattled.

I flattened myself against the cool brick wall and strained my eyes.

A fat shape waddled down the alley. The animal's striped tail waved lazily.

I blew out my breath. Another raccoon.

I hurried, head down, to my pickup. I'd just go home

and—

A shape reared up on my left.

I yelped, began to turn. Pain blazed in my skull. The world telescoped to a pinprick and went dark.

twenty-nine

Chocolate.

Its rich, bittersweet scent thickened the air.

A jackhammer banged in my skull. Groggy, I rolled onto my side and promptly threw up.

My arms were pinned behind me. Something hard bit into my wrists. Dazed, I looked around the chocolate storage room. I lay between the sorting table and a pallet laden with canvas bags of cocoa beans. Fake cocoa beans? Through the glass wall, the kitchen gleamed.

I wiped my chin on the shoulder of my hoodie and edged sideways. My butt thumped something soft.

I turned my head, gulping down my breath to stay quiet and not vomit again.

Sam lay sprawled on the wooden floor, his arms out flung, his face slack, his eyes slitted. He wore a zipped-up windbreaker and jeans.

"Hey," I said, hoarse, and nudged him with my knee. "Sam."

He gurgled.

"Wake up." My voice cracked. Fearful, I glanced into the kitchen but could see no one past metal cabinets and workstations.

Sam hadn't knocked me over the head and brought me here. He looked drugged.

So, who had brought me to Reign and why? In spite of what India apparently thought, I didn't have any secret knowledge about the killer.

I rolled to sitting. My wrists burned, the muscles in my arms aching. Gasping, I wriggled experimentally. Whatever pinioned my wrists was hard and sharp. Not metal. Plastic. Zip-ties?

I studied Sam's unbound, unmarked arms. Of the two of us, he had to be the more dangerous. The only reason someone would have left his arms unbound ...

My mouth went dry.

The only reason was to frame him for killing me. If he'd had marks on his wrists like I surely did, it would be clear we both were victims.

The disgruntled ex-employee made a perfect patsy. He had stalked India, picketed the store, been loud about his dislike for anyone and everyone associated with Reign.

I'd known he hadn't dunked me in the pool, and I'd told Jason. But the killer wouldn't know I'd cleared Sam, or that I'd told the cops about it.

I swayed, dizzy.

So why kill *me*? I thought, plaintive.

Cautiously, I raised myself onto my knees and peered through the window, past the metal workstations.

The kitchen was still empty.

I shivered in the chill room. Atticus had done a good job keeping up the facade, spending money to air-condition this room even though there were no real cocoa beans—or no usable ones—inside. But in spite of the cool air, sweat slicked my back.

Keeping low, I staggered to my feet and banged into the sorting table. My hoodie's zipper pinged against the metal edge. I froze at the noise.

When no one came, I rested my foot on Sam's shoulder and shook him lightly.

He groaned but didn't open his eyes.

I shuffled to the door and fumbled behind my back for the knob. My hands slipped on the metal. Finally, I caught it between my fingers and turned it.

Locked.

I muffled a curse. Of course it was locked. Whoever had brought us here wasn't going to make it easy to escape.

A low desk piled with plastic boxes of cocoa beans stood on the opposite side of the sorting table. I hurried to it and awkwardly pulled out the drawers. Maybe there was a knife or pair of scissors or *something*. But all I found were pens and scraps of paper.

No weapon. My hands bound. I was completely helpless. Swallowing my terror, I closed my eyes and took a breath. *Think!*

Dieter had demonstrated an unsuccessful zip-tie escape at the vigil. What had he done?

I closed my eyes, imagining the scene. Adele glowering at Dieter. Mason making awkward conversation. Lola on the gazebo steps holding a cordless mic, and Dieter bent double, beating his wrists against his low back.

I bent and raised my arms as high as I could behind me. Slammed them down.

Pain sparked through my wrists, and I gasped.

The ties remained clasped together.

What had Dieter been doing?

I closed my eyes. Think. *Think*. He'd said something about the ties facing the wrong way. I wriggled them around. Gritting my teeth, I tried again. Failed.

I blinked back tears of mingled pain and frustration. Dieter hadn't managed to free himself either.

I paced the small room, avoiding Sam's limp form.

Dieter had bent over.

I bowed again.

Lola had had a cordless mic at the vigil.

I slammed my wrists onto my lower back.

The firecracker had gone off by the sound equipment. And then there was the stampede.

I turned the zip-ties so the plastic tab faced toward me. Slammed my wrists onto my low back again.

The ties broke, my arms flying free.

"Oh!" Arms trembling, I sagged against the table and rubbed my reddened wrists.

Where had Lola gotten the cordless mic from? She hadn't been holding it earlier. She must have got it from somewhere, and the logical place was from where all the sound equipment was stacked on that picnic table— where the firecracker had gone off moments later.

Lola.

Lola who'd pushed me into believing Tilde was a crazed stalker, and then told me Sam was just as bad after Tilde had died.

I frowned. But India had also told me Sam was hanging around too much. India hadn't lied about Sam. But she could have gotten her news from Lola.

I rattled the doorknob again. And … it was still locked.

But why would Lola kill Atticus? Orson had a better motive for murder—to protect the business. But Lola had the same motive, didn't she? She'd certainly been enjoying the celebrity that came with being married to a star chocolate-maker. And the money.

My certainty grew.

Keeping my back toward the wall, I knelt beside Sam and pressed my fingers to his neck. His pulse was weak. Or maybe I was just terrible at checking pulses. But his chest rose and fell, even if his skin was grayish.

There had to be *something* that could get me out of here. I rummaged through the desk drawers a second time. Shifted plastic bins. Looked for a screwdriver. A hammer to break the thick glass. Anything. But I found nothing.

Doubtful, I stared at the glass. Could I jump through it? If it was safety glass, I'd be okay. If it wasn't …

Tilde had been stabbed through the heart. Lola was a molecular biologist; she would have known exactly where to jam that receipt spike into Tilde's chest. It wasn't conclusive evidence. I could probably find someone's heart. I just didn't think I'd be able to do it quite as efficiently.

If only I had my phone! I patted my pockets, confirming it was gone.

Sam muttered.

"Sam?"

He didn't respond.

Kneeling beside him, I felt the pockets of his windbreaker. They were empty.

Lola had told me she'd been with her husband at Reign when someone had been trying to drown me. But Orson had just asked me some odd questions about that day, as if he suspected … that Lola had lied? Had Orson figured it out? That might explain why he'd gone missing. Either Lola had gotten rid of him too, or he was heading for the hills with India.

Desperation growing, I patted the pockets of Sam's jeans, ran my hands up his chest.

And felt a lump.

I unzipped the windbreaker. An inside pocket!

Hands shaking, I reached inside and pulled out a phone. "Thank God," I whispered.

Crouching low, my hair falling in a wild tangle like a

mad woman's, I called Jason.

"This is Detective Hammer," Laurel said, her voice cautious.

"Laurel? I'd meant to—" Never mind! "It's Maddie," I whispered. "I'm at the chocolate shop."

The glass door rattled behind me, opened.

"Don't move," Lola said.

thirty

Praying she hadn't seen the phone beneath my hair, I slid my hand around the front of my neck. I dropped the phone down my blouse and raised shaky hands. "You don't have to do this, Lola," I said loudly.

Like Laurel would even care if she could hear me. She'd probably think this was a crank call.

"I'm sorry you got caught up in this," Lola said. "But I've gone too far to stop now. Stand up."

Unsteady, I got to my feet. Sam lay unmoving on the storage room's wooden floor.

"Turn around," she said.

I turned and gulped.

Camel slacks. Ivory turtleneck. A pearl-handled gun. She'd managed to match the weapon to her outfit, I thought hysterically.

"What I still don't understand," I croaked, "is why? Was it the money?" I edged away, my heel scraping the edge of the pallet. *Come on, Laurel. Hear me. Believe this.*

"I couldn't let Atticus ruin our image."

"Your image." My voice quavered.

"Image is everything. Atticus and his stupid principles. If people found out what Orson was doing to the chocolate, it would have ruined us all."

"You mean ... the Affaire chocolate? You killed two people to protect your brand?" I asked, incredulous.

Good God. Lola really was crazy. There was no way I was talking her out of anything. My fists clenched, my knuckles whitening.

"Do you know how much work I've put into curating my image? You can't outsource authenticity. And if people thought Orson and Atticus weren't authentic artisan chocolate-makers, my image would have been ruined. Not to mention all the money it provided."

"Curating ... ? I thought Atticus was the marketing guy. I thought you were overwhelmed with the job after he died."

"I've always been responsible for our social media."

"Our?" I asked, stalling. Laurel knew where I was. But would she come?

"Orson and me. After all, what's the use of being a happy couple if you don't post photos online?"

"You don't know," I said.

"Don't know what?"

"That Orson and India were having an affair."

She blanched. "What?"

"An affair. I thought for a while that that was why someone killed Atticus, but—"

"You're lying," she hissed, her hazel eyes narrowing.

"No." I shook my head and pain sparked from my neck to my scalp. "I overheard them talking about it. Later I assumed they were talking about Affaire, the chocolate company, but it was one of those Occam's Razor situations. The simplest answer was correct. They admitted it to me."

"No." Lola tossed her blond hair. "You're saying this to throw me off my game. You think I'll kill them instead."

I tasted something sour at the back of my tongue. Had I just made targets of two more people? "Of course not," I said. "It's too late for that. Besides, Orson already suspects you were the one who pushed me into the pool and tried to drown me." He'd seemed so relieved that I hadn't seen anyone at the pool. He must have been glad not to have his suspicions confirmed. "If India dies, he'll know the truth, and I don't think he's as concerned with image as you are."

Her eyes narrowed.

"Were you afraid I'd see the Affaire box and figure out your husband was peddling another company's chocolate as his own?" I continued. "Or did you think that when the police found my body in India's pool, they'd blame her?"

"I knew you'd seen the box, and drowning you seemed too good an opportunity. If the police found you floating in her pool, they'd peg her for Atticus's death." Lola's mouth twisted. "The spouse is always the most likely suspect." She stepped away from the glass door and waggled the gun in my direction. "Now move. Into the kitchen."

Come on, Laurel. Do the right thing!

Feet leaden, I walked through the open door. "It was you who tried to run me down in the alley last week. How did you get Atticus's car?"

"It was parked behind Reign," she said. "The keys were in his desk."

"Were you following me on foot too?"

She grinned. "Once. For fun. You were so funny, creeping around like a cartoon coyote." Her smile faded. "Now head to the melangers."

"But why come after me?"

"Are you joking? Do you have any idea how many times people told me about your past adventures in crime solving?"

"They did?" I said faintly.

"And sure enough, there you were, sticking your nose where it didn't belong. So I watched you. It was obvious you wouldn't figure out what I'd done. But when I overheard Tilde calling you, I knew I had to kill her."

Dread weighted my gut. She was going to kill me in front of the melangers and dump chocolate on me, like she'd done to Atticus. "But if you thought I was no threat, why bring me here now?"

"Because the entire town assumes you know something. Killing you provides the perfect setup. It will look like Sam killed you because you were onto him. I'll tell the police you were asking about him, and they'll believe you did something stupid. Sam makes an excellent killer, and he could have made a spare key to Reign. I'll leave one in his pocket."

I paused beside the roaster. "Sam will never admit to killing me."

"He won't have to. He'll kill himself, a murder-suicide."

"You've thought of everything," I said heavily. I was running out of stall tactics, and it might not matter anyway. How badly did Laurel hate me? "How did Tilde figure out you killed Atticus?"

Lola pressed the gun into the small of my back. "Tilde knew where the money was really being spent. She was the one who told Atticus about Affaire."

Laurel wasn't coming. A wave of nausea swamped me. "And then what?" I looked around the kitchen for a weapon, a diversion, anything. No handy butcher knives lay on the counters. No pots of boiling water sat heating. "Did she try to blackmail you?"

Lola poked me with the gun. "She wanted to ruin me!"

"I told the police that Sam couldn't have attacked me at India's house."

"You couldn't have. You didn't see who pushed you in, or you would have reported me."

She jammed the gun into my back, hard, and I stumbled forward, my shoes squeaking on the black fatigue mat.

"I drove to Sam's house right after it happened," I said. "He was at home."

"Alone, I'm sure. Not much of an alibi." Her voice dripped with derision. She shoved me forward, closer to the melangers. They hummed, melted cocoa swirling inside.

"And his car engine was cold," I said. "I told the police that too."

Another nudge. Another step. I stood beside the melangers now. Above them, uneven bricks of chocolate, two inches thick, lined the shelves in thick plastic bags. The metal counter opposite was clear. What kitchen doesn't have a single damn weapon in it?

"India saved me." My voice shook. "She pulled me from the pool and resuscitated me. She wouldn't have had time to save me *and* get rid of the box. The police know that too. That leaves you and Orson. And I don't think Orson's willing to go to jail to protect you. Not when he's in love with India. He always has been in love with her, you know. Atticus may have married her, but she was with Orson first, and he never forgot—"

"Stop it!"

Motion whispered behind me. Instinctively, I jerked away. Something hard struck my shoulder. I grabbed for the shelves above the melangers to steady myself. My fingers touched thick plastic. Gripping a bag, I swung blindly. The heavy chocolate brick connected solidly with Lola's head.

She grunted and collapsed in a tangle of blond hair.

The momentum of the ten-pound brick whirled me around. I staggered into a melanger. The chocolate brick flew from my hands. The melanger tipped. Chocolate cascaded to the black mat, splashed across Lola's still form, the gun.

The gun!

I kicked it away. It bounced off a low metal cabinet, skittered across the mat, and came to a halt in front of Laurel's cowgirl boots.

The detective lowered her gun, the muscles in her arms relaxing. "That cat better not be in here."

I pointed at Lola. "She's, uh … I hit her."

"Yeah. I saw." Laurel holstered her gun beneath her fringed leather jacket. She hurried to Lola, pressed two fingers to her neck.

"You came. I didn't think you'd come."

"Did you think I'd let you die?"

"Those messages—"

"As I told Jason, my damn phone was on the fritz and I didn't know it." She patted Lola down, carefully not meeting my gaze. "What the hell do you want from me? A signed affidavit?"

"No. Thanks. For coming, I mean."

She glared. Then a slow smile spread across her face.

"What?" I asked. "What's wrong?"

My feet heated. Wet. Gooey.

I looked down. I stood in an inch of chocolate. It was seeping into my canvas shoes.

"Nothing," she said, grinning. "Nothing at all."

thirty-one

"Your mom is so going to kill you." Adele curled in my gray-blue wing chair, her stockinged feet resting on a pile of magazines atop the coffee table. Pug snoozed in her lap, his breathing steady and clear.

My mother had been pretty mad. Relieved, but mad when she'd materialized at the chocolate shop in the middle of all those cops. If Jason hadn't agreed to come to dinner next week, I don't know what would have happened.

"Who would have thought chocolate could be so dangerous?" Harper agreed.

"It *was* a ten-pound block," I said.

"Who would have thought you could hit someone with a ten-pound block of chocolate?" Harper asked.

I made a face and reached for a slice of pizza. "I'm not that out of shape. I can lift ten pounds."

"This is the second killer you've disabled with food." Adele stroked her dog and he sighed. "Honestly, it must mean something."

Harper turned her laugh into a cough. "So, what happened to India and Orson?" she asked between mouthfuls.

"The police found them in Vegas."

Adele's feet clunked to the floor and Pug's eyes snapped open. "It's all right, baby," she cooed to him. "Are you telling us they ran off together?"

"According to Jason, India ran off. Orson was worried she might do something crazy, so in a fit of chivalry, he went after her."

Harper snorted. "Right. Chivalry."

"How'd the police find them so fast?" Adele asked. Pug's

head dropped to his paws and he closed his eyes, settling in.

"Orson took a picture of his meal at a Vegas hotel and posted it online," I said. "It was location tagged." Which just went to prove that social media was the devil's cocaine. I'd keep using it to promote the museum, but if my face never appeared online, it would be too soon. I pointed at Adele. "And speaking of incriminating photos, why did you really ask me to be your wedding's social media manager?"

"Because I can count on you," Adele said simply. "Formal photographs are great, but people open up to you. I want you to be taking pictures. Unless you'd rather not?"

How could I say no to that? I supposed social media had its good points. "I'd love to."

"What else has Jason told you?" Harper asked.

"Just that Lola's got a great lawyer and is still trying to blame everything on Sam. Sam doesn't remember anything from that night. And certainly not Lola injecting him with propofol."

"Where did she get propofol?" Harper asked.

"Lola studied molecular biology. Apparently she still had access to some chem lab in Sacramento. Her knowledge of biology also made it easier for her to kill Tilde." According to Jason, as I'd suspected, she'd stabbed the accountant in exactly the right spot.

Three times.

I shuddered.

"I thought you said Laurel recorded your conversation with Lola?" Adele asked. "How can she get out of this?"

I shifted in my chair. "No idea. And the police have Lola's cell phone. She snapped a picture of a hugging couple on her way to the picnic table the night of the vigil. It's time-stamped and puts her at the table in time to light the firecracker and get back to the gazebo for her speech. There were other photos, too, that put her near the scenes of Atticus and Tilde's murders." She'd been so obsessed with curating a perfect online life she'd ruined her own.

"Tell me about the molinillo," Adele said, changing the

subject.

I did. What I knew. What I guessed. But I didn't tell them about the shift in temperature in the museum, the new feeling of lightness in the Gallery. It was the sort of thing I should write up on the museum blog. But some experiences were just too personal.

Harper sighed. "Maybe the truth will set Felicitas free."

"Then I'll have an unhaunted molinillo," I groused. What good was that to the museum?

"But you'll have a great story," Adele said. "It's terrible the damage secrets can cause."

"Right," I said. "Are there any more I should know about?"

"Well ..." Adele toed the magazines on the table. "There was one more thing I was hoping you could do at our wedding."

"Oh?" I asked, wary.

"I wondered if you would lead the blessing at the reception. I'd ask Harper, but you know what a pagan she is."

"I am not," Harper laughed. "Mostly."

"I'm kidding," Adele said. "Well? Will you?"

Beads of sweat broke out on my forehead. All my friends, everyone I knew in San Benedetto, would be there, watching.

My community. Offline, in person, and in real life—a life that had nearly been cut short, and that I knew was getting better. The town was healing. Mason and Belle were rebuilding their family. My relationships with Jason, with Adele and Harper, and even with my mom were stronger. Deliver the blessing? I was already blessed, and my heart expanded. "I'll do it."

THE END

Note from Kirsten:
There actually was a case of two hipster artisan chocolate makers who were using less-than-artisan chocolate and calling it their own. And since I'm such a big chocolate lover, when I

heard the story, I couldn't resist turning it into a murder mystery.

And this book isn't really the end. I have to get Adele and Dieter to the altar, and I will in book 5, which… still doesn't have a name. But it has been plotted.

In the meantime…

Join the Society

Escape with *Fortune Favors the Grave*, a free novella in the Tea and Tarot series, by joining the Ravenous Society at KirstenWeiss.com

Plus, society members will get other free short stories and exclusive reads. Sign up and become a member today!

Here's a bit from Abigail about *Fortune Favors the Grave*:

Some people have the cockeyed idea running a tearoom is an elegant and genteel profession. *I'd* thought it would be elegant and genteel.

Some people haven't met my business partner, Hyperion Night.

In fairness, I can't entirely blame Hyperion for embroiling our tea and tarot room in a murder. After all, he was chained to the San Borromeo pier when California's most famous psychic, Trevor Amalfi, was killed.

And yet, here I am. And here we are. Embroiled.

Fortune Favors the Grave is an exclusive *Tea and Tarot* novella only for Raven(ous) Society Members!

OTHER BOOKS IN THE SERIES

ABOUT THE AUTHOR

Kirsten worked overseas for nearly fourteen years, in the fringes of the former USSR and deep in the Afghan war zone. Her experiences abroad not only gave her glimpses into the darker side of human nature, but also sparked an interest in the effects of mysticism and mythology, and how both are woven into our daily lives.

Now based in Colorado Springs, CO, she writes paranormal mysteries, blending her experiences and imagination to create a vivid world of magic and mayhem.

Kirsten has never met a dessert she didn't like, and her guilty pleasures are watching Ghost Whisperer reruns and drinking good wine.

You can connect with Kirsten through the social media sites below, and if the mood strikes you, send her an e-mail at: kweiss2001@kirstenweiss.com

Kirsten's Website: http://kirstenweiss.com

Made in United States
Orlando, FL
31 August 2023

36593226R00186